CELEBRATE THE 100th ANNIVERSARY!

YOU'LL HAVE A CHILLING CENTENNIAL AS YOU SHUDDER AT THE SIGHT OF JACK'S SECOND VICTIM—DARK ANNIE

"Look, Mum" I heard a child's sweet voice ring out. "Look, Mum, all 'er guts is streaming out."

"They's tied round 'er bloody neck!" another child said gaily.

I let the cover drop back over her body. Leave it to a child to speak the truth. Indeed, her intestines had been taken out and placed over her left shoulder. And there was blood this time, blood smeared like paint on her hands, blood on her swollen and bruised face, blood matting the wavy brown hair, blood on the skirts above where her sex had been cut out—but not enough blood, not nearly enough. The killer had to have been dripping in blood. *Where was it?*

YOURS TRULY, JACK THE RIPPER

"OUTSTANDING . . . WEST HAS GONE TO GREAT LENGTHS TO PROVIDE AUTHENTIC 19th CENTURY ATMOSPHERE, AND HER INTROSPECTIVE, ASTUTE INSPECTOR WEST IS A MARVEL."

—*Booklist*

Also by Pamela West

MADELEINE

Yours Truly, Jack the Ripper

PAMELA WEST

A DELL BOOK

Published by
Dell Publishing
a division of
The Bantam Doubleday Dell Publishing Group, Inc.
666 Fifth Avenue
New York, New York 10103

"A Joan Kahn Book."

For information address: St. Martin's Press, New York, New York.

The trademark Dell ® is registered in the U.S. Patent and Trademark
Office.

ISBN: 0-440-20259-0

Reprinted by arrangement with St. Martin's Press

Printed in the United States of America
Published simultaneously in Canada

February 1989

10 9 8 7 6 5 4 3 2 1

OPM

For Kenneth

The author would like to thank the staff of the Rare Book Room at Pattee Library, The Pennsylvania State University—especially Sandy Stelts—for arranging access to the library's Freemasonry collection. The author also appreciates the help provided by countless nameless librarians here and abroad: the Kew Public Record Office, the Colindale Newspaper Library, the British Museum Library, and the Library of Congress.

Author's Note

In reconstructing the events of 1888 every attempt has been made to achieve historical accuracy. Names have not been changed, except for those of very minor characters. Inspector John West (no relation to this author) really existed. So did Mary Kelly. Their personal relationship belongs to the realm of fiction, but the events that consumed them that autumn of 1888 really happened.

—P.W.

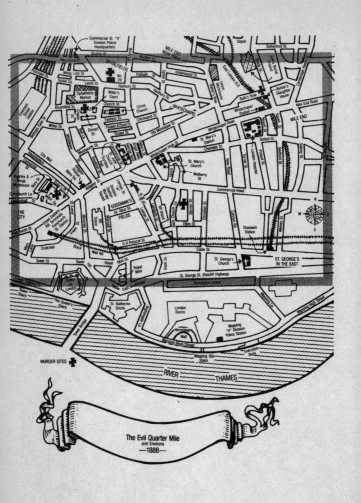

The Evil Quarter Mile
and Environs
—1888—

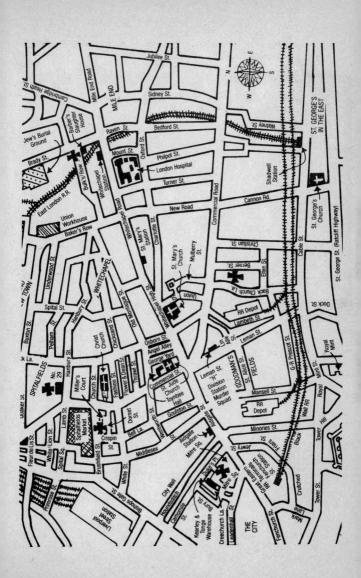

This New strange year of three eights—
never can it be written again!

—*Queen Victoria's correspondence, 1888*

Up and down the goddamn town
Policemen try to find me,
But I ain't a chap yet to drown
In drink, or Thames or sea.

I've no time to tell you how
I came to be a killer,
But you should know, as time will show
That I'm society's pillar.

I'm not a butcher
I'm not a Yid
Nor yet a foreign skipper,
But I'm your own light-hearted friend
Yours truly,
Jack the Ripper

—*Attributed, Jack the Ripper, 1888*

Suppose we catch the Whitechapel murderer, can we
not, before handing him over to the executioner or the
authorities at Broadmoor, make a really decent effort
to discover his antecedents, and his parentage, to trace
back every step of his career, every hereditary instinct,
every acquired taste, every moral slip, every mental
idiosyncrasy? Surely the time has come for such an
effort as this. We are face to face with some mysterious
and awful product of modern civilization.

—*Murder and Science, 1889*

Yours Truly,
Jack the Ripper

Wednesday, August 29, 1888

ʄ ʄ ʄ

Willy "Upright's" present on this, my fortieth birthday, has re-
minded me—as he knew it would—of my New Year's vow to
keep a journal.

"Now you can stop borrowing writing paper from my desk
every day," he said, handing the book to me unwrapped. "I got a
bargain because it's so late in the year, but you can use those
pages for scratching."

Good old Willy "Upright" Thicke, straight as a line and as
old-fashioned as the journal he has picked for me. It is grey with
large lined pages. The date is printed old style— *888.* How
strange it looks upon the page when I have been writing 8 since
the Jubilee. His birthday was last month, and though he has been
a staunch friend since I arrived at "H" Division, I failed to buy
him a present. No doubt he got this for a song, but I am nevertheless touched. And a trifle piqued at being called to task: If I do
not begin to write I cannot fail.

This year, 1888, the year of the Divine Mind come to earth, the
year of the three strange 8's, what does it hold in store for me?
How shall I begin? A poem? No, let us begin with the weather,
which tonight was sheer poetry.

* * *

For a week now, in spite of dark, wet days, we have been
having cherubic sunsets. This morn, when I drew the dimity curtains from the leaded lattice, I saw a dull grey sky with the sun
steeped in wet cloud. By noon the sky was opaque, the sun a
green sheen struggling to break through. It was muggy and close,
and the dinner I ordered to cheer myself on my birthday went
down so poorly I decided to skip supper with Hopkins at his
club. I worked in the office until the light went, then had a smoke
at the window and watched the sun set. The scene was quite

Hogarthian: a languid waiter in shirt sleeves looking out from his door, a cabman arranging a vase of posies in his yellow-wheeled hansom, the horse dozing. The lamplighter came round with his long pole, leaving a trail of yellow glowworms. As night fell, a dull blood-red band lingered on the horizon. The stars came out and I made a wish.

This year a milestone—millstone? Longevity runs in the West family, and I have always been rather smug about it, but suddenly it seems as if I have been spun blindfolded and that vast plain of time that lay always *before* me has shifted. The landscape now before me narrows precipitously. I found my first grey hairs today. High time I married and began a family.

Another smoke. That's when the glow in the west began. The sky grew pink and I could again see the street below.

"Fire!" someone shouted, and the people coming from the Beheading of John the Baptist Mass at Christ Church stopped where they tread; the storekeepers popped into their doorways; the street grew black with people. For a minute I thought I saw tongues of flame rising high over the West End. Then I realised it was the sun. A red wash of colour spread itself over the buildings and streets, the people's faces. My hand glowed red. Then the bloody red sheet was lifted as the sun set a second time. It grew very dark with great suddenness. The stars came out in a black sky.

A celestial phenomenon? It was like this five years ago when Krakatoa blew. The ash blotted out the sun's rays, producing a wintery summer charged with electrical currents. This summer we have had cyclones, hail, continuous rain—and glorious sunsets. Last week's *Gazette* reported on a volcanic explosion near Yokohama in early July. Could this weather be an aftereffect?

Now at midnight all is dark and clear. There are no clouds, only an overturned bowl of beamy stars.

Thursday, August 30, 1888

When we could endure no more upon the water, we [went] to a little ale-house on the Bankside, over against the Three Cranes, and there staid till it was dark almost, and saw the fire grow, and, as it grew darker, appeared more and more, and in corners and upon steeples, and between churches and houses as far as we could see up the hill of the City, in a most horrid malicious bloody flame, not like the fine flame of an ordinary fire. We staid till, it being darkish, we saw the fire as only one entire arch of fire from this to the other side the bridge, and in a bow up the hill for an arch of above a mile long; it made me weep to see it. The churches, houses and all on fire and flaming at once; and a horrid noise the flames made, and the cracking of houses at their ruine.

ƒ ƒ ƒ

Thus does Pepys describe the great fire of 1666 which began in the East End and melted the bells of all the churches. 1666–1888: Two hundred twenty-two years past, and his words are yet crisp and immediate.

The year of the three sixes, 1666, a year in which it was expected that many prodigies would be born, prodigies to fill the kingdom devastated by the bubonic plague of '65. It was the first day of September, a Saturday, and people were just beginning to return to the plague-scoured city. There were many empty houses, rough wooden affairs, their doors still painted with red crosses and crude great letters: LORD HAVE MERCY UPON US. Just past midnight a fire began. All of London went up in flames.

Tonight's fire was small in comparison, but it was still the biggest bonfire I've ever witnessed. Which tells one precisely nothing. *Small, biggest*—meaningless, empty, stale words! If I am to keep a journal, I had best take lessons from Pepys.

Begin at the beginning: an ordinary day in August. Rain. Sulky rain. The sun set in flames of purple, red, orange, and black. It stayed set.

Quiet on the streets. Only servants and magistrates are left in
London this time of year, and many a man is a temporary master
of a ring of keys until Michaelmas. Beginning Monday I am
standing in for Superintendent Arnold at HD, and while I am
dreading the division paperwork, I am glad of the prospect of
visits to the Yard. Visibility never hurt a man's chances for promotion. Hops picking began this morn, and at least 150,000 vaga-
bonds have padded the hoof to Sussex and are sleeping in barns
or under the stars. In the eve they'll have a sing-song and free-
and-easy, drink hopped beer by hop-bins crackling with fire. A
shilling for every seven bushels and all the beer you can drink;
miles of sweet berries on hedgerows, orchard apples. I wouldn't
mind going myself for a lark.

Shooting season begins Saturday. A day off and a dinner of
nice plump partridge would be sheer heaven, but for me there is
only the prospect of the pen. At least London is quiet with the
hoppers gone. I hear the yield is poor this year, though; only the
best will come home with pockets jingling. Most of the poor sods
will be padding the hoof home as well. Only the breweries will
profit.

It was brewery profit—of the illegal kind—that Willy Thicke
and I were talking about when the call came in. We were eating
ham and mushy peas in the mess; Jake McCormick came clam-
bering up the stairs. "An Aunt Maria at the London Docks.
West, Superintendent Arnold wants you and Thicke to go over
and see if Wapping Station needs any help. Assess the situation."

I went to the window. Another thermal phenomenon? No, this
time it smelled like fire. Besides, the sun had been down two
hours. Willy and I put on our bowlers and started south through
the fog-cloaked passageways of Whitechapel to the quay; as I got
closer I also smelled something else.

At the black iron warehouse gates two Wapping bluecoats were
manning a flimsy barricade of ashcans and packing crates. Beyond the gate brass-helmeted firemen aimed streams of water on
the flaming granite and brick-turreted warehouse.

"Looks like Dartmoor going up in flames," Willy said. "Anyone inside?"

The blue shook his head. "Staircases were blocked with packing crates. Couldn't be."

"We're going to need some sawhorses," I said. "And about five
more blues."

"I'll wire back to headquarters," Willy said. "Got any coppers?"

"Aye." I dug in my pocket and handed him some coins.

"It's Laughlin's warehouse," the other constable said.

"Spirits? So that's what I smelled."

"Hundreds of barrels of the Queen's finest."

Just then a series of rapid explosions shot sparks and thin blue petals of flame out of the iron-barred warehouse windows. Heat lapped out, and the heady bite of warmed alcohol.

"Is it the vaults?"

"No, just the barrels," the constable said. "If it burns down to the vaults, we'll never put it out."

"Willy, better get ten blues." I turned back to the constable. "Anything I can do?"

"Just keep back, sir."

I willingly retreated to Wapping Old Steps, where I could watch the tower of fire amongst the dark piles of the wharf.

"A blooming fireshow," a Cockney coster said, as he backed away from the scorching heat and almost bumped me. From the Thames the sirens of the Metro River Brigade sounded shrilly as its steamers' hoses began to mingle streams of water with those from the land engines. I inhaled the rich, deep fumes as from a snifter. Next to me a young woman in a blue shawl stood transfixed by the blaze, her face glistening.

"It's like a giant plum pudding," she said, to no one in particular.

I laughed. "A plum pudding fit for the Queen."

She looked at me, concern on her face. "Of course, there might be people in there."

"Not at this hour. Besides, they tell me the staircases were blocked with packing cases. Just brandy inside."

"And gin. I can smell it."

There was something in the situation that permitted easy congress. Nothing implied, just the camaraderie that arises during times of crisis. The light was apricot on her face, and the daisies on her velvet jerkin seemed to dance. Her eyes were deep blue— forget-me-not eyes, my mother would say. A nice mouth, soft lips. Kiss-and-come-again lips . . .

"You could get daft watching," she said.

For a moment I thought she'd caught me staring, but she was looking at the fire. "Yes," I said, "isn't it lovely?"

She turned to me and laughed, and her face softened. "I love a good fire!"

There were more explosions then, and the heat lapped closer; we retreated with the crowd, she letting me help her over a rough section of wharf.

"Do you know where you're standing?" I said.

"London Dock, I should think."

"Execution Dock."

"Go on."

I pointed to the large pillar by the wall. "They hung pirates here, let the rising tide wash their bodies three times. Captain Kidd was hung here in 1710—the pirate hunter turned pirate."

"Is that the truth?" She looked up at the wall where the tide line showed on the stones.

I placed my hand over my heart and nodded.

"What a thing to know," she said.

Willy Thicke came running up then with two blues. "John, we need you back at the gates. Can you—"

I tipped my hat and set off with them.

"Pretty lass," Willy said when we had gone a hundred feet.

"Very."

I looked for her again at eleven when the second Aunt Maria was called in at the Ratcliff Dry Docks, but she didn't appear. The fire broke out in Josten's coal warehouse and had spread to the masts and riggings of the ships in the harbour by the time I arrived. The pressure was low in the pumps from the Brigade's earlier drawing on the East End's supply, and the water gave out before they could put out the flames. They are letting it burn.

It is just past one now, and there is no water to wash with; the entire East End is illuminated in a hazy light, and though I have not lit my lamp I can see my hand smudge the page as I write.

The woman in blue has set me thinking again. A lovely face and figure, a soft pleasing voice. I am a horse for single harness— why continue to fall asleep in a section house to the sound of men snoring? I have enough capital saved for a modest beginning. I wonder if she is respectable.

Friday, August 31, 1888

ƒƒƒ

The sky was blue when I awoke this morning; I knew it even before I lifted the white curtain. It was the birds in the tulip tree on Fleur de Lis Street: I hadn't heard them for a fortnight. I sat up and stretched, then pulled back the curtain and watched a gusty little breeze scoot white clouds overhead; I could smell larkspur. I thought it eight from the light—an hour till I had to go on duty—but the sun surprised me; it was barely seven.

There was still no water; I daubed my face and hands with cologne, then shaved the best I could, studying the blueness of my shaven chin in the mirror. I needed a smoke. Willy's footsteps came down the hall, and he knocked loudly on my door. I opened it; he was already dressed: the same light checked suit he'd had on all week, though it seemed to be tighter than it had been on Monday. "Bit of a problem, John."

"What?"

"Arnold's gone off early on holiday."

"I thought he wasn't leaving till Sunday."

"He said not to wake you, but as you're acting division super—"

"What's wrong?"

"A woman had her throat slit over in 'J' Division last night, within whistling distance of our London Hospital fixed point. Bit of a nasty one. And we've had a robbery at the post office. Come on, put on a shirt, I'll give you the details over breakfast."

* * *

"Any tea?" A trickle of day-old tea slid into my cup.

Willy's bulldog head atop his six-foot-four frame sagged over the table; his walrus mustache drooped on the white cloth. "Probably won't have any all day. Do you smell anything cooking?"

"Bacon." I sniffed again. "Buttered eggs."

Willy's face brightened.

"Who's on the case for 'J'?"

"A chap named Helson," Willy said. "Bit of a twit."

"Did they find a weapon?"

Willy shook his head. "The Yard's sending Fred Abberline over to set up a murder squad. He wants to use his old offices at Leman Street for the operation."

"Ellisdon will have a fit." I smiled. "Come to think of it, that wouldn't be so bad."

"You think it's a link to our George Yard case?"

"Perhaps." We'd both been there at George Yard—an ugly bayonet murder three weeks past. We suspected her lover, a soldier, but had no proof. I ate my rasher and drank a jug of cream, then went down to Arnold's office and pulled the file. I read it, then sat staring at the mound of paper on the desk. Damn Arnold's eyes. You'd think he'd at least lick round the edge of the plate before leaving on holiday.

"Where you going?" Willy said as I passed him in the hall five minutes later.

"See if I can find this Helson."

"Want me to come?"

"No need."

He gave me a mock salute. "You're the gaffer."

I grinned. As far as "H" Division matters go, I am still wet. If not for Willy taking me under his wing, I would have made many more mistakes; I am grateful for his help. I tipped my hat, went down the stairs and out onto Commercial Street, past the gin distilleries, towards Whitechapel, London's broadest, a street as treacherous as the surface of the moon, with pocks, chasms, and lofty eminences of manure, over which a myriad of horse-drawn conveyances stampede. But the sky was a glorious ultramarine. Not a hint of sulphur left from last night. Two fires, now a murder. I might almost believe Old Jack Painter had risen from his grave.

On Whitechapel the hawkers' stalls lined both sides: apples, chestnuts, oysters, combs, brushes, cutlery, firewood. This section of Stepney is 95 per cent Hebrew, and the babble is deafening: a polyglot of languages dominated by Yiddish. The crossing sweeper was nowhere in sight; I picked my way carefully across two mammoth mounds of manure, reached a dry spot and looked for the next. A far cry from the sidewalks of "A" Division, but hadn't I learned more of thief taking in my six months in Babylon than in all my years on the force? The East End might not have a history of heroes, but its history of outlaws was legendary. Twenty-seven murders in the entire kingdom in '87 and a full quarter of them on these mean streets. Yes, it has been a learning experience, this school of criminals.

As I entered the labyrinth of crooked lanes, blind alleys, and grimy courts that make up the Evil Quarter Mile, the bells of Christ Church struck the hour. I quickened my pace. The smoke-blackened buildings seem to lean inwards here; the grime is denser, coating every surface like mourning garb. It is truly a place where the sun never shines.

* * *

The deadhouse is a shed behind the workhouse on Old Montague Street, nothing really but a hole and corner hovel. It is not surprising, I suppose, that the East End, with so much crime, does not have a decent mortuary. Stepney, the stepchild of the kingdom, filled with the off-scourings of the world's criminal population. The East End does without a newspaper, without a bookseller's shop, without concentrated wealth of any kind. Its only theatre is a cheap penny gaff. Entering the deadhouse, I felt part of a melodrama.

The door creaked loudly; I adjusted my eyes to the dimness, made out the marble slab. Detective Helson wasn't there, but in the corner the two attendants, Mann and Hatfield, stared at me with small black eyes. Like Liverpool rats, I thought, these scouses with their sharp noses and twitching nostrils. They had undressed the corpse and tossed her clothing in a pile, covered her body with a coarse grey canvas.

I studied the dull face; even the swelling of death could not hide the emaciated features. She might have been pretty once, but now her face was cold and waxen. A mole on her left cheek, soft mouse-coloured hair. Late thirties, I thought, but I have never been good at guessing women's ages. I leaned closer; there were small pinpricks of red in the skin around the eyes and a circular bruise on the lower edge of her jaw.

"Tsk, tsk." I'd never make a surgeon, I thought. It is not the blood or violence of the profession that bothers me, just some-

thing in the cool taciturnity of the clientele. I am good at my
profession because I am good with people. Nine-tenths of the
world will come along quietly if you just let them talk and don't
bully them. Isn't that what any bloke wants, just someone to
listen to his cares? This woman couldn't even tell me her name.

"Detective Helson been in?"

The older Dickey Sam twitched and gave me a surly grunt.
"He was here 'bout an hour past—went over to talk to the night
watchman at Barber's slaughterhouse."

"Did he get an identification on her? An address?"

"Bugger all. Just those bits and pieces."

They had set her effects upon the sill: a broken comb, a shard
of mirror, and a wafer of Sunlight soap. In the corner was a hat, a
shiny hat of glossy black straw with a cluster of red wax cherries
on the brim, brand-new—must have cost at least half a crown. I
picked it up and looked inside, but there was no label.

I peeled the canvas down to her shoulders and looked at the
black clotted pulp that had been her neck. Two cuts, the first
beginning below her ear and running for perhaps three inches,
the second just below the first and running ear to ear, deep
enough to sever the windpipe and gullet, cutting back to the
vertebrae. The hair beneath was matted with blood.

I knelt down and looked at the scattering of clothes, memoriz-
ing their order upon the floor. Then, like an archaeologist, I began sorting through the layers: Side-sprung boots and black
mealy-smelling woolen stockings off to one side. They had cut the
shirtwaist down the front and cut the bands of the petticoats,
peeled the clothes in layers from her body. Other than that, no
tears or rents. Blood on the bottom flannel petticoat, not a great
deal—at first I thought it her menses—another coarser petticoat,
darned but clean, a top petticoat, that one alone of once-decent
linen, close-ribbed brown stays, a cheap rusty-coloured ulster
with brass buttons, a black shawl. At the bottom of the pile was a
frayed red scarf, soaked through and quite stiff with blood. The
attendants had cut it off; I examined the knot. Then I went back
through the stack again. This time I didn't miss the stencil. On
the inner woolen petticoat was a launderer's mark: LAMBETH
WORKHOUSE.

The Lambeth casual ward on Prince's Street is a step below the
tuppenny tramp lodging kips. One goes there only when there is
nothing else. They strip you naked and bathe you and give you a

blanket before they lock you in a sleeping room; you get up at dawn the next day and eat your skilly and swill so you can work all day paying for your bed and bread. Hard work: breaking stone and pumping water. Still, if it weren't for the workhouses, many more of the wretched poor would have died this winter last.

I stood, turned back to the slab, and lifted the cloth to look at the body. And gasped. There were two horrid cuts: one deep and clean cut, crossing the intestines; the second jagged, running from her mousy thatch up to her navel—as if the killer had set about to disembowel her like a deer. The police surgeon obviously hadn't lifted her skirts.

The killer had.

"Pretty ugly, isn't it?"

I started and wheeled round. A short, sandy-haired man stood in the doorway, packing tobacco in his pipe with his thumb.

"You Detective Helson?" I said.

He nodded.

"I'm Chief Inspector West, 'H' Division."

"Heard the name."

"How could the surgeon miss this?"

Helson shrugged. "Maybe Llewellyn had something waiting back in bed."

"Any new clues?"

"Nary a one." He looked at his watch. "Well, I'm expecting the man from Central at the station. You stay as long as you like. Been over to the site yet?"

I shook my head.

"Not much there. Hardly any blood."

I raised my eyebrows, looked back at the corpse. "There had to be blood, lots of blood."

"You'd think so, wouldn't you?"

I looked back at the thin body on the slab. The George Yard victim, Martha Tabram, had been of ample architectural proportions and dressed in dark blue silk. The killer's bayonet had penetrated thirty-nine times, short violent rips through the cloth to the breast and stomach that had drained the body of blood. Thirty-nine stabs, and half as many buckets of water again to clean the carnage from the courtyard.

Saturday, September 1, 1888

ƒƒƒ

Inferno at the Yard today, yesterday's murder almost eclipsed. Our chief of detectives, James Monro, and Commissioner Warren are having it out like a pair of professional beauties, albeit from a distance, and everyone else is left at sixes and sevens.

> One fine day in the middle of the night,
> Two dead boys got up to fight.
> Back to back they faced each other,
> Drew their swords and shot each other.

Sir Charles is still at Cannes; telegrams, however, are flying. Monro's resignation has been accepted by the Home Secretary and his deputy, Anderson, placed in his office, but it is rumoured the chief will come back. Chief Constable Williamson is threatening to resign if he doesn't.

Inspector Abberline has set up his operations room at Leman and is directing inquiries. He's assigned "H" Division several dozen slaughterhouses to check out. I spent the morning filling out my first blue division report, dispatched it to the Yard. Then I went round to the Alexandra Room of the Working Lads' Institute on Whitechapel Road. Wynne Baxter, coroner for the northeast division of Middlesex, had the "J" Division surgeon Henry Llewellyn in the witness-box. Baxter was dressed in a dazzling white waistcoat, checked trousers and a crimson scarf—quite the dandy. Me, I don't think much about clothes as long as they're comfortable. I attribute much of my success as a "Tec" to this. I fit like an old glove wherever I go. I took a seat next to Ralph Helson.

"Get an identity on the victim yet?"

Helson leaned over. "The matron at Lambeth said the stencil is at least three months old. She said try the doss houses on Flower and Dean. We've got men on the inquiry now."

Frederick Abberline came into the hall and down the aisle, receiving greetings even from the jurors. Baxter paused, taking that moment to smooth his coppery muttonchop whiskers. Abberline stopped to say a word to a tall constable with a straw-coloured mustache.

"That's Neil," Helson said. "He found the body."

Inspector Abberline took the seat next to me, smoothed his trouser legs, and faced front. You'd never mark him for a Tec. He is portly and soft-spoken, more the appearance of a bank manager than a thief catcher. One of the first divisional C.I.D. inspectors, he served the last ten years in "H" Division as Detective Inspector before being promoted last year to the Yard. I took his place.

"The cause of death," Llewellyn was saying, "was the severing of the carotid artery. This wound and the others were made with a long pointed blade—"

"How long?"

"About six inches."

"A frontal attack?"

"Yes, and from the angle and direction of the wounds, I would say that the wielder of the instrument was left-handed."

"Was there much blood?" Baxter said.

"I examined the site at the time. Barely two wineglasses full."

"How do you account for the lack of blood?"

"I would say that she was killed somewhere else and then moved."

"Was she—er—interfered with?"

"I saw no evidence of such."

"The other wounds?"

"Those were made after death."

"Nevertheless, could you describe them?"

"She had bruises on her face. Her tongue had been cut out. There were two deep cuts in her abdomen. . . ."

Helson shook his head and leaned over and whispered. "I studied that site early yesterday. The ground was wet and muddy, yet there was no sign of dragging or resistance, no blood trail of any kind. I think he butchered her on the spot."

"I think you're right," I said. "Her clothes were clean—she wasn't dragged. But why so little blood?"

"Ah, that is the question," Abberline said. "It happens, I guess. Shock."

I stayed at the inquest until afternoon recess, and then went round to the murder site. A herd of bullocks was being driven down Whitechapel High Street to Barber's slaughterhouse, followed by a tattered regiment of barking dogs and small boys with sharp sticks; I had to wait while they filtered through the gateway and past the knacker's wagon into the row. The cattle were bellowing and thrashing about, and any trace of footsteps had long been obliterated. I sloshed my way through the muck; on the other side of the gateway leading to the stables stood a small crowd of onlookers. Behind them was the railway guardwall, a twenty-foot drop-off.

"Is this the place?"

An old woman pointed out the small brown stain on the ground just outside the wooden gateway. About the size of a man's hand, the stain. I looked round, trying to envision the body lying there. Constable Neil had reported she'd been facing east. To the north was the old Jewish cemetery, a crowded nest of aged marble vaults. Just beyond were the East London and District Railway embankments and lines, and, not fifty yards away, the gate to the Great Eastern Railway shunting yards. To the west stretched the slaughterhouse's companion industries: tanneries, gut-scraping and tripe-dressing sheds, tallow-melting and bone-boiling huts, all of which gave forth an effluvium of rotting flesh. The crowd had swelled now with the children who had come to watch the slaughtering. Now, while they waited for the drama within to begin, they danced round the spot, rooted there by the sense of adventure and danger.

"Is this where he did her in?" a ragged hollow-cheeked boy said.

The same old woman nodded.

"Were her eyes really open?"

She nodded. The lad shivered and grinned, walked forward and spat on the spot. Only when the animal cries began from within—piercing, haunting shrieks, one following another—did the children shift their attention from yesterday's death to today's dying and move forward and crowd round the slaughterhouse doors.

I took a deep breath; the air wasn't fresh, it smelled of tannery and distillery, but I was going inside where the air was worse. I pushed past the children and entered the slaughterhouse. Jake Barber himself came toward me, wiping his hands on his leather apron.

"I'm Inspector West, from 'H' Division," I said.

"The 'J' Division detectives have already been here twice. I've no time to waste. I'm a busy man."

"Mr. Barber, there was a woman butchered just outside your door. We're assisting in the investigation."

"What is it you want then?"

"I've never seen an animal slaughtered."

He raised an eyebrow, then nodded and took out a pack of smokes, offered me one. I accepted readily. "Over here, Inspector."

The ginger calf hung by its hind legs on a chain; it was bleating. Barber grabbed the chain and swung the animal towards the butcher in the bay. The butcher grabbed the calf's left ear, and holding the head steady, cut the throat with one deft stroke from left to right.

The calf seemed to scream a long time after. "Notice," Barber said proudly, "the windpipe is not severed."

The fact hadn't escaped me; the scream echoed in my head. I watched the butcher cut open the belly and take out the vitals; there wasn't as much blood as I'd expected, but there was more than two wineglasses full.

On the street I pondered it. A butcher would know what he was about; he was used to handling frightened animals. And he could walk down the street in his bloody leather apron—even with blood on his hands—and not be suspect. But why butcher a woman?

I stopped by Leman Street before going back to headquarters. The officer on duty directed me up the stairs to the murder squad. I found Fred Abberline in the interview room, tipped back in his chair, talking to a middle-aged woman who weighed at least fifteen stone.

"Mrs. Emily Holland here is missing a friend," Abberline said.

"Anyone show her the body?"

"Yeah. She says it's Polly."

"Polly who?"

"Don't know. Just Polly. Mrs. Holland, this is Inspector West. You want to start again—the night before the murder."

"Well, me and her was kipping together at Eighteen Thrawl

Street last week," she said. "Then we sort of lost track of each
other. I saw her last Friday night by the Frying Pan Public
House."

"When was that?" Abberline said.

"About half past two."

"Was she with anyone?"

"No, she was alone. I asked her to kip with me over on Flowery Dean—they sleeps men as well as women there." She smiled
a toothless smile and laughed. She had a vulgar laugh.

"Did you have a partner that night?" Abberline said.

"Course not. That's why I asked Polly. Only she hadn't any
lolly. I'd spent my last tuppence on a loaf of bread so I couldn't
lend her any. So we go over to see the proprietor—thought
maybe he'd advance her fourpence one night."

"Did he?"

"Hal? That heartless rotter? No lolly, no bed. But he liked
Polly, said even though it was closing, he'd keep the door unlocked another half hour. So she sets off to sell her bonnet, the
one with the cherries—that's the last I saw her. Poor old Polly."

"To sell her bonnet? Did she tell you how she'd got it?"

"A man had bought it for her the day before. I don't know
who he was. It was a gift."

"Did she ever mention any family to you?"

"I think she had a father in Sydenham. I know she worked at
Wandsworth 'til spring. But she didn't get on with the people. I
think she was married before that. She didn't much like to talk
about it. Poor Polly."

I leaned forward. "Do you know anyone who wished her ill?
Any enemies?"

"Polly? Nice as ninepence she was. No one hated Polly. If
anything she was too easygoing, too trusting."

When she'd gone out, Abberline laughed. "Poor Polly, indeed.
Out of the frying pan, into the fire."

I shook my head. "Vanity of vanities. She could have sold her
bonnet, but she only needed fourpence."

"And we all know what fourpence is the price of on Flower
and Dean," Abberline said. "Should've known when I saw she
had five front teeth missing." He snickered.

I coughed. Fourpence. These streets have their own rules, their
own regulars. The sisters of the abyss stake themselves out according to a hierarchy as rigid as that practised by their posher

Piccadilly and Haymarket sisters. The East End gaslit public houses and high streets are reserved for the younger, fresher girls, those who can command a guinea. Polly was a park woman, a doss-house drab who carried her possessions on her back, in summer slept in Christ Church's Itchy Park, the kind of woman who sold herself when the cold began for the price of a beer or a bed. Women like Emily and Polly belonged to the alleys and parks and gutters. They relied on the dark to hide their age and scars, plied their trade against stout wooden fences. But why kill her? Why slash her and cut out her tongue?

"Well, let's check out the domestic situation in Wandsworth," Abberline said. "I'll wire the station at Sydenham." He sighed deeply. "One more fallen angel."

Monday, September 3, 1888

ᚠᚠᚠ

The rain came down in buckets yesterday, and I did not write a word or go out, though I did work in my own way, reading over police reports on rapists, seducers, malicious wounders, and woman haters, looking for men who use knives. There is no new crime under the sun and no new criminals; surely this killing has a history. I got damn all out of my research; today I went back to work.

"Where's the man from the Yard?" I asked the duty sergeant when I entered Leman Station.

Sergeant Rack looked up from his papers. "Abberline? Down talking to the family Polly worked for in Wandsworth. Said he'd be back for the inquest. Did you see the *Globe*? Where'd they get that story about a trail of blood from the cemetery to Buck's Row?"

"I don't know. The *Post* had it too. Desperate for something to print, I'll wager."

"Oh, Ralph Helson was looking for you. Wait, I've got a message somewhere." He shuffled through the papers on his desk. "Helson found the father in Sydenham, a Mr. Marsten. Positive identification. Christian names: Mary Ann. She was married to a man named Nicholls, bore him three children. Last year wifey takes sick; the husband runs off with the woman brought in to nurse her. So, she farmed out her children and went to work. The last address the father had for her was in Wandsworth."

"That's gratitude for you."

"You ever nurse a sick wife?"

I laughed and shook my head.

"My wife won't let me in the room when she's sick. Throws things at me. Speaking of throwing things, you hear what happened to our new recruit Wensley?"

"Got his head coshed by a woman with his very own truncheon—yeah, Willy told me. He forgot the first lesson. Never try to arrest a woman if her man's within shouting range."

"There were three men. Not a good time to be a copper."

"Popular woman, eh?"

"One of our finest. You get anything with your inquiries?"

I shook my head. "Sweet Fanny Adams. We're going to start with the lodging houses next."

"It's got to be a Hebrew, don't you think? By their cemetery and all—with their big holies coming up—sort of spooky, what?"

"Maybe it's a ghoul. Climbed out of the vault and over the wall, then disappeared into thin air."

"I don't believe in ghouls, West."

"What about their holidays?"

"You know, slicing her up like—she was Catholic, you know. You know what they say about Hebrews and Gentile women. It could be some kind of blood penance. Besides, who else lives in Whitechapel?"

"Just about every outlaw in the kingdom."

"Yes, well—I say we'd better charge a Hebrew soon, killer or not, before the crowd ups and hangs one. Pretty ugly out there this morning."

"You talking about the weather or the people?"

"It's always ugly weather. Nope, I sure wouldn't want to be one of *them* today. Not with their big day coming and them spouting all that mumbo jumbo in the Temple."

"Rosh Hashona, isn't it? I don't know much about it."

"Begins sundown on Wednesday. Hey, you going over to the inquest?"

"For a while."

"Well, ask Fred to bring me some bloaters when he comes back. You want to know about their holies, ask him. He's been here so long he almost knows their lingo."

I walked to the inquest, making poor time but managing to avoid most of the mud. Whitechapel Road was a bedlam of grinding axles, stamping hooves, and cracking whips as gigs, phaetons, dog carts, and growlers all competed for high ground. The Alexandra Room was filled to the gills, but in contrast it was an oasis of calm. Abberline was already there; Henry Llewellyn was in the witness-box.

Abberline made room for me on the oak bench.

"Get anything?"

"Not much," he said.

"Why'd she quit?"

"Didn't. They fired her last Easter for stealing two dresses."

I looked up at the box, back at Abberline. "Didn't Llewellyn go over all this before?"

"No, it was a pointed blade," Llewellyn was saying. "Very sharp."

"Like a shoemaker's knife?" said Coroner Baxter.

"Or a cork cutter's, or a sailor's jackknife."

I turned round and surveyed the crowd. Towards the back, I saw the woman from the fire. She was wearing a maroon shawl over a dark green velvet bodice, a straw hat with a short veil. I had thought her in her teens; she looked older in the full light. She didn't see me, and I studied her as Llewellyn talked. Hair truly the colour of gold, red rosy cheeks. No makeup, just the blush of ripe youth. Testimony hardly fit for a woman, but she was listening intently—nary a blush.

At recess I strolled up to the front, had a word with a reporter I knew at the long table, then strolled down the far aisle, smiling when I came abreast. She cocked her head but then looked away; I could see she didn't recognize me. I had a smoke in the hall and was just going back in when I fairly collided with her at the doors.

"I'm sorry," she said. "I wasn't paying mind."

"It's me who's to blame. And I must apologize for being so bold inside," I said, tipping my hat. "Don't you recall—the gentleman from the fire? We spoke about plum pudding."

"And hangings. I remember. I was not quite myself that night."

"Who is it you were?"

She laughed, a tiny bell-like laugh that started inside her and rippled out, but she didn't introduce herself.

"Are you leaving?" I said.

"Time to get the supper." She was gone before I could think of anything else to say.

It is midnight now and I can't get her face out of my mind. Her eyes aren't blue; they are violet, rimmed with green.

Rack will be angry with me. I forgot all about his bloaters.

Wednesday, September 5, 1888

ʄʄʄ

"Is the battle still raging?" Willy asked when I returned from the Yard this morning.

"Aye." I laid the fat pay envelope in his hands. "Had to queue for half an hour. Our new AC has everyone moving furniture."

"Politics. Bah!" Willy spat into the spittoon. "Well, he'd not install himself too cozily in King Malcolm's space."

"Looked snug to me. Oh, rumour has it Commissioner Warren is cutting his Riviera holiday short."

"No doubt King Stork wants to skedaddle back and appropriate the blower before Anderson gets it."

"Too late. I heard it ring. No flies on him. He's even got his teapot set up. Not that I even got a 'Good morning.' A cold fish, I'd say."

"What do you expect from a barrister? He's certainly not the man to stand up to the Commissioner. Did you get to see Williamson?"

"The queue outside *his* office is an hour long." I picked up the papers Willy had been working on. "Want me to sign these?"

"It would help."

I tapped the top page. "No leave for Godley and McCormick. Williamson wants us to work round the clock on the Buck's Row case."

"Durward."

"What?"

"Didn't you hear? The residents voted to change the name of the street. It's Durward Street now. Eh, can I get out now? I've got something I want to follow up." He reached into the drawer and pulled out a yellow pad. "One of my noses says there's been this foreigner around here the last few months scaring women."

"What does that mean exactly?"

"He creeps up on them at night and abuses them . . ."

"Willy, be precise. Abuses them? How?"

"The nose wasn't sure. Some kind of blackmail. Threatens to harm them if they don't do what he wants."

"What does he want?"

"I'm no crystal ball reader, John. Maybe he's interested in their minds. I'd like to look for some of the women, though."

"Do you have names?"

"For a price."

"We'll pay it. And see if you can bring them in for a statement. I want to hear this one. Did you have your coffee yet? I was just thinking of going out."

He tossed me a coin. "Three sugars."

When I went to the corner, I could feel the strain. The pious Hebrews went diligently about their preparations for the High Holy Days. The abattoirs were on double shift; the smells of smoked sprats, brisket, and fried herring rose powerfully from the open windows, but there was an air of fear beneath, a feeling of waiting and watching. If the murder hadn't taken place next to the Hebrew cemetery, maybe it would have blown over; instead the newspapers have fanned the flame. The villains penned by the cartoonists all have Jewish faces. I saw a crowd of Irish roughs gather about a room-to-let sign that said NO ENGLISH NEED AP-PLY and tear it from its post. Things are getting ugly fast.

On the stairwell coming back up, slowly, so I wouldn't burn my hands with the hot brew, I heard Tim Godley and Jake Mc-Cormick in the hall.

"Give a Jew an inch and he'll put a bed in it."

"Yeah, and give him two and he'll take in lodgers." The men laughed, good healthy guffaws, just having fun. Why is it I have no sense of humour? The barb in every joke—intended for those outside the circle—always scratches me in passing. The poverty in Whitechapel is frightening, and it is true that these immigrants have cut wages and driven up rents by multiple lets, but their children are clean and polite and learning to read. Two weeks ago I called on a nose named Cohen who lives with his wife and two children in a two-room flat. One bed for all, the underside of which is a coop for twelve chickens. In the next room there are two hundred chickens, a terrifying stench. But the children! They are clean as new whistles, with bright eyes and immaculate clothes, as polite and well-spoken as any gentleman's children. Imagine! In this stew where vice is close-packed and lacks the room to turn, one is constantly being brought face to face with contradiction. In this dark, sunless place the odd encounter with truth and beauty shines like a beacon.

Perhaps the killer is a local, but I would not be surprised to learn otherwise. Jews might be gamblers; they might be slippery and evasive, but it is the subterfuge of the timid, not the cold depravity of a murderer.

I sent Willy off on his inquiry and spent the rest of the afternoon plowing through reports. Around half past five he came back with a slatternly looking crone in a yellow dress. She sat down on the stool and jutted out her chin at us.

"This is Iris," Willy said.

"Mrs. Paddyfont to you." She belched.

Willy laughed.

She gave him a scowl. "And it's bought and paid for, copper." She turned back to me. "Well, get on with it. You the Super?"

"The Acting Superintendent."

"Oh, ain't that bloody marvelous. Isn't anyone real round here?"

"Well, Detective Sergeant Thicke here is just himself." I laughed and she joined in, a toothless, raucous laugh. In a few minutes she relaxed, was even telling us about the budgie she'd had as a young girl. I got out my pad and pencil and lowered my voice. "We've heard that you've had a problem with a local character, a man."

"Men are always a problem. You got one in mind?"

"One who threatened you? Scared you?"

"Why do you want to know?" Her eyes glistened. "Do you think he's the killer?"

"We're investigating every lead, ma'am."

"Maybe he was. There wouldn't be a reward now, would there?"

I shook my head solemnly. "Sorry. Her Majesty's orders."

"The man gave me the willies." Iris shuddered loudly.

"Why?"

"I don't know. Just did. I was just coming out of the suck-crib with me pail of beer, on me way to the slap-bang, and I was—" She stopped, shook her head. "He made me hair stand on end."

I smiled and Willy grinned. "What did he look like, Mrs. Faddypont?"

"Paddyfont." She sighed. "He was a square-rigged sort of fellow, just above middle height, not bad looking. I thought at first he was drunk and had come in by mistake."

"What kind of clothing?" I said.

"A big coat, a slouch hat, old clothes, and inside the coat a leather apron."

"An apron? What kind?"

"Just an apron. White kid, new."

"You said he came 'in by mistake.' Came in where?"

"I don't go in for none of that business, you know."

"Mrs. Paddyfont, please, this man may have killed a woman. Just tell us straight."

She looked at me, then at Willy, then smiled and cackled. "That scummy little bastard sneaked up on me as I was using the closet, offered me half a crown if I would let him slap me bum while I piddled. When I said no, he threatened to report me to the police, said he'd tell you I'd set out to rob him; he said he was in with you like." She stared at me defiantly.

"What did you say?"

"I told you, I was having none of that. Not for no amount of push. Let him just try to sic you blue devils on me."

"Did he say anything else? Tell you his name?"

"Are you kidding? None of them have *names.*"

"How about his voice? Did he have an accent?"

"He wasn't English. Didn't look English and didn't sound English. I think he was a Kangar."

"But he spoke English?"

"He spoke like the Kangar at Katkov's cleaners. Only softer like."

"Do you remember when it was he approached you?"

"When? Last month? Hell. No—wait, yes, 'cause I'd gone that day to see me sister in Greenwich. To see the eclipse. It was the same day that driver was killed at Charing Cross Bridge."

* * *

"Well, what do you think?" Willy said when he had sent Iris back to the streets.

"A Jew who wears a leather apron? There must be five thousand East Enders who wear a leather apron and speak with a foreign accent."

"Didn't get much for our money, did we?"

"Just a minute," I said. "I'll be right back." I went and got my notebook from my desk.

"Katkov is a Russian Jew," Willy said, when I came back in. He rubbed his chin. "But the man at the counter's named Lieberman—German, isn't it? Never wears a leather apron, though. Let's see, who goes around on the street in a leather apron? Cobblers, smithies?"

"Well, we've run out of butchers. I'll ask Abberline if he wants us to try German cobblers next. And it might be worth bringing in these other women if we can find them. Draw some funds."

Willy smiled. "I've got two more names. Of course, there's a long way between paying to slap a woman's bum and slitting her throat."

"Aye, but—" I lifted the notebook. "The night the driver was killed on Charing Cross Bridge—that's the same night as the George Yard killing."

* * *

It is midnight now, and I am only just getting round to reading the evening *Gazette*. There is an article on marriage brokers. Why not answer an ad? Find some lovelorn lass who is pining for what I am. Here's one:

Young lady of 19, £20,000 invested in her behalf, desires to get away from friend's influence.

And accept my influence? What have I to offer a lady of means? A detective is a slave to his case: long hours, poor company, bad habits. To be a good shadower, he must drink like a criminal, think like a criminal, and live like a criminal. He is a sort of criminal himself, always asking questions of others and never telling the truth about his own intentions, learning to lie easily. And he always has an excuse for getting home late. Yes, more marriages have been killed by detective work than crimes solved.

I love my work.

What sort of woman would put up with such an obsession?

Thursday, September 6, 1888

THE CRACK OF DOOM

On the morning of the 15th of July the people of Bandaisan were startled by an unusually severe shock of earthquake. The frightened inhabitants rushed out of their houses and made for the foot of the mountain, which trembled and heaved beneath their feet. Suddenly a great, dense black pillar rose from the apex of the mountain, reaching the sky, which became as dark as night. The people stood in awe, and then, turning their eyes upwards for a moment, fell prone upon the heaving bosom of the earth, in mute terror. They fancied that the final destruction of the world by fire had come. Blacker and blacker grew the sky, the ground underneath their feet undulated like the sea; the fearful, roaring noises increased, noxious gases choked them, and the black pillar, alone in the sky, was seen to spread out like an umbrella over the whole horizon. Then red-hot ashes, massive stones, showers of sulphur, and volumes of boiling water descended, dealing instant and horrible death to the multitude.

—Report from the Shanghai
correspondent to the
Pall Mall Gazette

✦✦✦

They buried Mary Ann "Polly" Nicholls today. Her husband, William, and three children rented a shiny mourning coach and bore the polished elm coffin to Ilford Cemetery; the sun came out as she was lowered into place. There was a small crowd of onlookers, but her father did not appear.

"Poor Polly," I heard a woman say, walking away from the cemetery.

"Did you know her?" I asked.

"Polly? We sold nosegays together this spring. We'd get up at four to go to Covent Garden and get the best flowers. She had her baby with her; she was straight then."

"Did you know her real name?"

"She didn't want anyone to know who she was. I knew Polly wasn't it, that's all."

"Where did you sell flowers?"

"On the Strand."

"Do you still?"

"That I do."

"Did you know her long?"

"About a month. Until her laddie died in a paraffin lamp explosion. After that she wasn't the same, took to drinking. She tried to get me to take the flowers over to Piccadilly and sell them to the swells. You can get sixpence for a tuppenny bunch sometimes. I didn't want to. We lost touch when she went gay."

I handed her my handkerchief, and she wiped her eyes. "She loved that baby—it was all she had left."

I walked back to headquarters thinking of poor Polly. At the corner of Whitechapel Road, I stopped to buy a honey cake from the Jewish baker Leibowitz. He took me aside and whispered in my ear. "We've heard a rumour, talk of wholesale deportation."

I patted him on the back. "Nonsense, Mr. Leibowitz."

"And of a pogrom."

I could see from his face that he was serious. I shook my head. "Pogroms, smogroms, this is England, not the Steppes. We have not come to that yet."

"They said the same in Russia, not six years past."

"Russians are barbarians."

He shook his head sadly and pressed two warm cakes in my hand. I took out my purse, but he held up his hand.

"No, I'll pay, Mr. Leibowitz."

"A New Year's present. May you be inscribed in the book of life for a good year."

"Well, I suppose—"

"Eat and enjoy."

On the stairs to the station, a *Star* reporter stood waiting.

"Any arrests yet?"

"I can only give you the official reply: The Yard has forbidden interviews with reporters."

"Can you deny they found a message written in the yard that said 'Fifteen more and I give myself up'?"

"Sorry, no statement. I've orders."

"So you can't deny it? So it's true?"

Thus are rumours born.

A report on the volcanic eruption at Bandaisan in this evening's *Gazette*. No mention of my theory about the weather, but the explosion sounds even more dreadful than Krakatoa. "As terrible as Dante's inferno," the correspondent described it. Another article on marriage brokers. There are ten such agencies in London. They charge a nominal fee. Perhaps when this case is solved. . . .

Friday, September 7, 1888

None but a creature with a lust for blood and devoid of all sense of pity would, after killing his victim, mutilate her body. The Whitechapel murderer is as much a savage as an untamed Australian aborigine, yet utterly devoid of the courage which is often the savage's sole redeeming feature.

—*Pall Mall Gazette*

ƒ ƒ ƒ

Coming back from the Yard this afternoon, I stopped at Spitalfields Market to look for the muffin man. I don't know why it is, but the muffins on the tray under the green baize cloth always taste better than those you buy in the shop. I found him by the fruit vendor; he took the tray off his head and lifted the cloth. I ate the muffin on the spot, then haggled with the vendor over an orange; that's when I saw my woman in blue. She was in the aisle by the milliner's shop, where a row of white crinolines swung in the wind. She was struggling with a bulky framed canvas which kept catching in the wind and almost slipping from her hands. I caught up to her easily.

"May I help?"

"Do you like it?"

"Rather maudlin."

"Do you think?"

I looked at it closely: various shades of blue—a woman standing bare-armed by the sea, a small child swaddled in white reaching up to kiss her. In the background boats with sails. Something very sad about it. Signed Chasseriau.

"It's got a nick on the frame," she said. "It wasn't too dear. Do you really think it's maudlin?"

"It seems quite a good print. The colours are true, aren't they? What's it called?"

"The man said *Fisherman's Widow.*"

"I've heard of Chasseriau."

"Who?" She followed my gaze, but her face was blank.

"The painter." I pointed to his signature, then realized I had
embarrassed her; she could not read. "He's not very well known,
but I like him. Do you need any help getting it home?"

She smiled and shook her head emphatically. "No, but thank
you. Do you really like it?"

"Yes, I do."

"I've even got a nail ready over the mantelpiece. It's my birthday present, actually."

"Oh, is it today?"

"Tomorrow." She smiled.

"I've been trying to place the accent. Is it Welsh or Irish?"

She laughed. "Both. I was born in Limerick, but Papa moved
to Carmarthen when I was little." She stuck out her hand then
and gave me a kind of mock curtsy. "Mrs. Kelly."

"Mr. West. Well, I congratulate you on your purchase. If
you're ever in need of the services of the C.I.D. . . ."

She raised her hand in salute and turned.

"Wait."

"Why?"

I took the rose Chief Constable Williamson had placed in my
lapel and handed it to her. "Happy birthday, Mrs. Kelly."

She smiled and pressed the flower to her nose. "Mary Jane,
actually, but not since I left Limerick. Thank you—is it 'Sergeant'?"

"It's John. Inspector, actually."

"So young?"

"I hide my years."

"John West. That's a pilchard, you know."

"I know."

"I know all about fish." She made a face. "Well, I thank you
for the corsage, Inspector."

I smiled, watched her walk off into the saffron and violet sunset. How lovely she looked in the roseate veil of the sun. It is
midnight now, and I find myself hoping she is safe at home. Mary
Jane, what a lovely name. A poor girl, perhaps, but with a simple
natural beauty, nothing affected or imitative about her. Not one
bit like the girls you find in drawing rooms.

Might some poor honest girl tolerate such as I?

Annie had been sick all day, fever and chills, no stomach for a meal. Around nine she felt better, craved a bloater. She got up off the stoop, patted her black skirt into place and tidied her hair in the fragment of mirror she kept in her pocket. Her eyes were bloodshot, but the swelling had gone down. She counted the three copper coins in her pocket. A bloater, yes. But first a beer at Ringer's.

At midnight she still had not eaten. Though not for lack of coin. She patted her stomach. "Not so bad now, lass, is it? Aren't we still thirsty, though?" She eyed the door for a new john, weighed the waiting against the meal she'd promised herself. "To tell the truth," she told herself, "we could do with another beer." If she drank the coins in her pocket, she'd have to go out again. Unless she could find Hal or Sam, who might give her the price of the bed. She hadn't many regulars anymore. But there were a few, even some who still took her to a room instead of the park.

Her tongue played idly over the soft gum of her lower jaw. She'd been in the park six times so far, saying each trick would be her last—her doss money. "Oh, well, lucky in love I'm not, ducky. Still, it beats selling sweet lavender on the Strand. But why not have another drink before closing?" If she went now she'd just start scratching and lie awake. The coughing would begin.

Of course, she could have a short one and then share a bed with Bessie, who'd asked her. But she had her foolish pride. The bedbugs might have her, but she'd not share a common bed if she could buy one of her own. She nodded out for a moment then, and sleep would have won if the door had not opened and brought in two drunken sailors. One she knew from a leave past. Bessie had gone with him and he'd spent the night, bought her a hat. But Bessie was in the park now with a legionnaire.

She ordered a beer to wake her, keeping her eye on him. The sailor's pants were stiff and he was past caring who noticed; he fondled his balls absently as he drank the heavy tankard.

In five minutes they were in the yard, his pants pulled down round his knees.

It was half past when she got back, but she wasn't sleepy. "I could go all night—amazing I've had no food," she thought, ordering her tenth. It was just stout ale, no spirits, but the last made her sleepy. For a moment a wave of despair came over her and she laid her head on the bar and shed a tear. And then nodded out. The barmaid woke her after a few minutes, ordered her out. She was tuckered out, too tired to lift the glass to drain it, past thought of food. She felt in her pockets, but her fingers found only the thimble she kept there, the shard of mirror. She slid off the stool, looking right and left at the hard faces floating above their tankards. She crossed the street to the cheap lodging, searching the linings. Not even a farthing. When had she spent the last? Well, perhaps Donovan would give her credit.

But Tim Donovan shook his head and sent her back out the door. Fourpence or naught. "Hold my bed," she said, and started east in the fog along Whitechapel, slowly, as her feet were paining her. She paused briefly in the comfort of the next gaslight, resting her feet, twisting the rings on her finger. Not even worth pawning. Well, no use crying. She'd just do another. It wasn't two yet.

But she was on the street a long time. The half hour chimed and still she hadn't her bed money. Every once in a while a carriage passed, but none stopped. She huddled under a streetlamp, dodging the copper's rounds each half hour, afraid each time she had to shrink within the shadows that "the Whitechapel fiend" would approach her and drag her off. Only in the lamplight did she feel safe.

She jumped when the trick approached her, he came up on her so quietly, but then she saw his face and wasn't afraid. She sized him up as a foreigner, but he seemed clean. A neat mustache; maybe he had money.

"Did I startle you?"

"I thought for a moment you was 'him.'"

He laughed. "You'll be all right with me, lassie."

"A fine night, isn't it?" she said.

"A trifle cold, don't you think?"

"I could warm you up." Coyly, she reached out and touched his shoulder. He didn't object so she moved her hand lower.

"You're a well-shaped woman," he said, letting her fondle him. "I bet you've a fat bum."

She laughed. "Wouldn't you like to know?"

"I haven't much time."

"One and six," she said.

He laughed. "What would you do for that?" he said.

"Anything you'd like."

"I bet you would. All right," he said, surprising her. "Someplace dark. And anything I say."

"Of course, I know just the place. Coppers won't be back for twenty minutes. You can take your time."

He put his hand on her bum and pinched it.

"Oh, you devil. My, but you're the saucy one." She led him back behind the row. At the gate to the courtyard she paused and held out her hand.

"First the money, sir."

He paid at once, pressing the worn coins into her palm. She opened the gate and led him into the courtyard. There was grass there—and a stout wooden fence.

Saturday, September 8, 1888

There seems to be a tolerably realistic personification of Mr. Hyde at Whitechapel. The Savage of Civilization whom we are raising by the hundred thousand in our slum is quite as capable of bathing his hands in blood as any Sioux who ever scalped a foe. The police must look for a man who is animated by that mania of bloodthirsty cruelty which sometimes springs from the unbridled indulgences of the worst passions. We may have a plebeian Marquis de Sade at large in Whitechapel.

—*Pall Mall Gazette*

A nameless reprobate, half beast, half man, is at large in Whitechapel; a creature of hideous malice, deadly cunning, insatiable thirst for blood, a ghoul-like creature who is drunk with blood and will have more.

—*The Globe*

ƒƒƒ

There are some days in early autumn that are perfect. The air is crisp and blue and sharp as a whetted knife. Distant objects appear near and one feels the planet shifting on its axis. A body is one with the universe, whole. Today was such a day. As I hurried in the pink dawn along Commercial Street toward Hanbury, I knew it would be so. And I knew also that I would take no delight in the day.

Hanbury Street, just beyond Christ Church; the corner house is visible from the station steps. If you walk all the way down Hanbury, you come to the short row back of Whitechapel: Buck's Row, now Durward Street.

I saw the crowd as soon as I turned onto the narrow thoroughfare. Number 29 Hanbury, a stone's throw from another of Barber's slaughterhouses. A red hansom had just pulled away from the curb next to the Salvation Army refuge, and it came careening down the street past me. I jumped back, almost falling over the publican taking down his shutters. Number 29 Hanbury, just across the street from the soup kitchen yard where the Princess Beatrice opened this summer's charity bazaar. I was there and saw her: July 11, a benefit for Christ Church Hall and Club Rooms. You would have thought she arrived from another planet the way the people crowded round. Beatrice, stout and thirty, dressed like the Queen in a black frock—hardly the "flower of the flock," but still the "baby" of the family. Poor flower, forbidden to marry for so many years—finally allowed to wed only if she and her husband lived at the Palace. Perhaps she was glad to be out, for she stayed an hour and gave bonbons to all the children, kind smiles all around. I bought a snuffbox, an eye-shaped tin with the initial *W* within foliate borders, swags on the sides, and a gilt interior. Over a hundred years old, the dealer said. It came dear but the engraving was lovely, and besides, it was for charity's sake.

I crossed the street and made my way through the growing crowd. "It's a Kangar for sure," I heard a Cockney porter say. "Just let me get my hands on him and I'll scramble his brains." Inspector Chandler was standing behind a sawhorse and looking uneasy. Two helmeted blues were holding back the crowd.

"You get the call, Joseph?"

"Yes, sir. I'd just come on duty; one of the tenants ran in and brought me back. I wired Abberline and George Philips—he's bringing ambulance aid."

"So where's Abberline?"

"Didn't you see the hansom? He's been and gone."

"Nearly murdered me. Where's he going?"

"Back to round up reinforcements. We've got all the people in these buildings round locked in, but we've not enough men to question them."

"Back there?" I asked Chandler. I motioned with my head to the narrow green gate.

He nodded. "Constable Watson's there." His face was blanched, and I could see now that his unease lay with what was behind him, not the crowd round him. "Hold the barricades," I said, opening the gate. A narrow passageway ran down about twenty-five feet. I looked down as I traversed it, stopping three times to examine the ground. At the end of the passageway two steep stone steps led down into a square yard. From the steps I could see a pair of legs in red-and-white-striped stockings, black pointed boots.

The body lay against the fence on the stone-flagged courtyard, covered with sacking.

"The porter found her," Watson said, "coming out of the house at daybreak, still buttoning his trousers. Inspector Chandler put him under guard in the cat meat shop, but his story seems reasonable."

"Anyone around here recognize her?"

"Nothing so far. No one's missing from these dwellings." He tapped his truncheon against his beefy palm. "Most of them were still sleeping."

I walked across the yard and knelt beside the body.

"Sir?"

"Yes, Watson?" I looked back up; he was wiping his hands on his blue tunic; they were bloody.

"It's the most awful carnage I've ever seen, sir. That bloody demon—" His voice broke, and I saw the quiver of his hands. I lifted the rough cloth slowly from the face. From far above me I heard the sharp intake of breath.

I looked up, past Watson and the fence and rotted woodshed, to the tall three-storey brick buildings that lined the yard, made out the heads of some twenty people looking down from the sweatshop windows into the square court.

"Can you see it?" a woman's shrill voice said, being answered at once by a man's "Hish, woman."

"Can't you get those folk down, Watson?"

"You want me to try asking them real polite?"

"Don't suppose we can barricade their windows . . ."

"Bloody slummers," Watson said, "but what can we do? It's all Chandler can do to keep back the mobs on the street. Go on, may as well get a look before the children are all up."

I lifted the sacking back to the shoulders and swallowed hard.

She lay facing east, her eyes open, blue and glazed, as if transfixed by the rising sun. She had an odd face, I thought, the nose so flat, almost Negroid. There was a thumb-sized bruise on her jaw; she had a black eye, but that appeared to be old bruising. A red silk scarf had been tied round her throat; it was clotted with blood. Her neck had been cut left to right, ear to ear. And something more, something bloody and oozing and purpled, lay beside her throat.

"The scarf," I said softly, thinking of the scarf I'd seen on the floor of the deadhouse. The same sailor's knot.

"Looks like the killer tied it round afterwards to keep her head from falling off, doesn't it?" Watson said. "It gets worse, sir."

I knelt down and looked close at the scarf. The woman smelled of cheap jack. It was like the other scarf—red, silk, the lower edge frayed across. I looked up at Watson.

"You're wrong. He didn't put it round her to hold on her head. It was on when she was killed. Did you touch her, move her?"

"Blimey, sir, I didn't even lift her wrist to see if she was dead. Didn't touch a thing. But how do you figure that about the scarf?"

"The knife frayed the edge when it cut—see—"

He knelt down. "Blimey, you're right."

I reached inside her bodice. The skin was still warm.

"The only thing I touched was the apron, sir."

"What apron?"

"The one in the tap, sir. I went over thinking maybe it was a tarp I could cover her with. It had bloodstains. Inspector Abberline was pretty excited when he saw it. Thought maybe the Yard could tell if it was human blood."

"So he took it with him?"

"Uh-huh. A white one."

I almost smiled, the sleuth in me glad at the piece of the puzzle that fit. But why would he leave a clue?

The first fly of the day buzzed at my ear. I lifted the sacking and for a moment shut out the constable's voice and the voices from above, while I made a record with my eyes of the body: The woman lay facing east with one arm squared over her left breast; her feet were drawn up and planted squarely on the stony ground. Her black skirts were pushed up to her breasts.

"Look, Mum," I heard a child's sweet voice ring out. "Look, Mum, all 'er guts is streaming out."

"They's tied round 'er bloody neck!" another child said gaily.

I let the cover drop back over her body. Leave it to a child to speak the truth. Indeed, her intestines had been taken out and placed over her left shoulder. And there was blood this time, blood smeared like paint on her hands, blood on her swollen and bruised face, blood matting the wavy brown hair, blood on the red-and-white stockings she wore beneath her skirts, blood on the skirts above where her sex had been cut out—but not enough

blood, not nearly enough. On the hard, unevenly set stones there
was no pool. On the fence there were no spatters. Along the
passageway no drops. The killer had to have been dripping in
blood. Where was it?

"Did you look over the fence, Watson? Any sign of blood
there?"

"Inspector Abberline walked round. Nothing he could see."

I rose from my knees. They barely held me. The scene was too
perfect, too "clean" for the carnage that had been carved. It was
almost like the wax tableaux at Madame Tussaud's.

It was getting lighter now, and I looked round the court.
"What about this stuff here?" On the ground by the body was a
collection of coins, pennies mostly. In the centre lay two cheap
brass rings and two bright coins. Watson moved his toe and
shifted one of the worn pennies. He shrugged. "Sure ain't robbery."

"They seem arranged somehow—those half sovereigns set
apart. What do you think, Watson?"

"Fool's gold, sir."

"What?"

Watson laughed and reached down and scooped up the shiny
coins. "Best look closer. These aren't gold. These are farthings,
new from the mint. It's an old 'under and over' trick."

I replaced the coins on the ground and stepped back. "Don't
see new coins very often. Was it just like this?"

"I guess," Watson said. "They might have got shuffled some.
Those kennucks round there, the rings and two fadges inside."

"Hmm." I lifted the sacking again, intent on the left hand that
was squared across her breast. Two of the fingers were banded
with blue, the kind of stain given off by cheap copper; the knuck-
les were bruised—had the killer wrenched them off? I looked at
the victim's face. A saturnine expression that told me nothing;
woeful eyes staring. In them, a shimmer of the sun and the reflec-
tion of a face. A man's face. Mine? Or the face she saw before she
died?

Was that possible? I looked again: a dull image, very distant. I
reeled back and looked her full in the face. The mouth was
slightly open and her tongue protruded. For a mad instant, despite the carnage, I expected her to speak. Then a breeze arose
and the smell of cat meat came from the house and I gagged and
would have lost my stomach if Watson had not at that moment

offered me his flask. The brandy burned beautifully in my charred throat.

"No Englishman could have done anything so horrible," Watson said. He spat and looked up.

I looked up too. The children had been pulled in and three puffy-eyed bearded Hebrew faces glowered down at us. They had all been asleep upstairs while the killer performed. If only houses could talk . . . what chilling tales they might tell. Protestant Huguenots of narrow religious persuasion had once lived in this yard, Huguenot families who won their acceptance by weaving and spinning intricate Spitalfields silk tapestries for the rich. In their heyday more than a hundred thousand weaving looms would be going at one time. Cheap power did them in. Today's tenants are tailors.

I dropped the canvas and made my way out of the yard and past the curious crowds. A young man ran up to me in the street and grasped my sleeve, thrust a brand-new press card in my face. "Sergeant, can you tell us what's in there?"

"It's Inspector, young man." I shook my head. "Just Sergeant Death."

As I made my way down the street, I saw the morning newsboys hit the pavement. " 'orrible murder! 'orrible murder! Paper! —'ere y'are, guv'nor—" He took my penny and handed me a pale red *Sun*. " 'orrible murder! Paper!"

* * *

The body had been stripped and washed when Police Surgeon George Bagster Philips entered the postmortem room.

"Who did this?" Philips roared. He is a tall, lanthorn-jawed man with red hair, and this was the first time I had seen him angry.

The attendant shrugged. "Guess them charity ladies."

"Damn all do-gooders! Get out of here and don't let them back in." Philips spat and picked up a surgical blade. I took the farthest chair and turned it round, sat astride. They had closed the victim's eyes—was the image still there? I heard the cartilage splitting as Philips cut down alongside the breastbone. He talked as he worked, his voice very low and deliberate:

"Carotid artery severed . . . at least a six-inch blade, pointed . . . wielder of blade left-handed . . . victim lying on the

ground when the other wounds were inflicted . . . intestines re
moved after death . . . vagina and uterus and ovaries missing.'
He wiped the autopsy knife with alcohol and set it on the tray.

"Shouldn't there have been more blood?" My voice came ou
high and squeaky, and I swallowed and spat.

"Yes? What's your point?"

"I don't know. It bothers me. I can't figure it."

Philips shrugged. "Death plays strange tricks."

"What about the tongue? The last victim—"

"First thing I checked," Philips said. "It's there."

I hesitated, then told Philips about the image I had seen re
flected in the victim's eyes. He lifted the lids and shone a light or
the pupils. "Yes, I see it too. A man's face. Remarkable."

"Could a photographic image be obtained?"

"It would be a difficult technique," Philips said. "If the image
does not fade, perhaps photographs could be taken of each layer
of the retina."

"Will you try?"

He nodded gravely. I went back to headquarters and made
myself a cup of strong tea, drank it, then had a smoke in Arnold's
chair. It was a long shot, but what else did we have? If the image
of the killer emerged out of the photographer's chemical bath, I
would be the hero, the giant-killer. If not, I would be a laughing
stock.

Willy came in, shaking his beefy head and carrying a telegram.
"You'll never believe this."

"What won't I believe?"

"It's from the Yard. Our new C.I.D. head has taken sick as of
six this morning. Dr. Anderson's physician has prescribed the air
of Switzerland to effect a cure."

I laughed. "You mean *no one's* in charge at the Yard?"

"Exactly. That should bring King Stork running."

I sat down to the morning reports. "Poor Williamson."

"Eh, can you spare me?" Willy said.

"I could use help with this," I said, staring ruefully at the stack
of papers piled on my desk.

He shifted on his feet. "I'm on to something, John."

"Go then. I can see you're chomping at the bit."

"Thanks." He was off before I could say Jack Sprat.

I turned back to my papers, but my heart wasn't in it. I'm a
shadower, not an administrator. I should be out on the streets

sleuthing, not locked in an office with a pen. I sighed, dipped the nib, and smoothed the blue paper:

I beg to report that at 5.40 this A.M. Detective Chandler, the officer on duty in Commercial Street, was summoned to 29 Hanbury Street, Whitechapel, where he found the body of a woman. . . .

Respectfully submitted. Jn. West, Acting Supt.

The report ran three pages and took me an hour; I shall have to learn to do better. I dispatched it to Williamson and then walked over to the Leman Street station.

"Inspector Abberline's gone to the Yard," the duty sergeant said. "Didn't he wire you from the mortuary?"

I shook my head.

"He's got an identification on your body. Found a drinking partner name of Bessie from the Ten Bells who had bedded with her in a doss on Thrawl. The victim called herself Dark Annie."

"This Bessie gay?"

"Looked like a harlot to me."

* * *

Now, as I lay myself down to attempt sleep, the day reels out behind me, an intricate tapestry of murder. Outside the stars are unusually numerous and bright, but I cannot lose the picture in my brain: The square courtyard. The red-and-white stockings. The open eyes. Two prostitutes with red scarves tied tightly round their slashed throats. Park women, doss-house gays, drabs without hearth or home. "One more unfortunate, weary of breath, rashly importune, gone to her death." Was this trail already cold? Or had the killer left clues? The apron? The trumpery articles placed round? Two shiny farthings?

I last saw such coins on Thursday. Two to close Polly's eyes in her coffin. Could it be? He must be a monster, a butcher, and yet —no monster is capable of compassion. A man? But what kind of man? What kind of man lays out farthings to close a victim's eyes and then carries her vagina away in his pocket?

Sunday, September 9, 1888

Dr. Anderson will have an admirable opportunity of show-
ing that wits sharpened by reflections upon the deeper problems of "Human Destiny" and the millennium are capable
of grappling with mundane problems of detection of crime.
                                                —*Pall Mall Gazette*

The series of shocking crimes perpetrated in Whitechapel,
which on Saturday culminated in the murder of another victim, is something so distinctly outside the ordinary range of
human experience that it has created a kind of stupor ex-
tending far beyond the district where the murders were committed. One may search the ghastliest efforts of fiction and
fail to find anything to surpass these crimes in diabolical
audacity. The mind travels back to the pages of De Quincey
for an equal display of scientific delight in the details of
butchery.

                                                —*The Times*

ʄʄʄ

When I entered the Yard it was all a bustle: a jumble of horses,
loungers, and peelers. The bells were ringing and the Salvation
Army band was playing a marching song. I shall miss it when
Metro moves next year, miss the history of this yard. Here, a
thousand years ago, Edgar the Peaceful selected a tract of high
terrain clear of the marsh to build a palace for the Scottish kings;
here Duncan and Malcolm walked. I patted a magnificent black
gelding tied to the chain railing and waved across at Abberline,
who was just coming out the back door. He turned and waited for
me to cross the cobblestones.

"The newspapers are going to raise merry hell when they find
out who's running this place," I said.

"Who's running this place?" Abberline said.

I laughed. "The Home Office, I suppose. I tell you, we'd better
take good care of Williamson." I opened my coat and showed

him the box of Beecham's. "I'm taking this in to the old man and making him drink it whether he needs it or not."

"He needs it, but no one's ever made him do anything."

"How's his heart?"

"He'll never say. But I see him touch the spot now and then, not in pain, only as if checking. There's a lot more silver in his hair. You going to breakfast?"

"Yes. Aren't you?"

Abberline patted his portly stomach. "Martha made me eat this morning. No telling when I'll be able to next. No, I'm skipping, but come by Leman Street later. And good luck with the Beecham's—he's in a beastly mood."

I wasn't too worried. Chief Constable Adolphus "Dolly" Williamson is phlegmatic and obstinate, but underneath his gruff exterior there beats a Scotsman's kind heart. I am told he also has the redheaded temper, but I have never seen it. I knocked on the chief's door.

"Go away, Pennefather," Williamson boomed.

"It's Inspector West, sir."

"Well, come in then." Williamson was standing at the table, wearing the same ill-fitting black coat he has on every time I see him; he was arranging a bowl of roses, pink today. He cut one off and turned round, a cherubic smile on his leonine face.

"Morning, West. How goes it?"

"Not very well at all, sir."

"I see you have lost your sense of humour. Well, get it back." He brought the rose and pinned it to my lapel. "We're all short-handed. Come on, you've not lost your appetite as well, have you?" He motioned me towards the white-clothed table set for two. I leaned forward and smelled the overflowing roses.

"Grow 'em with my own hands," he said. He held out his hands and then dried them on his trousers.

Honest hands, not large, with silvery hair, like his beard. A Scot from crown of head to sole of foot, and the Scot in me warms to him. Warren and Anderson and Monro are all of the new socialite-soldier-lawyer school. Only Dolly Williamson is a thief catcher. Son of a superintendent, he rose through the ranks to senior detective. But that was before the C.I.D. He doesn't have much book learning; it is rumoured he can barely write a legible report, but he knows more about the game of detection than any other man alive. He was running the force when Abberline started on the beat, when I was still in knickers.

Williamson rang the bell, and breakfast was brought in on silver platters.

"Thank your lucky stars you've got Fred Abberline on the murder case. He knows every nook and cranny in Whitechapel."

"Yes, I'm grateful."

"Superintendent Dunlap's offered to send a few clerks over from 'A' Division to help in the office. We'll find you a few extra blues here and there."

"Bless him. I could use ten."

"Well, Abberline will need two. I could detail you—let's say one crack clerk."

"I accept. And thank Superintendent Dunlap for me."

"Why not walk round and thank him yourself?" He motioned towards the "A" Division offices at the back of the building.

I shrugged. Perhaps I have a chip on my shoulder. At five feet nine and a half I am half an inch shy of our crack division's height cutoff. "H" Division, never "A." Sour grapes, pure and simple. At least I shall have a tall clerk.

"I shall write him a note of thanks."

"Ach, if you have the time. After, though—first we eat." He lifted the lid of the nearest serving dish. Steam poured out.

"No man can think on an empty stomach. That's the trouble with these new recruits—coffee and a roll—they're off—die halfway through. Cuppa tea?"

"Yes, please." What followed was one of Dolly Williamson's famous Scottish haggis, sausage, bacon and eggs and potato scones Sunday breakfasts. I ate slowly, enjoying my surroundings. You'd never know from the rooms on this floor that quarters at the Yard are so cramped; it is in the basement detectives' room that the men sit in cubicles. This room is massive, with high panelled wainscotting and cream-coloured frieze, a ceiling of raised plasterwork. Commissioner Warren's room next door is even larger.

"So," Williamson said, when he had wiped the last bit of egg from his plate and downed his third cup of tea. "It is a bit of a mystery, is it not?"

"More than a bit. Two park women. It's almost as if it's—"

"Random?"

"Exactly."

He nodded. "Two women who make their livings by sailing along on their bottoms, both down and out, drunk, helpless. It's like a lion cutting out its prey. He picks the weakest."

"But why mutilate the bodies?"

"Perversion?"

"A plebeian Marquis de Sade, like the papers suggest?"

"Perhaps. Have you checked for men with bloodstained garments at the common lodging houses?"

"We've asked at a hundred so far. Another hundred and thirty to go. If there were a reward—"

"I know, I know. But there's to be no reward."

I walked over to the window and looked down at the bustle in the square. When we move to The Embankment next year, Malcolm and Duncan's courtyard will house more mundane activities. I shall miss the old stable with its hanging red tile roof and wooden balustrades, miss the shade of the black-trunked plane trees. There will be no yard there at all, and the stables will be separate. There will never be anything homey about the new red Dartmoor granite baronial keep; it lacks grace. Even with a Norman Shaw design it shall look forever like a prison.

I turned back and faced the room. "Have you heard anything further on Anderson's condition?"

"Influenza, I am told. But I am not told much," Williamson said. "I think a mild strain, though." He shrugged. "He should have followed my advice and avoided that daily constitutional."

"Meanwhile we're the headless horseman."

Williamson laughed. "And I'm the horse's ass—all the work and none of the glory. How about you, got writer's cramp yet?"

"My hand is stained permanently blue."

"Getting any sleep?"

"Not enough."

"Well, don't be an adjective fool. You never know when you'll have to go three days without. Get all the sleep you can."

"It's only the paperwork that gets me down. I need to be out there, talking to people."

"Ah, lad, don't you know? This detection is a game of blindman's buff—with your hands tied and your eyes bandaged with tape."

"Aye, red tape."

He laughed. "I'll try to get the clerk for you today." Williamson massaged his writing hand. "The nerves go dead." He sighed and rose. "Well, since, against all odds, the direction of detectives —in absence of our head, resigned, and our new head, not yet fitted upon his shoulders—has somehow devolved upon me, I suppose I must muddle through."

I took the signal to rise, thanked him.

"Just one thing, West," he said, when I had my hat and was starting out the door.

I turned back. "Yes?"

"Never give up."

I rode back from Whitehall to the East End in a decrepit hansom that was poor protection from the lashing rain.

"How's old Dolly?" Willy wanted to know when I dragged myself into the section house.

"Looks fit. Serves.a bang-up breakfast."

"You should have known him before."

"Before his heart attack?"

Willy shook his head. "That hasn't changed him. No, I mean before the birth of this miserable system of checks and balances we call the department."

"Oh, that. You mean the De Goncourt scandal."

"He's been a shattered man since."

"Well," I said, "Dolly's lift still goes to the top floor. He says more in ten words than most supervisors do in ten hours."

"So? What's he think?"

"Frankly, he's as baffled as we are."

"Well, I've got a lead, John."

" 'Leather Apron'?"

"I don't know. Helson's been interviewing cork cutters; he put me on to this grass. The grass says he has something on a Polish cobbler who keeps a lot of knives."

"Local?"

Willy nodded. "Jewish. He disappeared right after Hanbury Street, hasn't shown up for work. I've got Godley and Pearce working on it with me."

"Keep at it. I've got to stop by the murder squad to see Abberline. Wire me if you need me."

"Want to share a cab?"

I smiled at Willy's beefy frame. Sharing a cab with him was always a bruising experience.

"No, I think I'll walk. Get the lead out of my stomach."

"That good, eh?" He licked his lips.

"You bet."

* * *

I walked down Commercial, thinking of Williamson. It's a sad story, Williamson's; it was his men, up to and including his Chief Detective Inspector, Druscovitch, like a son to him, who betrayed him in the turf fraud scandal. It was Druscovitch, to whom he had entrusted the entire inquiry, who gave him the Judas kiss. Williamson was the last to know what had been worked behind his back under the cloak of Masonic secrecy and by then it was too late; the department lay in ruins. They say he has taken it upon himself over the last ten years to pay back Countess de Goncourt every penny she lost. The guilty were out in two years. And yet Williamson bears no grudge against the Masons, though he has never, unlike most of his superiors, joined himself.

My own prejudice against the group is entirely personal. I find it foolish for grown men to be playing pretend games of any sort. On one occasion a colleague invited me to think about becoming a Mason and said that if I was interested he would be pleased to propose me, but no pressure was brought to bear and I let the matter drop. Abberline has told me it may hurt my chances for promotion, but I'll take my chances. If I make Superintendent, at least I'll know I've done it upon my own merits, and not through influence.

* * *

My trouser cuffs were soaked through by the time I reached Leman Street. I propped my umbrella in the hall and went upstairs to the squad room.

"Have a nice breakfast?" Fred Abberline said. Ralph Helson was sprawled in the visitor's chair, smoking a clay pipe.

"I had two nice breakfasts." I patted my stomach. "Did I miss anything?"

"No suspects yet. We're in a right fix," Abberline said.

Helson inhaled deeply on his pipe and exhaled a blue cloud. "We've got a new theory, West. It's a Malay seaman, syphilitic."

"The jackknife would fit, but where'd you get the mad Malay?"

"Not so farfetched. The Malay remedy for syphilitic sores is to apply the female sex organs as a poultice. To suck up the virus."

"That sure is ugly, Helson. You sure you got it right? Maybe they don't cut them off."

Helson laughed.

"Hey, you've spruced the place up," I said. I walked over to the large map covering the side wall: the East End, two red tacks to mark the two last victims.

Abberline smiled. "And we've got surnames for both now."

"So, I *did* miss something."

"While you were breakfasting we found a drab named Ivy Miller who knew our Dark Annie. Knew her as 'Sievy,' though. She knew all about the black eye; says a woman named Eliza gave it to her last week for eyeing her man. Annie used to live on Dorset Street with a sievemaker named O'Hara. We brought him in and he gave us a positive identification."

"Married?"

"Not to him. O'Hara says Annie's married to a coachman at Windsor named Chapman. We're checking that out. He says she used to make antimacassars and sell them; when she couldn't get the material, she sold matches; when she couldn't get matches, she sold herself . . . that's when he kicked her out. A wee drinking problem as well."

"Anything else?"

"Inspector Pinhorn's found a woman who saw a couple talking on Hanbury Street about the time of the crime. She's in the interview room waiting to be questioned. I was about to go over. Oh, and the publican's wife at the Prince Albert on Brushfield is sure she saw the murderer when she opened up Saturday morning. Says a man came in and ordered a pint of four-ale, drank it down in one gulp."

"That's a crime?"

"She says he made her hair stand on end."

"Did she see any blood? Did he say anything?"

"No, but he gave her a dirty look, frightened her."

"Wonderful."

"Intuition—women invented it." Abberline got to his feet. "Well, I suppose you have to get back to your reports—I just wanted to catch you up. Anything at your end?"

"A few disturbances. Some ruckus about blood sacrifices. We've checked a few Jews into the hospital with cuts and bruises.

Oh, and Thicke's got a lead. A Polish Jew—could be our Leather Apron. Hey, speaking of leather aprons, where's that leather apron you found at Hanbury? I wanted to take a look at it."

"I dropped it off at Central for analysis. You know them. May be weeks. No label though, I checked. Well, tell Thicke to keep on the trail. Who knows, we might actually have an identity parade before the weekend's out. You coming, Helson?"

"An arrest would be better," Helson said. He emptied his pipe and pocketed it, but didn't move from the chair.

"It's getting uglier by the minute, that's for sure," I said.

"And with their day of Atonement coming up, it could get much worse." Abberline opened the door to the hall.

I took out my watch. "I've got some time. Mind if I sit in?"

"Not at all, West. Not at all. You coming, Helson?"

"By all means, let's go talk to the park keeper's wife."

The park keeper's wife, Elizabeth Long, was fiddling with the twist-turned arms of the mahogany chair when we entered. She looked up and bobbed her grey head.

Abberline took the chair behind the desk. "You taking notes, Helson?"

"Why not?" He took up pad and pencil.

Abberline tented his hands on the desk. "Now, Mrs. Long, start from when you left your house in Spitalfields that night."

The woman swallowed and blinked. "I'd just left our cottage in Church Row and I was on my way to market."

"What time was it?" Abberline said.

"Just past five."

"Was it light?"

"No, not quite. But the fog had lifted and the moon was up and I could see quite clearly. Mostly night people out—I'm an early riser. And a slow walker."

"Go on. What did you see?"

"I saw a man standing out front of Twenty-nine Hanbury, talking to a scorcher, the same one that's lying in the shell."

"What made you notice them?"

"They was loud."

"Arguing?"

"I wouldn't say that. No, he was kissing and cuddling her and she was laughing. And then I heard the man say, 'Will you?' and the woman she says, 'Yes,' and then they went through the gates."

"The gates leading to the yard?"

"Yes. Number Twenty-nine."

"Can you describe the man?"

She shook her head. "I couldn't see his face; he had a hat pulled down over his eyes. No beard, though."

"What kind of hat?"

"One of them plaid deerstalkers with a little feather. He was wearing travelling clothes—sort of a cape."

"How old would you say he was?"

"I don't know. Twenty and some. Not thirty yet."

"English?"

She shook her head. "He sounded foreign."

"Jewish?"

"Maybe."

"Thank you, Mrs. Long, that will be all for now. You've been very helpful." Abberline rose.

I leaned forward. "Mind if I ask a question?"

"Fire away," Abberline said.

I faced Mrs. Long. "Madam, did he have a mustache?"

"I told you, I couldn't see his face."

"Gloves?"

"I don't recall."

"Did you form an impression as to what class he was?"

"Oh, sort of shabby genteel. A man who's known better days." She laughed. "Of course, that could describe many a poor soul."

I smiled. Myself included. What was a detective if not shabby genteel? Second sons of second sons, men who would never achieve true elegance.

"Just one more question, would you recognize him?"

She shook her head slowly. "I might."

* * *

"You going to circulate the description?" I asked Abberline when Mrs. Long had gone.

"Let's hold it back a while. Run it by Thicke and see if his Jew fits the bill." He drew out his watch and wound it. "Well, West, you've stayed this long. You may as well stay and see your brain pictures."

"Philips has them?"

"Don't get too excited. It may be nothing. He'll be here soon."

"I'll just have a smoke then. The paperwork will wait."

Halfway through my smoke, George Philips came in. He shook his head and flipped a manilla folder on the desk. Abberline took it up and withdrew the plate; he sighed.

"Sorry, gentlemen, but it failed. I took three photographs using the latest physiological techniques: one of the illuminated eyes plain, one with the eyes illuminated and charged with electrical current, and one with the eyes charged but not illuminated. Then I superimposed the pictures onto one plate."

I walked over and looked over Abberline's shoulder. The paper was black.

I crushed out my cigarette. "I've been thinking, Mr. Philips," I said. "About the lack of blood."

Abberline looked round. "You have a theory?"

"Well, no one heard either woman cry out. If he strangled them first, and *then* cut their throats—?"

"But the report concludes that death was caused by the severing of the carotid artery," Abberline said.

I looked at Philips. "Is it possible, Mr. Philips? It would explain the neatness."

"Maybe he's a vampire," Helson said.

"Well, is it possible?"

"Anything's possible," Philips said. "In any case, the severing of the neck would destroy all evidence of strangulation. Frankly, I wasn't looking for such evidence."

I left Leman Street deep in thought. The temptation was always to accept the obvious. The throat was severed. The knife became at once the murder weapon. Every prostitute was on the alert for a man with a knife, none for a man who worked with his hands.

When I got to my office, I closed the door and buried myself in paperwork. The light was fading by the time I finished. I leaned my head against the cool wood of the desk. One killer against 14,000 police. We should be able to find one killer. But how am I to know who if I do not know why? Damnation, I do not even know *how*.

What was it Doyle's Sherlock Holmes said? "There is no crime to detect these days, or at most some bungling villainy with a motive so transparent that even a Scotland Yard official can see through it."

Where are you now, Hound of Justice? I could use that rapier-like brain. I laughed out loud. If you were real, Sherlock, you would be sitting there eating your hat.

"John?"

I raised my head. "Yes?"

Willy opened the door. "Why are you sitting here in the dark?"

"Thinking."

He snapped on the light, and I saw that he was beaming.

"We've found him, John."

"Leather Apron?"

"His name's Pizer. He's holed up in a house on Mulberry Street. We've got it under surveillance."

Monday, September 10, 1888

Strange, almost incredible though it appears, it was in the very midst of the series of murders at Whitechapel that the internal disputes which for some time past paralyzed the efficiency of the metropolitan police came to a head, and in so doing decapitated the Criminal Investigation Department. Mr. Monro, who for the last four years has acted as the chief of detectives, resigned. His successor is Dr. Robert Anderson: a millenarian and writer of religious books. But although Dr. Anderson is nominally at the head of the C.I.D. he is only there in spirit. At a time when all the world is ringing with outcries against the officials who allow murder to stalk unchecked through the most densely crowded quarter of the metropolis, the chief official is as invisible to Londoners as the murderer himself. You may seek for Dr. Anderson in Scotland-yard, you may look for him in Whitehall-place, but you will not find him, for he is not there. Dr. Anderson, with all the arduous duties of his office still to learn, is preparing himself for his apprenticeship by taking a pleasant holiday in Switzerland!

—*Pall Mall Gazette*

ƑƑƑ

Just before dawn this overcast day, Willy drove the Black Maria to arrest the suspect John Pizer, alias "Leather Apron," in his brother Gabriel's house at No. 22 Mulberry Street. A predawn raid is always the safest. A man's defences are down and his mind and body are muddled. He rarely puts up resistance. In this case, we had a double reason. We wanted to be sure the suspect made it alive to the station.

I was with Abberline at Leman when the Black Maria pulled up, a small crowd bringing up the rear. Willy quickly ushered Pizer into the charge room, but the *Globe* reporter was in the hall so the newspapers will be hawking the story shortly. John Pizer is a short man, not five feet and three inches, with an olive-hued sullen face and dark watery eyes; he stumbled on the doorstep as he entered, shied like a colt and almost upset the spittoon. He was crying as we made him sign his name. He signed with his right hand.

"You're going to deport me?" he said, his voice shaking.

Abberline went over and looked down at him. "No, we're going to charge you, you scum."

"For what?"

"The murder of two women."

"I never murder anyone, Constable."

"Inspector, Inspector Abberline, Scotland Yard. You are known by the name 'Leather Apron'?"

"Yes."

"Charge him," Abberline said to the sergeant.

"I never murder anyone, Inspector." He looked round wildly, then met my gaze. "Believe me." He touched his phylacteries and closed his eyes.

Abberline motioned for Willy and me to follow him to the corridor. Pizer watched us through slitted eyes as we left.

"Turn up anything on the house search, Thicke?"

"We found about half a dozen knives under his bed. He was making a pair of pink ballet slippers when we nabbed him. There was a white leather apron on the workbench."

"New?" said I.

Willy shook his head. "Pretty well worn."

"Oh, jolly good," Abberline said. "A killer who makes pink dancing shoes. What about the knives, Thicke? Anything that looks like a murder weapon?"

"Nothing over four inches."

"Hmm," Abberline said. "West, you want to question him? He doesn't seem to like me much. Besides, I've got to go round the Yard."

"Sure. Willy?"

"I've got my pad and pencil."

We took seats in the interview room. Pizer sat stiffly on his wooden chair.

"How long have you been in the country, Mr. Pizer?"

"Nine months."

"You come from Warsaw, don't you?"

He nodded.

"What is it you do for a living, Mr. Pizer?"

He rubbed his hands. "I'm a finisher."

"Explain, please."

"When I got off the boat I worked as a greener; three months they make me a clicker and I got to pattern and cut out the leather; now I close the uppers, shaping and stitching the leather pieces into slippers. That is all."

"Do you spend any of your money on women?"

He sighed. "For the last three months I have been working eighteen hours a day, six days a week. For that they pay me eighteen shillings a week. I am too tired for women."

"You work until late at night, don't you?"

"It's the season, of course I do. From dawn until midnight usually. I'm a finisher."

"Where were you on Friday night?"

"At my brother Gabriel's."

"Why did you go there, abandon your job?"

"There were rumours of a pogrom. I feared being deported. I was afraid."

"Are you a socialist?"

"I am a nothing. I told you, Detective, I make ballet slippers."

"We have witnesses who say you have threatened them with a knife, taken advantage of them."

"They lie!" The little man jumped up and then sat down. He was quiet again.

"You've never gone up to a woman and asked her if she would let you slap her bum?"

Pizer turned his head to the wall. I watched his body shake. At last he turned and his face and voice were controlled. "Show this woman to me. Let her accuse me to my face!"

"We have another witness who saw the last victim with a man who looked like you."

"I told you, I was at my brother's. I do not go out on the Sabbath. Oh, why me? If the newspapers print my name, I'll be ruined. I've already lost a week's work. Why me?"

"You never go out on the Sabbath? Never?"

"On that day I rest. Always."

"You wear a leather apron?"

"To protect myself from the knives, if they slip."

"Let me see your hands."

He hesitated, then held them out. They were a workman's

hands, calloused, as a cobbler's hands should be. There were dark red stains on the palms.

"That is the fruit of the mulberry."

I pressed my palms together, then released the tension, turned them over. "I, too, like mulberries, Mr. Pizer."

He smiled when he saw the purple-red palms.

"I am not a killer, Mr. Detective. I am not."

"Would you like a cup of coffee, Mr. Pizer?"

For the first time since I had approached him, Pizer's hands stopped shaking. He nodded, slowly, not taking his eyes from me. I brought three mugs and set them on the desk. Willy put away his pad. Pizer sipped and an involuntary sigh escaped his lips.

"At the sweatshop, they give us coffee for breakfast. Phoo! It is muddy water. And worse, they won't even let you sip it. 'What's all this?' the foreman says if you don't down it in gulps. 'A coffee-house? A restaurant? On Shabbas you'll have plenty of time to drink coffee.' "

We left him sipping, went out the front door and stood under its arched frame. The day was cold and a mass of heavy rain clouds the colour of unbleached linen hung on the horizon. Eight A.M. and the street was busy, men and women going in and out of public houses for their matinal moistenings, imbibing a drain of max or a ha'penny of coffee. From the bakery on Scarborough came the smell of hot cakes. The first paper boy hit the streets, began hawking pink *Globes:* "Special! Murder! Paper! Got 'im! 'ere y'are—Paper!"

"What do you think, Willy?"

"I've had my doubts since I found the knives."

"And he's right-handed."

"I noticed." Willy looked crestfallen.

"Well, let's see what the witnesses say. Hungry?"

"Not very."

"Well, I'm going to buy a paper."

"Ah, maybe just one hot cross bun."

I had to stand in line to buy a *Globe;* this case was certainly a boon to the papers. They described Pizer as satanic with grizzly strips of hair on a dark face. Soon there'd be a mob. For the first time I wished Arnold were here.

At nine we ran Pizer in an identity parade, but neither Mrs. Paddyfont nor the park keeper's wife picked him out. "Taller," they both said. "Younger."

"I think Mr. Pizer's telling the truth, Willy," I said when the blues had taken him back to his cell.

Willy went to the window and looked out at the crowd. "Now we just have to convince *them.*"

"I'll go give him the news."

Pizer was sitting cross-legged on the cot when I opened the door. I could see from his eyes that he had been crying. The breakfast he had been served sat uneaten in the corner. He saw me looking and shuddered. *"Trafeh,"* he said.

"What?"

"It's forbidden, not kosher."

"There's no pork."

"I know."

I shrugged. I lit a cigarette and offered it, and he took it quickly.

"Well, looks like you're not the leather apron we're looking for, Mr. Pizer. You passed."

"Then I may go?" He was on his feet.

"Er, I'm afraid not. There's a few things we have to sort out."

"But I'm innocent."

"And alive. We want to keep you that way. When things die down a bit, we'll release you."

"Is my name in the papers?"

"I'm afraid so."

"They accuse me of the murders?"

I nodded.

He crushed out the cigarette and sat down on the pallet, rocked back and forth. After a bit he stopped and looked up at me with deep wisdom and great weariness. He held his hands out towards me. "I wasn't a cobbler always. In Warsaw I worked for a rich man; these hands held fine leather books, books only rich men can afford."

I nodded.

"I'm not a well man," he said. "I've a carbuncle on my neck and my bowels are in an uproar. How long must I sit in this Stygian darkness?"

"I don't know. Until we can guarantee your safety."

"I'll sue the papers. I'm not a killer. I've never touched a Gentile woman in my life."

"Mr. Pizer, I believe you. But if I let you go now, you wouldn't make it fifty feet. You're safer here. If I can get you anything?"

"No."

"I'll tell your brother to bring in your meals. That's all I can do."

He nodded.

I handed him my cigarette pack and a box of brimstones, let myself out. On the way to the inquest, I had a handful of mulberries, staining my hands darker. Symbol of the devil—the white fruit turning black with sin, bloody with juice. Blood washes out easier, I thought. I thought of Ovid then, Ovid with his five thousand cures for love. And the story of the doomed Babylonian lovers Thisbe and Pyramus: the tomb beside the white mulberry tree where they agreed to tryst.

The girl Thisbe arrives first, breathless. Alone, she comes upon a young lion, fresh from the kill, the blood still on its jaws. She is frightened. She runs. And her scarf is snagged upon a tree. She does not turn back to see the great cat seize upon it and work it with his teeth.

Enter Pyramus. He sees the scarf and the blood. No Thisbe. His life is not worth living. He takes up his knife and plunges it into his heart.

Thisbe returns, sees him dead, takes up the knife, and follows him in death.

And the roots of the tree, stained with the lovers' blood, forever after yielded up the bloody fruit of the *Morus nigra.* I can understand dying for love. Or hate. I cannot understand murder without motive. What did Doyle write in his *Study in Scarlet?* "There was something so methodical and incomprehensible about the deeds of this unknown assassin, that it imparted a fresh ghastliness to his crimes." I could use a consultation. What had the killer done with that which he carried away—bagged it and thrown it out as one does the offal of a deer? Saved it? For what purpose? Would the missing portions be spoken of today at the inquest? Would the papers print it? Would my Mrs. Kelly be shocked and blush? I imagine she is pretty when she blushes.

* * *

"Oyez! Oyez!" the bailiff said, calling for the crowd to rise. Wynne Baxter entered, walked slowly down the aisle to his coroner's podium, arranged his white tie. I shifted in my seat next to Willy, uncomfortable in my starched shirt and very much aware that I was serving for the first time in official capacity as "H" Division Chief. Baxter rapped the gavel. His voice rolled out: "You good men of this district summoned to appear here this day to inquire for our Sovereign Lady the Queen, when, how, and by what means Ann Chapman came to her death, answer your names." When he had lifted the heavy roll book and called out the jurors' names, he came to the centre of the room and looked soberly at the plaque over the large oak table that held the eleven jurors. The papers had mentioned the plaque last year when young Prince Eddy had dedicated the room to the cheers of his Toynbee Hall friends.

" 'What doth the Lord require of thee, but to do justly, and to love mercy, and to walk humbly with thy God?' " Baxter read in a minister's sonorous voice. The room stilled and the jurors shifted in their sturdy oak chairs. Baxter turned from the jury to the audience: fashionably and not so fashionably dressed spectators, women as well as men; reporters with pens in their hats; Metropolitan bluecoats and plainclothes detectives in bowlers.

"As Coroner of Whitechapel, I want to express the Crown's thanks for providing us with these facilities. The Working Lads' Club has been most generous in letting us use these quarters." He smiled sardonically and stroked his copper sideburns. The penny-copy newspaper reporters scrawled furiously. "Of course, if this were the West End, no doubt the Crown would have its *own* facilities." He spun and walked back to his chair. "The Crown even must sit on borrowed chairs to dispense justice."

The audience laughed. Baxter pulled a large silk handkerchief from his pocket and dabbed at his beaded forehead. "I want to announce that in the absence of a reward from the Crown, the jury foreman has given twenty-five pounds out of pocket towards a reward. You can bet if the victim had been a rich person, the Crown itself would be offering a reward. After all," he said, "this poor woman had a soul like anyone else. When that Judas approached her, she was one of us." He turned to the jurors and nodded at the foreman. "Jurors, all rise."

While the jurors were out viewing the body in its shell, I took the opportunity to scan the room. Towards the back I saw Mrs. Kelly sitting next to a young woman with a sleeping infant. I got up and went back. She was wearing blue again today, a dark blue skirt with a moss-coloured velvet jerkin over crisply starched white puffsleeves. She had a small book upon her lap; I caught a glimpse of ankle and white hose.

"Morning, Mrs. Kelly."

"Morning to you, Mr. West." She smiled, a smile of genuine womanly feeling, and smoothed her skirts. "Isn't it horrible, her being in the same shell and all?"

"Likely she's not minding," I said gently.

"She'll not ever mind anything again, will she?"

It is strange how in a court of law as in a hospital certain liberties are permitted that would never be admissible in polite society. Here we were discussing an unnatural indelicacy with great intimacy—as we had done at the dock fire. I could say anything to her.

"How was your birthday?"

"Oh, nothing much. The picture looks grand, though."

So much to say. How the dress she wore complemented her violet eyes. "Well," I said, "perhaps we will meet again. If I can ever be of service, please don't hesitate to call upon me."

"I'll remember."

"Well, good day then." I went back to my seat next to Willy. He gave me a wink. The jurors came back and the inquest resumed. Baxter called Inspector Chandler to the box.

"Inspector, you were the first officer on the scene. Tell us what you saw when you entered the yard."

"Well, it's a square court with an outhouse and a tall fence. The body was lying to one side."

"How high is the fence?"

Chandler shrugged, held his hand across his second button.

"Didn't you measure?"

"No, I—" He broke off and looked at me.

Coroner Baxter turned to me. "Acting Superintendent West, do you have a scale drawing of the site?"

"I'm sorry, sir; no."

"This Court is handicapped enough without having to rely on approximations. We'll dismiss this witness for now and recall him after you can provide us with a drawing. Next witness."

Mrs. Long took the stand. I nudged Willy. "Want to come with me?"

"Sure." We took our hats and ducked out.

"I thought Abberline would have had that done," Willy said.

"Well, let's get on with it. Don't mind Baxter; he's all bark."

"Is he?"

On the stairs a blue came running up, telegram in hand. I opened it. "It's from Abberline. From Gravesend: he's arrested a suspect named William Pigott; the man had blood on his clothes and a bite mark on his hand. He admits to being in Buck's Row the night of the first murder. He'll bring him in tomorrow."

"Gravesend. I was there once on an outing."

"Me, too." In the burial yard of St. George's parish church lies the gravestone of Pocahontas; foreign visitors are greeted there; it is the starting point of all expeditions. "I hope his expedition bears fruit," I said.

We took a hansom to the site, threading our way round green omnibuses and four-wheelers. Number Twenty-nine Hanbury was deserted today. I took the measurements while Willy sketched the plan. "Height of fence, five feet, two inches. Length. . . ." Not halfway through, a small, ragged urchin tugged on my trousers. I looked down into a pair of doleful brown eyes.

"Mister, you a copper?"

"Aye."

She tugged at my leg to follow her, then scampered off. I shrugged; Willy and I followed her round the dividing fence into the yard of No. 27 Hanbury; she pointed her thin, dirty finger at the fence. Stains. At first I thought it was urine. I wet my handkerchief and dabbed, saw the telltale hue of pink. Bloodstains, splatters ranging from the size of a pinhead to that of a sixpence, as if someone had taken a bloody coat and slapped it against the fence. I looked round the yard: a rubbish dump of old cans and leaves; it hadn't been cleaned in aeons.

"Over here," Willy said. "Abberline must have missed it in the dark." He handed me a pale yellow sheet of newspaper smeared with dark blood. The *Echo,* a ha'penny rag founded by a philanthropist.

"Looks like the killer wiped his hands on it." I unfolded the paper and looked at the date. "The evening before the murder."

"And look here. Damn!" Willy was on an ashcan, looking down into No. 25 Hanbury. "There's a trail of blood here. He must have escaped this way. If we'd had bloodhounds, we could have tracked him!"

"If we'd known there was a trail we might have had hounds. What a cock-up."

When we got back to the inquest, the landlady, Mrs. Richardson, was in the box.

"Did you know that your yard was sometimes used for immoral purposes?" Baxter was saying.

"Certainly not. I'd never have stood for such a shocking thing," the woman said.

"Did you hear anything that night out of the ordinary?"

"Not a thing."

Baxter asked her a few more questions, then called her son and put the same questions to him.

"Of course I knew what the courtyard was used for," said he. "It's common knowledge. That yard was a favourite place for trysts."

"Son!"

"Mother, I'm under oath."

When the laughing died down, Baxter cleared his throat. "You told the officers that the apron found in the tap was yours, did you not?"

"Yes, I washed and left it there Thursday night."

"Thursday night. Almost thirty-six hours before the crime?"

"Yes."

"Hmm. Let us enter the apron as Exhibit C." He turned to the bailiff. "Let the jury see the exhibit."

"But, sir—"

"Yes?"

The bailiff approached the bench and whispered in Baxter's ear.

"Well, where the deuce is it? Acting Superintendent West, do you know the apron's whereabouts?"

I stood. "Inspector Abberline informed me that it was in analysis at the Yard. Isn't it?"

"Apparently not. Now, how are we to show Mr. Richardson an apron to identify if there is no apron? Very well, Mr. Richardson, you may step down. We will ask you to return when our laboratory has found the missing apron. We'll break now for dinner."

* * *

"Strange isn't it, about the apron?" I said to Willy over a meat pie.

"What's strange about incompetence?"

"Not that. I meant what Richardson said about it. Thirty-six hours he said the apron lay in the sink. You know a piece of string cannot go unclaimed on Whitechapel for three minutes."

"Unless it's tied down."

I laughed. "But it's true. Even a bit of blackened apple core is salvaged and eaten; children crack open the pits of discarded greengages to eat the kernels; anything that can be eaten or sold for a penny is fair game for the petty pilferers. And yet an apron worth a shilling remains for two days in a sink? It doesn't make sense."

"You think the chap was lying?"

"I don't know. Why would he?"

"Dunno. Hey, here comes Helson, let's ask him."

"No, it's probably nothing."

"Have you heard about the big reward?" Helson said when he was still ten feet off.

"Did the Queen change her mind?"

"Oh, it's not the Crown's money. Seems a bunch of Hebes formed a vigilante today in the Crown Public House. If we can't catch him, they will, they're saying. They've started collecting for a hundred-pound pot."

"A vigilante?"

"A vigilance society. A butcher, a baker, a cigar maker. Chairman's a Mr. George Lusk."

"Well, good luck to them."

"You think a Hebe'd turn in a Hebe?" He pulled his mustache. "Come to think of it, it might work. Thirty pieces of silver. . . ."

"Come on, Willy, let's get back to the inquest. You coming, Helson?"

"Nah, got some sleuthing to do."

The first witness called when the court reconvened was Albert Cadoche. I had been expecting George Philips' medical testimony.

"My name is Albert Cadoche," the grey-haired man said. "I live next door to Twenty-nine Hanbury—Number Thirty-one."

"Tell us what transpired the morning of eight September."

"I woke up that morning and went out back. That's when I heard a woman crying out 'No! No!' over the tall fence, then the sound of a scuffle. Then a loud bump against the fence and silence."

"What did you do then?"

"Why, nothing, sir."

"You weren't concerned that a crime was being committed?"

"No. I thought little of it 'til I heard the news. I often hear such things."

"Were you on your way to work, Mr. Cadoche?"

"No, I had just gone out."

"Why?"

"To relieve myself, sir."

"Ah, yes. You may step down."

* * *

An ordinary night in Stepney.

* * *

When I got back to the station, I wired the Yard about the apron. In half an hour I received an answer:

NO SIGN OF APRON IN ANALYSIS OR ANYWHERE ELSE
STOP ADVISE CORONER IT IS LOST STOP
MY REGRETS STOP A F WILLIAMSON

"Damnation!" I said it so loud Willy came running.

"Just call us the 'defective department,' the men in blue shining with crapulous decrepitude. Can't we do anything right—just once?"

Willy patted me on my back and asked if I'd had my supper. I hadn't. Even when I did, it didn't help.

* * *

In the *Gazette* tonight is the long-awaited Conan Doyle story. I find I cannot read it. Last Yuletime I devoured his *Study in Scarlet* in *Beeton's* with the utmost absorption. Now, even with the coincidence of the character's name, James West, I have no appetite.

I, James Fothergill West . . . have endeavoured in the ensuing pages to lay my statement before the public in a concise and business-like fashion. . . .

I find myself instead thinking back to Sherlock Holmes—what
he said about a man's brain:

> . . . you have to stock it with such furniture as you choose.
> A fool takes in all the lumber of every sort that he comes
> across, so that the knowledge which might be useful to him
> gets crowded out, or at best is jumbled up with a lot of other
> things. . . . Now the skilful workman is very careful in-
> deed as to what he takes into his brain-attic. He will have
> nothing but the tools which may help him in doing his work,
> but of these he has a large assortment, all in the most perfect
> order. It is a mistake to think that that little room has elastic
> walls and can distend to any extent.

According to Doyle's story, the best tool is knowledge of what
has come before:

> There is a strong family resemblance about misdeeds, and if
> you have all the details of a thousand at your finger ends, it
> is odd if you can't unravel the thousand and first.

Was there ever a crime like this?
The Ratcliff Highway murders? Perhaps. Seventy-seven years
ago almost to the month since John Williams made his debut on
the stage of Ratcliff and executed those murders which De Quincey says make the connoisseur in murder very fastidious in his
taste, murders so deeply crimson as to make all other murders
pale. An entire family cut to pieces, the baby bludgeoned in its
crib. And then he did it again—and the killer turned out to be the
most benevolent soft-voiced gentleman you would want to meet.
Ratcliff. A strange thought comes to me—the dock fires the
night of the first murder. Very strange, for the first fire blazed up
not a stone's throw from the site of the first Ratcliff slaughter, the
second but a skip and jump from the site of the second. Coincidence? Or deliberate? Some sort of diversion—or herald? I am
stuck. Have we a competitor here? Some highflier on our hands, a
connoisseur of crime determined to make the Ratcliff murders
pale? The kingdom has outlaws and dodgers aplenty but only a
handful of artful assassins. The Ratcliff highwayman is legend;
we applaud the young Glasgow lass Madeleine Smith, who mur-

dered her French seducer with arsenic and *belles lettres*. There
are not many more.

I cannot sleep so I turn again to Doyle's story, but I still cannot read. I am too caught up in my own murder for fiction. My
brain is on edge, as acutely tuned as a safecracker's fingers. It
goes over and over the details, sifting and sorting. Is he leaving us
clues?

When Sherlock Holmes was called to the scene, he found a
locked room and a dead man inside. On the corner wall the
murderer had written in blood the word "RACHE."

He must have been starting to write the female name Rachel,
the detective surmised. "No," said Holmes, " 'Rache' is the German for 'revenge.' " He then described the killer.

What can I tell you about our killer? A shabby genteel sort of
fellow in a deerstalker hat. He wiped his bloody knife and hands
upon an *Echo*—the newspaper Sherlock Holmes reads—and disappeared into the labyrinth.

Tuesday, September 11, 1888

It is to be hoped that the police and their amateur assistants are not confining their attention to those who look like "horrid ruffians." Many of the occupants of the Chamber of Horrors look like local preachers, members of Parliament, or monthly nurses. We incline to the belief that the murderer is a victim of erotic mania which often takes the shape of an uncontrollable taste for blood. The Marquis de Sade, who died in a lunatic asylum at the age of seventy-four, after a life spent in qualifying for admission to gaol and escaping from prison, was an amiable-looking gentleman, and so, possibly enough, may be the Whitechapel murderer.

—*Pall Mall Gazette*

ʄʄʄ

Under the wooden Grosvenor wharf this morning a group of children found what they thought was the carcass of a small fat white dog. The flies were buzzing round it, and, as children do, one of them picked up a pebble and amused himself by having a go at it.

They had "killed" it many times over when a workman named Moore heard what he thought was chanting. He had been lounging on a bench upon the small green strip of Pimlico Gardens beside the Gibson statue; the noise had disturbed his reverie and he had risen and walked past the statue of the classic nude figure in the bath and gone down to Ebury Bridge to see what was about. He thought it was a dog, too, and he chased the children away. The target turned out to be an arm, a human arm.

The "A" Division surgeon, Mr. Neville, who served as a medical officer in the Crimean War and therefore has great experience with such matters, pronounced it a medical school prank. As he has known quite a few medical students, it is highly possible. Ask any surgeon about his medical school days: Constant exposure to death creates a callow kind of humour, an objectiveness about the subject of flesh and blood and bones that mere mortals often find offensive. In any event, there are no "vital parts" and there will be no inquest. I sent George Philips over to "A" for a look—who knows these days when you will find a body to go with an arm?

Philips wired me from Neville's surgery to meet him at Abberline's office.

"It is the right arm of a well-nourished, nervous, fair-skinned brunette," Philips said, drawing deeply on his pipe. "She was perhaps twenty-one, and she was alive three days ago. The arm was severed after death."

"Quite amazing," I said. "Go on."

"I don't think it was a student's prank."

"Everyone is a Sherlock Holmes these days, don't you think, West?" Abberline rocked back in his chair. "So how do you make such a deduction, Mr. Philips?"

"Logic."

Abberline laughed. "You've left out her profession and her name."

"Not a labourer, perhaps a woman of means," Philips said. "Her name I can't tell you."

I whistled. "How in the deuce do you deduce all that? You've got a stinking swollen arm that's been battered with stones."

"Her hands are not worn, and the skin on her arms is smooth and white, if plump. A workingwoman bares her arm for work, uses her hands, gets freckles and calluses. The length of the bone tells me she is not a child. The hair under the armpit tells me she is a woman and a dark-haired one at that. No moles or age marks, and the skin is taut—she is not middle-aged. She bites her fingernails." He took a breath, bowed.

"What about the medical school prank? You said you doubted Neville."

"I'm not sure. The arm appears to have been severed from the socket more with force than with the care of the operating room. Anatomical skill, yes, but precision, no. We know it was severed after death because of the lack of muscle contraction."

"Perhaps a beginning student?" Abberline said.

"Perhaps. It is hard to say after three days, but my guess is that the arm was separated immediately after death. You might ask Openshaw to have a look. He's the expert. In any case, if there's a student running round with a board loose in his barn, Openshaw's sure to know his name."

"Good idea," Abberline said. He looked at his watch. "West,

I've got a meeting at Whitehall. Why don't you wire Openshaw and see if he can spare you a few minutes."

* * *

As I walked down Commercial towards Whitechapel, I thought of all the medical students I'd known. One who'd killed himself by jumping off a bridge. One who cut off his finger. Perhaps our killer was one. A medical student would know that if he strangled her first there would be less blood. He would know how to cut and dissect. He wouldn't shake and quiver and give himself away just because he had sliced human flesh. Myself, I couldn't do it. Oh, I can understand murder—after all, I'm a copper. At George's Yard I saw gore and passion without blanching. The hate in those wounds! The blood. The overturned flowerpots and scuffled earth. But the cold clinical dismembering of an anonymous victim? I have always preached getting to know your victim. When you know your victim you will know who killed her. Look to the victim and the person next to her, look to those who loved her enough to hate her. The trail grows cold so quickly when the victim does not know her murderer.

All I do know is that neither of the men we are holding behind bars did the deed. William Pigott is a lunatic. Two hours after Abberline brought him back from Gravesend and put him in a cell, he was ranting and raving and fighting off invisible bugs and snakes. He has also confessed to impregnating Queen Victoria and killing the Prince Consort. He shall be off in an hour under a light escort to the asylum at Bow. We shall release Pizer tomorrow.

I'd missed my elevenses. Might as well miss dinner. I took a hansom over to Pimlico and had a look round the foreshore of The Embankment. The houses are quite nice, neat creamy stucco. The dock itself is old, and the pebbles under it dirty; sewage and dead fish float up on the tide. On the Strand coming back, I saw a woman selling flowers and bid the driver to stop. I gave her sixpence for her bouquet of violets, Chinese asters, and pink roses. She smiled and thanked me. It was Polly and Annie I was thinking of, women downtrodden by life itself, happy to get an extra fourpence, grasping the last rung of respectability.

My appointment at London Hospital was for half past three. As I approached, the chimes sounded from the clock tower. An endless day. The long, dusty front of the hospital stretches the whole block. It is built on a slight rise—the debris of the Great Fire—and one must climb a mountain of steps to the front door. To the left is the old cholera wing that covers the bones of a plague pit from the same year. They built the pits after the churchyards swelled up and began heaving out bodies, such was the destruction of the Black Death, the plague, spread by fleas on rats. Ignorant, they killed the cats that killed the rats, and the Black Death bloomed. Thousands and thousands perished.

I walked in and downstairs to the Pathological Museum. Thomas Horrocks Openshaw was at a microscope, looking at a slide.

"Well, Dr. Openshaw, have we another victim or a hoax?"

"I haven't seen the arm so I won't venture a judgement."

"But it could be a prank?"

"Certainly."

"Would a medical student have access to such a part?"

"At a price."

"What would it cost?"

"The price of a corpse is three pound five. You can purchase a corpse at the postmortem room twelve hours after death."

"Can one buy a part?"

"You can buy an arm or a leg or a head and neck for fifteen shillings."

"I thought Burke and Hare got eight quid for their bodies."

"You're right. That was before they changed the laws. Now it's legal to sell bodies."

"Do you have any students who might pull such a prank?"

"Oh, many."

"And any who might murder?"

"We had a student last year who was quite crackers—name of John Sanders—he dropped out. And another dotty fellow by the name of Fitzroy. I think he lived at St. Johns Wood. But that was two years ago. Believe he went abroad. Not much help, I know. I'll drop by and look at the arm if you like. By the way, will you see Mr. Merrick today?"

I looked at my watch. I had only visited the Elephant Man twice, the first time out of curiosity, the second time out of pity.

"He had a good night. He'll be glad of a visit," Openshaw said.

"I'll be glad to see him for a few minutes." I rose to go and

then turned back. "Tell me, what about the other parts . . .
those . . . parts the killer took away? Can you buy those, too?"

"Those flaccid parts can be had for the asking at any postmortem room."

* * *

I climbed the spiral stairway to the sixth floor and knocked at
the blue door. John Merrick opened it; he had just combed his
hair and the first thing I smelled was pomade. Inside, the light
was a pale rose, filtered by a lamp with a veil of pink tissue. It is a
shock each time, but I find that within minutes I have forgotten
the creature and see only the urbane man.

He speaks softly.

"Mr. West, how kind of you to honour me with a visit." He
offered his right hand and I took it and squeezed gently. The skin
is white and delicate, a hand any woman would envy. The hand
he holds behind his back is loathsome, the fingers thick and tu-
berous, grown over with a pendulant brown cauliflower mass—
more a fin than a hand.

"Please sit down, Mr. West, and excuse me for standing."

I met his good brown eye, the single mark of humanity in his
gnarled giant head, nodded and sat. His condition makes it very
painful for him to sit or sleep; he stands—I suppose one must say
stoops, for the weight of his head bows him down greatly—with
his right side angled out. The left side is monstrous: the eye oc-
cluded by the funguslike osseous growth of his forehead, a bony
mass as large as a bread loaf.

"Do you mind if I smoke?" I said.

"No, please do. I'm sorry I don't have any of your cigarettes. I
remembered last time, but I had another visitor."

"I've my own. No need for you to trouble yourself." I took out
a fag and lit it, inhaled deeply.

He stood leaning against the high windowsill, the gnarled eye
looking out, the good eye turned to me. "Dr. Openshaw says you
have quite a case on your hands."

"It's baffling. No discernible motive."

"I was awake here at the window that first night. But it was
dark. I'm afraid I saw nothing."

I rose and walked to the window, looked down. There was a

clear view of the street and the alley leading to the slaughter-house.

"I didn't expect you to have seen anything."

"Those poor women . . ." He turned full and his face quivered, the pink stump that was his mouth opening and closing. "I wish there were something I could do."

"We all do, Mr. Merrick. Pray to God we find him before he commits another."

The quivering stopped. "I pray thus every night. But now let me make you tea, Mr. West. I can make it quite well."

Tea was the last thing I wanted, for his body gave off an odious stench; I feared offending him, though, so assented and took a chair. I watched him prepare the tea with his good hand, his dropsical form hovering anxiously over the burner, the finlike hand moving now and then to aid the other.

Merrick watched me as I drank my tea. "You hold your cup like *she* does. It's not too hot, is it?"

"No, not at all." I sipped noisily.

"She says it's always too hot, but that she likes it that way."

His voice was a lover's voice, full of the loved one. I knew he was talking about Alexandra, Princess of Wales, future Queen of England. It is his favourite subject; the last time I visited, he showed me the shrines in the spartan room. "That pillow there, her little dog sat upon it. And the bone-china cup on the sideboard; that is hers." He is, one might say, obsessed with her.

We all love our Royalty, hold their lives as a kind of national treasure we're all entitled to speak about and live through vicariously. They may not even be English, but they rule us by destiny. They are our fairy tales. We all have our favourites. Frankly, I prefer the old Queen with all her regal mystery. I garner great pleasure from knowing that in her castle she breakfasts spartanly on a boiled egg—even if she does eat it from a golden cup with a golden spoon. The thought of her riding out in her open barouche, her dour face framed by her antediluvian bonnet, fills me with peace and complacency. She is the Monarch.

In contrast, Victoria's son is an arch vulgarian, less than nothing in my eyes, with all the old Hanoverian flaws; his nickname, "Spuds," is an applicable one, and I always think of him as an enormous potato ready for the pot. Yet he is popular—I suppose because he exemplifies all the vices Englishmen are so fond of. Love them or hate them, they are ours, these Hanoverians and

Guelphs. Alexandra may be lame and deaf and her beauty more enamel than natural; the future King may be a glutton and professional lover and bad friend; the young swan-necked heir Prince Eddy, an enigma even unto himself; his sisters ugly ducklings—but they lead charmed lives. They are ours.

"They say she is very bewitching," I said.

Merrick made a noise that was half cry, half sigh. "The Princess is the most perfect woman in the world. She is so fair, and she never grows old. Did you notice that? It's ironic, isn't it?"

"What is, Mr. Merrick?"

"My being able to sit and talk with her. She sat right where you are sitting, her little Pekinese in her lap, and told me a delightful story about her cockatoo mimicking one of her American friends. 'Cocky,' he is called."

"The American?"

Merrick laughed, then sobered. "If I'd been a normal man, I would never have known her." His mouth quivered. "I might . . . almost . . . make such a trade."

He lowered his head, then walked to the window and looked out. "She is a saint—when I had my last operation she came and held my hand, told me of her own surgery and how the knife had saved her life, told me how she has had to go through life half-deaf and half-lame. How brave she has been!"

"Was she ill recently?"

"Oh, this was long past. She had an attack of the 'king's evil.' Like Charles II, the lymph nodes swelled up so badly she couldn't breathe. It left a horrible scar. The ladies think it's fashionable, but she hates to wear those high collars. Prince Albert Victor also suffered the operation when he was but a lad of fourteen—typhoid. Now he too must wear high collars forever. Do you know, she's coming home soon? She and her daughters have been visiting her family in Copenhagen. She has promised a visit on her way to the countryside."

A strange sight they must make together, the Elephant Man and our Queen of Hearts, foulest and fairest.

"Do you think Prince Eddy will marry soon?" I said. "Tuesday's *Court Circular* certainly suggested romance."

"Romance in bloom for Albert Victor? That would be delightful. The House of Hesse is an ancient one. It goes all the way back to Charlemagne. But his mother says he is really just a child."

"At four and twenty?"

"She says he is a dear, sweet child, though he smokes too much, but not yet ready for marriage. Like you, Mr. West, one end used to light the next."

I ground out my cigarette in the potted plant. "You're right. It's a vile habit. Well, who knows? They say his cousin is pretty as a picture. Blond and sweet sixteen."

"Have you seen a photograph?"

"Not yet."

We parted with a handshake. Strange, I was used to him now, to the point where now the white hand seemed the deformed freak of nature.

The air was fresh and pure outside, and a gusty breeze made the women's parasols dip and dance. The lass on the corner smiled at me. "Apples, fine apples, ha'penny a lot." I smiled back. Even the mudlarks seemed clean. I gulped large breaths and practically danced my way back to the station in the flickering windblown sunlight of the waning afternoon. To be shut forever in that room, to have to rely on the world to come to you—I should hang myself in a minute! Such a gentle man, so graced with goodness. Perhaps God has granted him the goodness in direct proportion to the hideousness without. I should visit him more often.

When I leave Merrick I am always pensive. We all have our deformities, our dark sides we reveal to none. He must wear his as a face. Which meant, since God rules in heaven, our sinister killer might have the face and form of an angel.

My hand strays to my throat, lingers. Both of them, mother and son, hiding the life-giving scars below scarf and collar. I wonder how it feels to have your throat cut. I wonder what kind of scar it leaves. Royalty can at least change fashion itself to hide the wounds.

Wednesday, September 12, 1888

As an advertisement nothing is so effective as one which is printed in capitals all gory red with human blood. Terrible crimes have their uses, like pestilences, earthquakes and other revelations of the unseen forces which in ordinary times slumber unnoticed in our midst.

—Pall Mall Gazette

ʄʄʄ

I signed Pizer's release as soon as I had finished the morning reports, took it over to Leman Street and personally unlocked the cell. Pizer was sitting on his cot eating a plate of wizened herrings. He looked smaller than he had last time, but as soon as he was out of the cell door he seemed to swell up; his courage returned.

"I'll sue every last one of you," he was telling the reporters as he made his way past the crowd and down the steps.

Helson was just coming up. "Letting the Hebe go, eh?"

"About time."

"I still say it has to be one of them." Helson spat into the spittoon.

"Why has to?"

"It has to be a local, that's how I see it. How else could he know the back alleys and courts? And since this area is ninety-five per cent Hebe. . . ."

"Two flaws in your argument. First, he wouldn't have to know anything except how to pick up a whore on the high street. They know the back alleys; they even know the police schedules. Besides, yesterday you were saying it was a Siberian surgeon."

"Yeah, well, 'Y' Division telegraphed. They're holding the Russian all right—in a straitjacket. Not our 'butcher.' What's the second flaw?"

"We live here, don't we? I don't see any sidelocks on your face. And there's plenty others who aren't Jews. Especially at night."

"Sure, Indians, Malays—coloureds. I still think it's a Hebe, though. You know, the highest Hebe holy day falls this weekend: The Day of Atonement, Yom Kippur. I'd bet good money he's going to strike again."

"If he does, will it prove he is Jewish?"

"Ah, West. Hey, Fred, what do you think?"

Fred Abberline came in and pulled out a chair.

"Frankly," Abberline said, "I'm hoping he's not Jewish. We'd have a hard time holding this station against a determined crowd."

"You know what Rack told me," Helson said. "If a Hebe has sex with a Gentile woman he has to kill her to purify himself."

"But why butcher her?" I said.

"Got me. Who knows? Probably just a cheap bastard wouldn't pay for his fun, then she cut up nasty like, and he did her in."

I shook my head. "You know anything about these holidays, Abberline?"

"Just what I've seen over the years. This is a big one. But all they do is pray all day. And stop eating."

Helson grinned. "Yeah, and make these blood sacrifices to the devil and such."

"Oh, stubble it, Helson." I turned back to Abberline. "Who could tell me about them?"

"Well, you could talk to the Ashkenazi rabbi. I've been thinking it might not hurt to contact him."

"The what rabbi?"

"Their chief, over at the Great Synagogue on Duke Street. If you've got time you could kill two birds with one stone. Get a lesson on the holidays and feel him out about this Old Testament sacrifice talk."

"I'll make time."

"Don't worry," Helson said, "your paperwork will still be there when you get back."

"Thanks."

I went out and down the stairs onto Leman. Two six-year-old girls and their infant charges were sitting on the stoop playing the button-counting game.

"Rich man, poor man, beggarman, thief," said the urchin in the grey sack. They both laughed.

"Now count mine!"

"Rich man, poor man, beggarman, thief, doctor, lawyer, Indian chief. Rich man—! Ah, lucky you."

They looked up as I passed and then returned to their game. I walked north in glum silence through the clogged streets. The day was dark and dull, dun-coloured. Dun skies, dun streets, dun buildings, dun lives—now emblazoned by this meaningless game of death. We still do not know who or why. Rich man, poor man, beggarman, thief, doctor, lawyer, Indian chief? The papers are howling for blood: Commissioner Warren's, Home Secretary Matthews', even Prime Minister Salisbury's. As if they were to blame. Of course, there has been incompetency, but it is more than that: Without a motive the killer can slip like a cat into the shadows, fade away. If only I knew *why* I might begin to know *who*.

Halfway down Duke Street I saw a knot of people looking in at the showcase window of a photographer's studio. From their cries of admiration I was sure it was another bare-legged actress, but when I pressed close I saw it was a photographic print of Princess Alix of Hesse, the young woman who is perhaps at this very moment partaking of tea with the Queen and her grandson. On the blue velvet cloth next to her is a photograph of her "intended," the young heir Prince Albert Victor Christian Edward, known since birth as "Eddy." Aquiline features, a long neck rising from a high white starched collar, doe-shaped dark eyes, receding hairline. Stiff, bespatted, like a tailor's dummy, he sits, something of the air of a sleepwalker about him, hand resting just below his thick gold watch chain, practised in the genteel conduct of the cane, an *arbiter elegantiarum*.

Perhaps he has taken this moment to press his suit, to touch his cousin's glove, or perhaps even to steal a kiss while the old lady is not looking. She is a lovely lass with rosy cheeks and golden hair. Not unlike another I know but have vowed not to think of so.

I walked on; ahead of me rose the stately facade of the Great Synagogue, once upon a time a Wesleyan chapel.

Rabbi Adler was lighting the gas in the fish-tail burner when I entered his office behind the Temple. He looked like an English clergyman; only the skullcap on his balding head distinguished him as a Jew.

"Chief Inspector West," Adler said, giving me a firm handshake. His accent was Etonian. "I was expecting you. You really must appeal to your superiors to do something. We have had assaults every day since Sunday."

"We've a quarter of our men on foot patrol."

"It's not enough. We've already had heads bashed; someone is going to get killed."

"And the newspapers don't think we have enough men tracking the killer. We can't please everyone, Rabbi. I did want you to know that we released Mr. Pizer about an hour ago, gave him an escort home."

"And I thank you for that. But what is the poor man to do now? He's lost his job and is afraid to set foot upon the street. If there's another murder, the crowd is liable to come hunting him with a rope. He'll sue, you know."

"He might win."

"Can't you appeal to your superiors for extra men?"

"The Yard is in a bit of a tangle at the moment. It would require special funding. Not that we don't need them. That's why I came. I'd like your help in finding the killer."

"How can I help? The killer is not Jewish."

"Then why did he pick the Jewish section of London? Why did he kill on your Jewish Holy Days? It's hard to think there is no connexion. Frankly, I'm afraid about this weekend. I understand that Friday is the beginning of your day of sacrifice."

He nodded. "And I fear for my people."

"That's why you must help me. If there's a killing on this day, it is your people who will suffer."

"I will tell you one thing. If—*if* he is a man born Jewish—and I do not believe he is—then he is a Jew who has turned his back on God—not a man who observes the rites. If he is a Jew, he is a Jew who no longer calls himself Jewish—one of those socialists! You know, if there is a killing on the Day of Atonement, I can tell you exactly where to look. Not here. Not in Temple."

"Where?"

"Go look at their headquarters, Forty Berner Street. There are men born Jewish there who reserve their *particular* scorn for this Holy Day, who would as soon desecrate it as spit. If he's a Jew he'll be there at the working man's clubhouse, eating pork pies and listening to cart-end haranguers denounce the Lord."

"Can you tell me a little bit about this weekend's holiday."

"Yom Kippur? Yom Kippur is the Day of Atonement, the Sabbath of Sabbaths, a day of solemn rest and fasting, of ritual cleansing—of sins, of debts, of old enmities—a day of forgiveness. It begins at dusk with the singing of the Kol Nidre."

"You use a different calendar?"

"Yes. Yom Kippur is the tenth day of Tishri, the first month of our civil calendar. We use the old Egyptian calendar; I believe your Masonic lodges use it as well."

"Is there any ritual sacrifice connected with it, Rabbi?"

Adler scratched his smooth chin and looked at me hard. "We are always to blame, wherever we go. Yes, there is a sacrifice or used to be."

"What kind? Human?"

He looked at me with disgust. "A goat. A scapegoat."

"Rabbi, I'm just trying to prevent another death, not persecute anyone. I've got two sacrificial victims; it might be a motive."

"I'll do all I can to aid the police in understanding, but the killer is not one of ours."

"You don't know that." I waved my hand in the direction of the street. "There are so many demented out there—you can't know them all. I'm just looking for some pattern, I'm looking to *disprove* as much as I can. I'm not trying to fit some design upon anyone. I need to understand."

"You need a scapegoat."

"I want to stop another killing. It's my job."

He nodded. "Very well. Yom Kippur is the day Moses came down from the mountain with the tablets and pardoned the people for the sin of the golden calf. A goat is sacrificed; under our ancient law, two goats, one to the Lord and one to Azazel. Our people abstain from food and drink . . . and from sexual relations. At the end of the holiday the Neilah is sung; the day ends with a single blast on the shophar."

"Who performs the sacrifice—the slaughterman, your sochey?"

"Sochet."

"What if a sochet went mad? He would have the knowledge of anatomy, the tool . . ."

"I find that a difficult proposition to accept."

"Why?"

"To begin with, the papers say these women were killed with a pointed blade. The khalef knife used for slaughtering bullocks is single-edged. No point."

"Are you sure?"

"I can have a man bring one by the station. Single-edged. Your detectives have talked to every sochet in Whitechapel. Didn't they observe that simple fact?"

I swallowed. Damnation! The men had sent back their reports on six-inch blades and failed to remark on the one small detail that mattered. One more for the defective department!

"How does the sochet kill the goat, Rabbi? What did you say, two goats, one for the Lord and one for—?"

"Azazel, the demon Satan. He hobbles it with ropes and then cuts its throat. The knife must be perfect, without blemish."

"Does he sever the windpipe?"

"No, he does not."

"And the blood?"

"He lets it drain from the throat."

"He doesn't save it, take it away?"

"No, it is not that kind of sacrifice." He sighed. "Do you know why Jews soak meat in salt water before they cook it?"

I shook my head.

"To drain more blood. Because there is nothing a Jew abhors more than the sight of bloody meat. The blood is the seat of life, don't you see? It *is* the life. The whole system of shehitah revolves round that. From the moment he is born, a Jew is taught taboos against consuming blood."

"I—"

"And there is nothing a Jew is taught to view with greater horror than the mutilation of a dead body."

"A dead Jewish body?"

"Any body, be it Jew or Gentile."

I sighed. "There are so many stories. So much fear. Tell me, Rabbi, what is a golem?"

He smiled. "A golem? Is he being accused as well?"

"It was just a story I heard, an old Polish woman in the market who said the killer had special powers, that he was invisible."

"It is a legend. The great Judah Loew created a golem to serve him; only it ran amok and became a killer. But there are many golems."

"Any that are connected with ritual murders?"

"Only in modern literature. The true golem is mentioned in the Bible—Adam is called a golem. It means a body without a soul, as Adam's was during the first half day. It means something unformed, imperfect. A sort of a homunculus."

"A what?"

"A creature, one made in an artificial way, perhaps by virtue of magic. It has to do with the creative power of the letters of the name of God, the Kabala."

I smiled. "Sometimes I really think he is a phantom. I can't imagine a man doing what he does."

"But you can imagine a Jew?"

"Damnation, that's not fair, Rabbi. Of course it's a man. And it's my job to ask questions, even those you might consider indelicate."

"Ask what you will."

"All right, I will. Someone down at the station said he'd heard how a Jew who sleeps with a Gentile is considered soiled; he has sinned, and—"

"It is a sin to look at any woman with lust."

I raised an eyebrow, pursued my thought. "—that only by killing her can he become pure again."

"No, Inspector. It's not true."

"There's another rumour." I hesitated. "It's about an elixir vitae."

"Well, tell me your story and I will try very hard not to get angry."

"I heard it from a German baker over on Commercial. He tells me there is a story about a special candle made by Jews whose fumes will render anyone unconscious. It is made from a . . . a uterus."

Adler suddenly turned red. He rose and strode across the room. "Peasants, stupid peasants. Do you see what poverty does? Shall we never get out of the Dark Ages?" He hit the table and then turned to me. "Next thing you know, they'll claim there was no blood because a Jew drank it. You know, if I were sleuthing, I'd look at your own earnest churchgoers. It's not our temples that are preaching doomsday. Go this weekend to any church and you'll hear talk of the Anti-Christ, of the Second Coming. Listen to your own Dr. Robert Anderson preach on the coming of the end of the world."

"Then why does the killer pick the Jewish section?"

"You're the detective, not me."

"And I've much to learn. Just one more question. You said something about sacrificing two goats, one to the Lord and one to —I can't remember."

"Azazel. Azazel the arch demon, the fallen angel. In the Bible, when the sons of God began to marry the daughters of men, Azazel was their leader. The Flood was the world's punishment."

"Genesis 6. 'There were giants in the earth in those days . . . when the sons of God came in unto the daughters of men, and they bare children to them . . .' "

Adler smiled. "I see you know your Old Testament. Azazel—or a scapegoat—must die in order to purify the Holy of Holies."

"Holy of Holies?"

"The Sanctum Sanctorum. The Temple."

"But, Rabbi, doesn't that scripture suggest punishment for sleeping with one not of your kind?"

He nodded, smiled benignly. "You should study Talmud, Inspector."

"What about that other word, *Neilah?*"

"The Neilah celebrates the closing of the gate of the Temple, as the final judgement is sealed."

I thought of the gates then, the gate at Buck's Row and the gate leading into Hanbury. Both had been closed. Coincidence? I leaned forward. "There's another line of scripture that keeps coming back to me, Rabbi. 'Ye shall hate the harlot and make her desolate and naked and shall eat her flesh . . .' "

"Ezekiel."

"Couldn't it be a fanatic? Some earnest Old Testament religionist with the delusion that he has a mission to extirpate vice by killing whores? It wouldn't even have to be a Jew."

"Not likely. According to the Old Testament, you kill a harlot by strangulation or stoning, never by cutting her throat."

"What?"

He nodded, smiled smugly. "And these women had their throats cut, didn't they?"

I walked back to the station deep in thought. "There's the scarlet threat of murder running through the colourless skein of life"—and I must unravel it, isolate it, expose every inch of it. You kill a harlot by strangulation, never by cutting her throat. I was right. The knife comes after. The murderer didn't sneak up on his prey; he coddled up to them. No warning knife. No struggle. No scream.

But why mutilate her afterwards? What kind of man kills a woman and carries away her sex? Why? It is a mystery. A riddle. Had the sphinx posed a more difficult one? I had to smile—and the sphinx strangled those who could not answer the riddle.

"Ye shall hate the harlot and make her desolate and naked and shall eat her flesh. . . ." A harlot killer? The scarlet thread hangs loose and I grasp one end and pull. Did they die because of what they were? Because they were fallen angels? The thread will not pull out; it is snagged within the skein. A blood sacrifice? One for the Lord and one for Azazel. If so, perhaps the sacrifice has been made; perhaps the evil is over.

Just then my reverie was broken as I stepped in a pile of fresh manure. I looked up and round at the blackened buildings: gin houses, flash houses, doss houses, slap-bangs, lurks—all filled with the wretches of humanity: screevers, shofulmen, snakesmen, speelers, stickmen, dollymops, mumpers, and macers. There was much talk of appealing to the Crown to cleanse this blight. I sighed and scraped my foot against the curbstone. It would take a deluge of forty days to cleanse the dirt from the Evil Quarter Mile.

And God saw that the wickedness of man was great in the earth, and that every imagination of the thoughts of his heart was only evil continually. . . . And the Lord said, I will destroy man whom I have created from the face of the earth, both man, and beast, and the creeping thing, and the fowls of the air; for it repenteth me that I have made them.

Friday, September 14, 1888

𝓕 𝓕 𝓕

They buried Annie Chapman today. Two years ago she was a coachman's wife in Windsor, secure in a vine-covered cottage. Now she lies six feet under.

The Day of Atonement began this eve at sundown. The streets were deserted, the familiar smells of herring and kippers missing from the wind.

Williamson has cancelled all leaves and every man was on the street tonight.

Two A.M. now and I must grab what sleep I can. Orders to wake me at the first sound of trouble.

Sunday, September 16, 1888

In a paper read before the Bombay Natural History Society, Mr. Inverarity, a noted shikari, discussed the habits of the tiger, and especially the mode in which it kills and eats its prey. Some think he seizes by the throat, others by the nape of the neck from above. Mr. Inverarity has examined scores of slain animals and in every case but one the throat was seized from below. The tiger kills by pressure on the windpipe, without breaking the skin; it is only by accident, if at all, that tigers in killing sever any important vein or artery, and no blood to speak of flows from the throat wounds. . . . Mr. Inverarity believes that animals killed by tigers suffer little beyond the panic of a few seconds. The shock produces a stupor and dreaminess in which there is no sense of pain or feeling of terror. . . . Natives have a belief that the ghosts of the man-eater's victims ride in his head and warn him of danger, or point the way to fresh victims.

—*Pall Mall Gazette*

ʄʄʄ

No body for anyone to atone for this weekend. Some of the tension has lifted; in Petticoat Lane it was business as usual this morn. Perhaps better than usual, for this past week of sunny days has brightened everyone's mood. I walked down Middlesex Street between the rows of carts and stands: card-sharpers, thimble-riggers, fan gamblers—the noise was astonishing. The crowd was three deep around the cheap jack and cordial sellers; there were loafers on every corner and each corner was packed more densely than the one before.

Last night at sundown I listened to the shophar sound its mournful judgement. Today is Stabat Mater, the day of the Sorrowful Mother Standing, the day Mary stood in her station and watched her Son pass. From Christ Church this morning came the hymn of the Virgin, and I found myself humming it as I pushed and shoved my way to the front of a swag dealer's table. Ten stanzas of six trochaic lines. I used to know all the words.

A card-sharp worked next to me, his shill a tall man with a top hat. A fortnight ago I would have given the nod to the constable on stationary for the nick. Today I had larger prey to hunt and merely watched the shill lose three times in rapid succession. The tall man had disappeared now, and a short Jewish-looking man had taken the bait. The sharp let him win once, then took him for all he had in his pockets. I wonder—If Jesus were to pass there, would He make a scourge of small cords and drive out the dealers, would He overturn the tables?

Ten years ago this area was a ghost yard. Then came the influx of Jews; a few Jews took to opening their storefronts on Sunday and selling old clothes. Today the streets are impassable. It has become popular to come bargain hunting in the slums on Sunday. It's also a popular hunting ground for pickpockets, which means we must station extra patrols. I bought a boxwood peg top for Willy's nephew. His birthday was last week, and Willy brought the lad round the station; he took a liking to me.

I was on my way back to the station when I heard the rumour. "Have you heard?" a woman in queue for the omnibus told her neighbor. "Canon Barnett says the killer is a socialist." I heard the same story on the high street. Not a mad Talmud student or crazed millenialist, but a sane killer who believes he has a divine purpose to expose the plight of the poor. A scientific humanitarian.

Commissioner Warren arrives back at the Yard tomorrow. Perhaps now the investigation will gather steam; Sir Charles is ever keen to do battle with the socialists.

Monday, September 17, 1888

The real criminal is the vicious bourgeois system, which, based upon class injustice, condemns thousands to poverty, vice, and crime.

—The Star

ͰͰͰ

As I approached St. Jude's, I saw a garbed clergyman come out of the vicarage and down the white pebble path to the church. In his hand was a large white envelope.

"Canon Barnett?"

He turned round and squinted. Sunlight gleamed on his high forehead. "Ah, yes, you must be Chief Inspector West. Got your telegram. Do come along." He held the door open.

The interior was a surprise: apple-green walls stencilled in hunter's green, red-and-gold curtains, scarlet pillars fluted with gold leaf. On the walls were photographs and prints: the Parthenon, Spanish-looking country landscapes, religious themes.

"My friend William Morris designed the colours," the Canon said, leading me down the aisle towards the altar. "Do you like it?"

"Very much. I've heard a great deal about him." I turned round and took in the whole room. "Very uplifting."

"I mentioned that very point yesterday in my sermon. You know, that is the great want of the East End, the reason people begin to shrivel up: lack of beauty. Morris's whole life is dedicated to it. Pays not a lick of care to his person, looks like a sailor in old clothes. And yet everything he touches—"

Barnett went past the pulpit towards a small door. "We'll go and meet Dame Barnett, but first I must see to this envelope's safekeeping." He lifted it and I heard the jingle of coin. Barnett whistled merrily. "We've more contributions in a fortnight than I had all of last year. Anonymous donors." He raised his head and looked back at the crucifix. "The Lord works in mysterious ways. Do you like Velásquez, Inspector?"

"I don't know much about art."

"That painting there, *The Coronation of the Virgin*—it's a favourite of mine."

"I'm afraid my own room is bare. I don't pay much mind to my walls."

"It's a feminine virtue, one we could use more of. Morris always says: 'Have nothing in your home that you do not know to be useful or believe to be beautiful.' It's women mostly who see to the beautiful."

"Perhaps when I have a home of my own." I thought then of the *Fisherman's Widow* print that hung above Mary Kelly's mantel and of the two of them, she and her spouse, sitting by the hearth, the kettle on the hob humming a song of domestic peace, she lifting the cozy and making his tea.

I had nothing in my "home" that was not useful. Had I anything that was beautiful?

"Well, I'm ready now. Dame Barnett will have the tea set out. And we've a friend visiting, a young Fabian journalist—Irish. Came for a copy of my sermon and invited himself for tea. I hope you don't mind. He's promised not to talk politics."

"Not at all. And I'd like a copy myself. Your sermon's caused quite a stir."

"I meant it as a parable, but, yes, it has rather caught the public fancy. I'm thinking of sending it to *The Times*." We came to the end of the path, and he opened a heavy wooden door and ushered me into a large hall.

"Henrietta?"

A handsome woman of forty answered his call. She kissed his cheek and took my hand in greeting. "Please excuse the untidiness. We've only just returned from Ireland." She led the way into a large room decorated in warm shades of red.

A thin man in his early thirties rose from the settee; he was dressed in a rather shabby square-cut frock coat.

"Mr. West, may I present Bernard Shaw."

"We have met," he said, giving me a crisp handshake. "At Princess Beatrice's bazaar this summer. I was on assignment for the *World*. You bought a snuffbox and gave me a quotation for my article. I'm sure you don't remember."

"But I do. You were wearing a cap?"

"This one," he said, lifting the cap from the seat beside him and placing it at a rakish angle atop his auburn hair.

"Actually, I don't use snuff," I said, "but the engraving was unusual." I took a seat, smiling. I am not half as bad as I make myself out to be. There *is* something in my house that I have merely for its beauty.

"Bernard, take off your cap," Dame Henrietta said. "And I see you've finished all the chocolate cherries."

"Delicious." He took off his cap and smoothed the part in his hair.

"Well, I'll bring tea," Dame Barnett said.

"Reverend," I said when the tea had been served, "tell me about your sermon yesterday."

"Well, as I said, I meant it as a parable. Only now I'm beginning to take myself seriously. There has been a great deal of good generated by this killer's actions, intended or not. Why not a thinking man? A reformer who kills for the people."

I shuddered. "Somehow it's much more terrible. I'd rather have evil incarnate."

Barnett stood up and began pacing the room. "It's horrible to say, but the crucifixion of those poor lost souls may be the salvation of this district. Why, these murders have done more to advance our cause than I've been able to do in all my years here, more than three dozen Royal speeches to Parliament. Half of our children die before the age of five. We don't want charity balls and free dinners. We want real reform. If this brings it about—"

Mr. Shaw rubbed his scraggly auburn beard and leaned forward. "We need a few more, actually. The blood money has just begun to flow."

"That's terrible, George," Dame Henrietta said.

"You know I dislike being Georged."

"I'll 'George' you when you're wicked. One woman of the people sacrificed is too many."

"That's not what your husband is saying."

"I don't always take Mr. Barnett's part. Look at the worst abandoned dreg of the street and there is still the *chance* of repentance. Only get to know her and you will find compassion and trust and, yea, even divinity." She poured second cups. "I am sorry for the man, whoever he is. But sorrier for those poor women. They are your martyrs."

"All in an inn, guests for the night, not children in their Father's house—yes, we must pray for their souls." Canon Barnett bowed his head and we were silent a moment. Then he resumed his pacing.

Shaw crossed his leg and swung it. "We need lights yet, Dame Barnett. The Lord Mayor is still talking peace and prosperity—the public conscience is as hardened as a millstone."

"The Lord Mayor is a silly fool. Peace and prosperity indeed!" Canon Barnett stopped and looked out the window. "We are doing what we can, but what is needed is the entire rebuilding of this whole bad quarter. We need at least two thousand pounds. I've got a committee looking into the finances. I think there is four per cent in it for an investor. What do you think, Bernard?"

"Vice pays the rent now. No reason you can't promise four per cent." Shaw rubbed his beard. "If only the habits of duchesses admitted of their being decoyed into backyards, a single experiment in slaughterhouse anatomy might save the sacrificing of a woman of the people."

"Perhaps he has already dispensed with a duchess," I said.

"Do you mean the Pimlico discovery?"

"No one knows who the woman was," I said.

Dame Barnett sighed. "We pay such a price. Those poor children. Have you seen them on the street playing games of murder? There is no talking of anything but blood and gore." She turned to Shaw. "You newspapermen are as much to blame as anyone else—printing the ghastly details. Vultures."

Mr. Shaw held up his hands. "I only review art."

"And we must get rid of the slaughterhouses. Why not have your editor write on that? Or on the noble settlement efforts of our young Cambridge and Oxford graduates?"

"Toynbee Hall charity works don't make good copy," Shaw said. "Now if they were to form a vigilante, perhaps. We do need to sell papers. Unless you want a new charity case on the street."

Dame Barnett laughed. "Not likely we'll see you on the streets, Bernard."

"No, I meant my mother, poor soul." He picked up his cap. "Well, I've a speech at Southwark tonight. I plan to walk to save the fare."

I rose. "I must be off as well."

"Inspector, we plan to revive our weekly 'at homes,' " Dame Barnett said, handing me my hat. "If you'd like to, do drop by."

"That would be a pleasure. Perhaps when we've solved this case."

"Well, solve it swiftly," Dame Barnett said. "Before another poor creature is cut down."

Canon Barnett walked us out to the steps of the vicarage. It was just past six and the sun was outdoing itself. "I must say," he said, "these glorious sunsets lighting the blackened walls into gold—if the Anti-Christ were to come, it *would* make a rather good Valley of Jehosaphat. You know, it is the harlot who must be destroyed before the Anti-Christ can reign in the Valley of Jehosaphat."

Mr. Shaw smiled. "Metaphorically, it works nicely. A deep ravine in Babylon, an abyss separating Jerusalem in the East from the Mount of Olives. Isn't the Evil Quarter often called an abyss? Ask any of the down-and-out, once you scrape bottom, you don't come back up again. And we often speak of Whitechapel as Jerusalem—it *is* a popular metaphor."

"What would be the Mount of Olives?" I said.

Shaw gave me a roguish wink and waved a grand hand in the direction of the setting sun. "Let's say the whole propertied class."

Canon Barnett laughed. "A Fabian fable! You would make politics out of breakfast porridge, Bernard." He drew out his watch and opened the case. "Well, gentlemen, I must bid you adieu. Go in peace."

"Are you walking?" said Shaw as we turned and went down the stairs. "I've got to stop by Forty Berner for my lecture notes."

I nodded. "Do you smoke?" I had refrained inside but now drew out my pack and lit one.

Shaw shook his head. "I've enough other vices." He turned round and walked a few paces backwards, looking at the sunset. "Well, maybe we'll get our lights. Blood money for Whitechapel. They're scared, you know. Scared the East End will erupt like a bloody volcano. It could happen."

"We're a long way from that, don't you think?"

"Not at all. With Bloody Sunday not even a year past? If I were a killer who wanted to start a revolution, I'd pick that day for the next act."

"You're really walking all the way to Southwark? What's your speech?"

"Really." He dug a toothpick out of his pocket and bit the end. "I'm giving a talk to the federation, on socialism. No admission if you want to come." He winked. "It's a good place to meet women."

I laughed. "But why not take a cab?"

He reached in his pockets and pulled them out.

"And I thought they paid critics rather well."

"Actually I'm only a part-timer filling in for the real critic who's—"

"—on holiday," I supplied. "Well, I'm only a fill-in superintendent."

Shaw laughed. "Then we shall get on. Actually, I began as leader writer," he said. "Lasted three weeks. There I was, thirty years old, my first job—my poor mother wept. But it was necessary, a matter of principle. Tay Pay, however, took pity on my mother and has given me an odd assignment. Last month I reviewed Mansfield at the Lyceum. Have you seen the performance?"

"No time," I said.

"He's astounding. And Stevenson is a genius." He laughed and when I looked at him he laughed again. "Stevenson," he said, "is one of the two people on earth who actually paid a shilling for my last novel."

"Who's the other?"

"My mother, of course." He winked.

I laughed. "I've often thought I'd like to write."

"It's highly unprofitable. Maybe I should write plays." He shuddered. "I hate that novel with my soul."

"What's it called?"

"*Cashel Byron's Profession,* the majority of copies in cheap binding. Actually, it's sold rather well; of course, it was a very small edition."

"Are you working on another?"

"I've no intention of lowering myself to the level of Bruce's spider. The last tomfoolery was enough. But go ahead, don't let me discourage you. Write. You're not damned till they begin to pay you for it."

"That hardly sounds like damnation."

"You must be starving to be an artist. You must be half mad. Or better yet, mad as a hatter—like that mad Dutch painter Van Gogh; he clipped off his ear and sent it to his lover—to make an artistic point. There's a self-portrait he did just this year, bandaged ear and all. Ah, art!"

"If your theory were right, there should be artists all around."

"But there are. You know, the best performance I ever heard was played by an itinerant artist outside a public house on Clapstone Street. The man played the Pilgrim of Love, with great pathos and taste. And any Salvation Army band gives an excellent performance."

We turned onto Berner Street and stopped outside the green gateway.

"Well, don't give up," said Shaw, pushing open the gate. "Catch the downstart."

"It might be easier to catch the devil. Mr. Shaw, do you believe in the devil?"

He smiled. "Karl Marx said there's no such thing as the devil. It's just God when he's drunk."

I laughed. We shook hands. I turned to go and then turned back. "Are the women pretty?"

"All socialist women are beautiful. Smart, too."

"You tempt me, Mr. Shaw."

"The Reading Room of the British Museum is also very good." He tipped his cap.

As I walked, I found myself thinking of the devil. My grandmother taught me about him at her knee. This is what I know:

He was once an angel, Lucifer, the Angel of Light, the fourth Archangel. After the Fall he became Satan, the Prince of Darkness, evil incarnate. Satan can assume any shape, any face, any name. He loves the night and hates the day, fleeing when the cock crows. He rides backwards on a black horse, and on his buttocks is a tattoo of a woman's face. He lives in the North where it is dark and perpetually cold. I remember my grandmother taking me to church, teaching me that the church faces east, away from hell.

"How do you fight the devil, Granny?" I remember asking.

"Constantly," she said.

"But how?"

"There's a secret. To fight the devil you should write the Lord's Prayer in Jew's blood and throw it in the fire."

"What if you can't get Jew's blood?"

"Then you must whistle, for the devil abhors music. Whistle with all your might."

As I turned onto Commercial and entered the Evil Quarter Mile, I began to whistle.

Thursday, September 20, 1888

Sir Charles Warren presiding over the C.I.D. is like a hen attempting to suckle kittens. He doesn't know the ABC of the business.

—*Pall Mall Gazette*

ƒƒƒ

Full moon today. I expected it to be clear and bright, and it was. The fog burned off by ten, and then a bright ebullient sun stole the day. As I was finishing the morning reports, Willy came in.

"You're looking peaked, John. Why don't you get a bit of fresh air while the sun's still out? I can handle that stack."

"You're a saint, Willy. I could do with a breather."

"Things getting you down?"

"King Stork and his infernal red tape. All he's done since he got back is meddle."

"Bad, eh?"

"You know my plan to put some of our blues in plainclothes? Denied. And those extra blues we were promised—where are they? We're still at half force. Warren doesn't seem to comprehend we've a murderer to catch here."

"It's more than that, John. You know he won't ask Pennefather for the time of day, let alone extra funding."

"Well, let the Home Office appropriate the funds. Lord knows we need some help. You can bet if this was a socialist gathering in the park, he'd get the funds right quick. Ballocks!" I slapped the paper in front of me. "I've enough on my plate with a division to run. Look at this incident sheet: fights and stabbings and robberies. It never ends."

"Just lick round the edge, that's all they care about. Keep the fringe clean where the rich have to walk. No one cares what the poor do to each other."

"Ain't that the truth? Now, if he was killing them in 'A' Division, we'd have troops aplenty. And a reward."

"The Home Office still refuses?"

"It's not the money. According to our Home Secretary, Her Majesty believes that rewards in such cases only encourage vice. Can you believe that?"

Willy shook his head, spat into the spittoon. "Don't think I've ever seen you so worked up, John. Come on, get out of here. You'll be pissing red tape soon."

I grabbed my hat. "I won't be long. Thanks, Willy."

He took my chair and set his hobnailed boots on the desk. "Take your time."

I caught the next dark-green city-bound omnibus, clambered up to the roof and took one of the knifeboard seats, bracing my boots against the iron railing, not even bothering with the canvas lap cover. We waited while one of the grey mares deposited its load of manure (they say each horse in London produces two bushels a day!), then set off, making our way from Blackfriars Bridge to London Bridge, then north to Fleet Street, Newgate, Cheapside, the old City. For a while at least I put politics and personal frustrations out of mind and focused on the blue sky.

A man atop an omnibus is lifted from the cramped vision of the pavement. He becomes one with the pulsating beat of the city, merged in a kaleidoscope of dissolving patterns and shadows. We passed a square with its church, rode level with the overshot windows and jade tops of plane trees, the horses striding in unison—*clip clip, clop clop,* round and round the beat, round and down the road. This morning I turned the teacup three times round and studied the dregs, promised myself that when this is over I would marry. I make a decent living and even have a small sum saved. As a senior officer I would be eligible for accommodations. There are several families with daughters who have invited me more than once. I might fulfill my social obligation to rise in the world. So why is it all I can think about are Mary Kelly's kiss-and-come-again lips? A sudden answering in my loins. But she is another's.

Better perhaps to escape over politics. I took up a newspaper from the seat beside me and read studiously. The image of Warren as a fat hen made me laugh. Warren is the perfect bird-man: "King Stork," a hen, a great stuffed penguin in a monocle, blown up with his own importance. He is all huff and puff; someone must pierce him and let out the hot air. The *Gazette* is certainly doing its best.

A hen attempting to suckle kittens. Very apt, really. And me the poor kitten. I smiled and folded the newspaper. What was it Dolly Williamson once said to me? "A cat can usually catch a mouse, but not if he is wearing gloves." I smiled. An idea had come to me.

When the omnibus drew up again at my boarding stop, I climbed down. I walked across the street and stopped at a stand and bought tuppence worth of short nails; at the next stand I bought three India rubber bicycle tires.

"What you got there?" Willy said.

"Secret weapons."

I took them to the back room and set to work. First, I got out the sturdy blade I keep to cut twine. I cut a slit from inside the tire all round, laid the tire rubber flat on the table, took off my boot and used it as a pattern. When I was done, I tacked the cushion onto my boot. Then I did the same with my left.

I got up and walked round the room. Rubber soles. The papers have called the killer a ghoul, a ghost. How to catch a phantom? By being one.

I took up my supplies, walked down the hall and up behind Willy, who was taking a drink from the fountain.

"Heigh ho."

He wheeled round, spilling water from the cup.

I smiled and held up my foot, handed him a bicycle tire and the shears. "Full moon tonight, Willy. I want every man on to be wearing these."

"You think he's going to strike again?"

"If the moon can affect the tide's flow and change the weather, might it also not affect a man's mind?"

"Who's paying?"

"I am."

"Out of pocket?"

"I'm not going to risk submitting the idea only to have Warren veto it. Yes, out of pocket."

* * *

Midnight now and so far all is quiet. Outside, the street shimmers in moonlight. "It is the very error of the moon; she comes more near the earth than she was wont, and makes men mad."

The error of the moon: I have heard it said that all literature and all religion were born of one celestial error, that the moon once hung round in the sky every night. Then something happened: a comet, an earthquake, some celestial collision—the moon was struck from its orbit. A world mourned as it watched heavenward. Fourteen days passed, and then a sliver of silver appeared on the horizon. The god waxed full again, only to wane and die. And be reborn. Man created myth to tell about it; myth became religion.

Two A.M. Perhaps he strikes only under cover of fog. Perhaps he is done killing. I keep plucking at the threads, seeking one that will unravel the skein. It is as if the mystery existed simultaneously on various nonintersecting planes.

Murder as art? Reality refined and heightened for the sake of an audience, to please the connoisseur? Murder as an advertisement? Killing one to help the many? To contemplate it is fine, but it still requires a man who can with his bare hands snuff the life from a fellow human and then carve the corpse. Does the blood in some men's veins flow differently?

Was it sexual? He takes each woman to a dark corner; round her throat he ties a red scarf. The satyr's urgency rules him now. He throttles her. The knife cuts a red gash. The knife enters her—

Not a carnal lust, more of the mind, the symbolic replacing the whole. I can understand the origins: the woman's ankle triggers the male lust, becomes the woman. But beyond erotica to bestiality? I have only literature to guide me.

From Flaubert's erotic sensibility:

> My heart begins to pound every time I see one of those women in low-cut dresses walking under the lamplight in the rain, just as monks in their corded robes have always excited some deep, ascetic corner of my soul. The idea of prostitution is a meeting place of so many elements—lust, bitterness, complete absence of human contact, muscular frenzy, the clink of gold—that to peer into it deeply makes one reel.

. . . to De Sade's chambers:

> She threw herself upon the kneeling stool, and while in a loud voice she poured out her heart to the Eternal, Roland tortured her still more cruelly. He scourged her with a ham-

mer studded with steel spikes, every blow of which forced
the blood to spurt and spatter into his face. . . .

"You must die, Therese, I told you so, didn't I?" He
gripped her arms and, tying them to her legs, passed round
her neck a black silk cord, both ends of which he held in his
hands. At will, he was able to tighten the cord around her
neck and choke her to death. "This torture, Therese," he
said, "is sweeter than you think. You will feel death through
exquisite sensations of pleasure. . . . This delightful operation, Therese, will just about redouble my own pleasure
too."

How does a man fall down that depraved path? The blue de-
mons rule me tonight. Is he a slummer? According to "Walter,"
there are many who live such *Secret Lives,* slumming for the thrill
of it—or to save a few coppers. I know I will not sleep until
dawn. My loins are tense. I can hear my heart pounding in my
chest. I am waiting. Waiting for the next body.

Saturday, September 22, 1888

ϝϝϝ

The sun enters Libra today as the equinox falls upon us. The solstice's scales weigh even as the gates of heaven are opened. Day equals night. Soon we will see the first frost.

In the mail today arrived a small brown parcel. Inside were two slim volumes: *Cashel Byron's Profession* and *The Unsocial Socialist.* Not the cheap yellow railway novel bindings but blue book cloth.

The Buck's Row inquest on Mary Nicholls closed today. Verdict: Willful murder. Weapon: knife. The Hanbury inquest is rolling towards the same conclusion: Willful murder by a six-inch blade. Only the matter of the missing organs is left to be revealed to the public.

I wonder. So often in this case it is not the clue left upon the ground that is vital, but the lack of it. No sign of struggle. No footprints upon the ground. No screams. Absences become presences. I must hold the pieces to the mirror before I can see.

On the street it is business as usual. The prostitutes have again begun walking about singly; the veil of fear has lifted. There was even a suggestion from the Yard today that we reduce our patrols. I am not getting used to being Superintendent. The paperwork is frightening, and my time is eaten up in small bites. Nine A.M.: Prepare "Morning Report of Occurrences." Ten A.M.: "Morning State of Divisions." Half past ten: "Morning Report of Crime." Eleven: "Supplemental Report." Twelve: Meet with Abberline at Leman Street to coordinate inquiries. One: Budget. Two: Answer correspondence. I ache to be outside, talking with a thousand different people, mingling and listening. I would trade places with Willy in a minute.

Two new pictures in the photographer's window this afternoon. "Oohs" and "aahs" from the women and soft chuckles of appreciation from the men. The Royal romance has caught the public fancy. The photograph of Alix ("Alicky," they say the Queen calls her) is a dandy. She wears a crisp white voile dress with lace trim and high standup collar and looks fresh out of a bandbox. A genuine beauty, her face brimming with youth and natural gaiety, a worthy rival for our own "Queen of Hearts," Alexandra.

Prince Eddy's picture is a shooting pose, taken before he grew in his mustache. He stands in a grouse butt, a Purdy held to his shoulder. There is a photograph today of the younger brother, George, as well: a short lad with a childish face; he is wearing his naval uniform.

An article in tonight's paper on royal maladies of the Hapsburgs and Guelphs: premature and still births, liver ailments, obesity. Could it be that so much inbreeding weakens the line—just as with dogs? What was it my rude uncle used to say? "Before Victoria England was ruled by a profligate, a buffoon, and a fool. And she only got to the throne because none of her uncles could whelp anything but bastards." The Curse of the Coburgs? If it exists, it seems to have bypassed this generation at least, for the young folk are the picture of health. I am cheering for the match to come off. The House of Hesse is the oldest of the royal houses and carries with it a proud history. In recent years, however, great tragedies have befallen it. Poor Princess Alix, losing her mother so young. This Royal match could bring a reversal. It certainly appears serious. Thrice now the prince has been to his grandmother's castle to see the young princess. Picture her there in her white lace dress at the falls of Corriemulzie. The picnic tea is spread upon the grass in the Linn of Dee, and she smiles and slowly twirls her parasol. Above, the sky spreads out as it can do only in Scotland, perfectly scaled for a soaring heart. Enter the handsome young Prince on his charger, tall, dark, and dashing in his cavalry boots and sword and new mustache. There in the misty Scottish wilds, the waterfall splashing round them, he woos her—they pledge their troth.

The Royal romance makes me think of my own empty life. No soft hand to remove the tea cozy and soothe the furrows from my brow. It is my fault alone. Somehow I thought that a woman made all the moves, steered the man to the altar. Somehow I thought Fate arranged it all.

For want of sleep, I shall read Mr. Shaw. I open the book. He has signed it in red ink: "Yours in Socialism, G. Bernard Shaw."

In the dark of an October evening, a sensible looking woman of forty came out through an oaken door to a broad landing on the first floor of an old English country-house.

That's the trouble with socialists; they have no sense of romance. Who wants to enter the life of a sensible woman of forty on a dark October evening? I would rather count sheep.

Tuesday, September 25, 1888

⸙ ⸙ ⸙

Dolly Williamson was facing the window, uttering guttural sounds, when I entered.

"Are you all right, sir?"

"I am practising German, West. I'm still encountering some difficulties."

"At your age, sir, is it possible to learn a language?"

"I taught myself French at forty."

"But German. I applaud you. I'm terrible with different tongues." I took my usual chair.

"I got your report on your meeting with Canon Barnett. You write well."

"Thank you, sir. Thank you very much."

"Hmm. Murder as art. Blood as advertising. Bismarck's theory of creating the psychological moment—wasn't that what you said? Do you buy it?"

"I'm not sure. He does appear to deliberately pick women who are beyond redemption."

"Or does he merely pick the weakest from the pack?"

I nodded. "In any case, there's planning involved. He's not just some creature run amok."

"What do you mean, planning?"

"He seems to know our schedules. And I think *he* brings the scarlet scarf, ties it on his victims, uses it to strangle them."

"Hmm. The knot, eh? Interesting theory. You know, a scarlet scarf used to be a sign of a streetwalker. Before your time, though. Anyhow, I've been asking Sweeney over in Political about the social reformer bit. After all the dynamite plots, he tends to see things with green-tinted glasses, but he's got the names of some very troublesome men."

"Any who think they are Christ?"

Williamson laughed. "At least half of them. That's why I called you in, actually. Take a look at this letter."

The letter was penned in red ink on good bond paper:

Mr. Stead, Editor, *Pall Mall Gazette.*
Dear Honoured Sir and Editor:
    I must confess that I am the Whitechapel murderer. I am the one who put those poor women out of their misery. I will not quit till every court is lighted and every child has a full stomach.

Yours in Socialism,
J. Christ

"A prank, surely."

"That's what Mr. Stead thought. Until one day he got talking with the editor at the *Star*. Seems that there are a few other letters from this J. Christ fellow floating about. So he decided to give us a call. What do you think?"

"Hmm."

"You want to go round, see what O'Campbell at the *Star* has? It might be a lead."

* * *

T. P. O'Campbell was sitting in his office on Stonecutter Street smoking a cheroot when I entered.

"I just might have something for you. It came last Wednesday." He handed me a copy of a handwritten letter on foolscap. Red ink.

19 September. Sky Parlor
    Sir—Why do you try to put the Whitechapel murders on me? Sir Charles Warren is quite right not to catch the unfortunate murderer, whose conviction and punishment would be conducted on my father's old lines of an eye for an eye, which I have always repudiated. As to the eighteen centuries of what you call Christianity, I have nothing to do with it. When I see my name mixed up with it in your excellent paper, I feel as if nails were going into me—and I know what that sensation is like better than you do. Trusting that you

will excuse this intrusion on your valuable space, I am, sir&co.

J.C.

" 'Sky parlor'?"

"Heaven, I suppose."

"Did it come in the mail?"

"I imagine. I don't sort the mail."

I studied the envelope. "Then how come there's no frank?"

"Huh? I don't know. Bernard sorted the mail last week. You'll have to ask him."

"Bernard Shaw?"

"The very one. But he's at a meeting or some such thing over at Forty Berner."

Forty Berner, just one of many wooden two-storey houses on the narrow thoroughfare off Commercial, but in other ways unique. This house, nestled between the homes of respectable cigarette makers on the edge of the Quarter Mile, is the headquarters of socialism in London, the hub of the radical and trade union movement. Think of 10 Downing Street and you think of a certain kind of power; think of socialism and this is the address.

I passed through the big green wooden gate and went up the walk to the door. It was unlocked, and I went in, walked across a long spacious room filled with hundreds of chairs. This is where the workers rallied on Bloody Monday, the day they stormed the Mall. That day got us a military martinet as commissioner. This is where they met last Bloody Sunday, before beginning the march on Trafalgar Square. This is where they came back to lick their wounds after Warren thrashed them.

On a small stage at the back there were three men and a woman. A short man with a cigar sat holding a script in the front row. They were rehearsing a Stepniak play.

"Mr. Shaw about?"

The short man nodded and motioned to the door on the side of the stage. I could hear the printing press when I opened the door. A young man was printing copies of the daily *Arbeter Fraint*.

"Seen Mr. Shaw?" I said, shouting to be heard.

He nodded and pointed to an open door at the back. Inside at a small desk behind a stack of pamphlets sat Bernard Shaw writing with red ink.

"Heigh ho!" he said. "What brings you here, Mr. West?"

"Looking for you."

"I'm deep into my notes for my lecture to the Fabian Society—just a tick." He jotted down a few more words, then put down his pen, and held out an ink-stained hand. "Nice of you to visit."

I held out the letter. "Know anything about this letter sent last week to the *Star*? Your editor says you took it in."

"This letter?" He laughed. "You think it might have come from the killer?"

"It's possible. Murder as art and drama—more publicity. The *Gazette* got one, too."

Shaw laughed, so hard he had to double over and grab hold of a chair. When he caught his breath, he lowered his voice. "I wrote those letters, West."

"I suspected as much. Why?"

"It was your fault. You set me thinking about the martyr bit. And just a bit of the devil in me. I like to shock people." He smiled and gave me a large wink. "You going to charge me?"

"Only if you won't promise not to do it again. I've enough wild geese to chase, Mr. Shaw."

"Any new leads?"

"You're it."

"Well, I'm sorry I'm not your man. If you arrested me it would probably make me a celebrity. If it's any consolation, I am rooting for you. Usually I root for the giant in these matters, but I'm making an exception. Good luck to the giant killer."

"You think this man's a giant? Is everyone now going to condone the two sacrifices?"

"Perhaps. If he doesn't do it again."

"And if he does?"

"Then he's carried it too far. No one would forgive another."

I stuffed the letter back in my pocket. "Promise to lay off the letter writing?"

Shaw raised his right hand and laid it over his heart. "I swear I will not write any more letters."

"Very well then." I started to go, then turned back. "I almost forgot. Thanks for the books."

"Have you read them?"

"Well, not yet, I've been—"

He put up a hand. "No need. They're horrid."

* * *

A column in tonight's paper on the Princess of Wales and her brood. They arrived today at Marlborough House and were greeted by Prince Eddy. Tomorrow the women depart for the Highland Castle. Poor John Merrick, I fear, will be disappointed.

Wednesday, September 26, 1888

ϟϟϟ

When I arrived at the inquest, Coroner Baxter had just recalled Police Surgeon George Philips to the witness-box. I saw Mary Kelly in the back sitting next to the girl with the sleeping baby; I raised a hand in greeting.

"Now, you told the jury at the first session that the cause of Annie Chapman's death was a severed carotid artery, is that correct?"

"That is correct, Coroner," Philips said, leaning on the railing.

"Were there other wounds?"

"Yes."

"Please describe them."

Philips cleared his throat, looked out at the sea of faces. "I . . . I really don't think such a report is proper for a mixed audience."

Baxter leaned forward, tenting his hands. "I feel I must insist that the report be given."

"I feel as strongly that it need not." Philips' mouth was set.

"Mr. Philips. As coroner of this jurisdiction, I demand that the evidence be given. We are here to decide the cause of death and have a right to hear all." He looked out at the reporters. "Whether this information is made public or not rests with the press, but the police surgeon has no right to withhold evidence from a coroner."

Philips rose, sighed. "I am in the hands of the court. But what you ask for took place *after* death."

"That is a matter of opinion. You know that medical men differ." He smiled. "But perhaps it would be better if we cleared the court of women and children."

Mary Kelly waved when she left. I could see by her face that she was disappointed. I, though, could only feel relief. What the surgeon had to say was not for delicate ears.

When the doors were closed, Philips cleared his throat, shook his head. "I still think it a great pity that I should have to give this evidence. . . ." He opened his notebook and read:

"The abdomen had been entirely laid open; the intestines, severed from their mesenteric attachments, had been lifted out of the body and placed on the shoulder of the corpse; whilst from the pelvis the uterus and its appendages, with the upper portion of the vagina and the posterior two-thirds of the bladder, had been entirely removed."

The cold clinical delivery punched a shock wave through the audience.

Baxter looked up. "No trace of these organs was found?"

"Nary a trace."

"They are small, aren't they? Could not they have been overlooked?"

Philips paused. "Yes, if a thorough examination had not been made, they could have been. They would fill barely a single teacup. But a thorough and searching examination *was* made."

"Tell us, was the level of skill with which these incisions were made that of a surgeon?"

"The pelvic organs were severed with one clean sweep of the knife. I would say that this showed anatomical knowledge but not necessarily surgical skill. A butcher or hunter—one familiar with dissecting carcasses—might have made the cuts. I can tell you that the cuts were cleanly made, dividing the vagina low enough to avoid injury to the cervix uteri, cutting cleanly round the rectum."

"Could you tell by the incisions which hand the killer used?"

"The incisions ran from left to right; they appear to have been made from the front by a left-handed person. The victim was most likely placed prone when the injuries were inflicted."

"And what sort of knife was used?"

"A sharp five- or six-inch pointed blade."

"Such as a surgeon might use? An autopsy knife, for example?"

Philips made a face. "Yes, but it is a common length. Sailors' jackknives are similar in—"

"Thank you, Mr. Philips. You may step down now."

Baxter looked at his watch. He nodded and spoke, his voice deeper; the reporters sat up.

"But, gentlemen, strange as it may seem, there was a market for the missing organs!"

When the room had quieted again, he spoke. "Some days past, I received a call from an official of one of our great medical schools. This man was a subcurator of the pathological museum and in that capacity had been called upon by an American doctor asking him to procure a number of specimens of that organ. He offered the man twenty pounds apiece for such."

Philips' mouth was open. "Who would pay that money and why, Mr. Baxter?"

Baxter shook his head. "That is the remarkable part, Mr. Philips. This American was writing a treatise on female disorders and he planned to issue an actual specimen with each copy."

"A spirit bottle in each book? Rubbish."

"He planned to preserve each specimen in glycerine, actually, to preserve the flaccid condition." Baxter looked at his watch again. In five minutes the court was dismissed, just in time to make the deadline for the evening edition. Only *The Times* decided not to print the testimony, and only *The Times* had copies left upon the stands.

"Paper! Murder! Burke and Hare! Paper!" I heard the chants going round before the sun had set. A body snatcher? Another Burke and Hare case? Is this the absence that provides the motive —the missing parts? Is this the key to the puzzle? A purely entrepreneurial motive? But twenty pounds for a quiff? When an entire corpse can be bought for three quid? And those particular organs—as Openshaw says, they can be had for the asking in any autopsy room. Of course, the autopsy is not done until twelve hours after death. Is the deterioration of that soft tissue so rapid that a freshly removed specimen could command a sixfold increase?

Thursday, September 27, 1888

The coroner's summing up in the case of the Whitechapel murder is a very remarkable document. His theory of the murder is that it was done by a doctor for the sake of £20 offered by a mysterious American who in vain attempted to buy that portion of a woman's body. This suggestion caps all the others for its gruesome horrors. Talk about scalps after this! The worst Red Indian atrocity fades into insignificance compared with this market quotation for "actual specimens."

—*Pall Mall Gazette*

ƒ ƒ ƒ

A letter written in red ink on both sides of a sheet of foolscap was sent today from East Central London station to the Central News Agency. Webster Higgins wired me to come round and have a look. I smell a rat.

Tuesday, September 25
Dear Boss
   I keep on hearing the police have caught me, but they won't fix me just yet. I have laughed when they look so clever and talk about being on the right track. That joke about Leather Apron gave me real fits. I am down on whores and shant quit ripping them till I do get buckled. Grand work the last job was. I gave the lady no time to squeal. How can they catch me now. I love my work and want to start again. You will soon hear of me with my funny little games. I saved some of the proper red stuff in a ginger beer bottle over the last job to write with but it went thick like glue and I cant use it. Red ink is fit enough I hope *ha, ha*. The next job I do I shall clip the lady's ears off and send to the police officers just for jolly wouldn't you. Keep this letter back till I do a bit more work then give it out straight.

My knife's so nice and sharp I want to get to work right
away if I get a chance. Good luck.

> Yours truly
> Jack the Ripper

Dont mind me giving the trade name
Wasnt good enough to post this before I got all the red ink
off my hands curse it. No luck yet. They say I'm a doctor
now *ha ha.*

"What do you think?" Higgins said. "A practical joker? Looks
like he added the postscript after the inquest."

"And disguised his hand."

"What?"

"I think I know who wrote this."

I went straight round from Higgins's office to the *Star* and
stomped into Shaw's cubicle.

"This is too much, Shaw! You gave me your word."

"What in Heaven's name are you talking about?"

"You know very well. Had you already *written* it? Is that the
way you got round your pledge not to write any more letters?"

"Damnation, man, what are you talking about?"

"Your last work of art, Jack the Ripper. Red ink and all."

"You're spouting rubbish, man."

"I saw you writing with red ink."

"I use red ink for my speech notecards, what of it? Who's this
Jack the Ripper, anyhow?" He grabbed a stack of red-penned
cards and thrust them at me.

"And for letters to the editor," I said.

"I gave you my word. Listen, if the whole propertied class had
one throat, I would gladly cut it—but a single human? I don't
even kill my own bedbugs."

It took him an hour to convince me. Shaw is not the author of
this letter.

Jack the Ripper. Just a joker? Or could he be genuine? Jack? A
jack is a saucy fellow. *Jack:* from Latin, Greek, and Hebrew,
Jacke, Jakke, often used as a term of reproach, as in Chaucer's
Jakke Fool. A detective is a jack. A John is a Jack. A sailor is a
jack; any damn Englishman you please is a Union Jack. Jack
Shepherd, Spring-heeled Jack, Slippery Jack, Jack the Painter.
All our criminals are jacks. If we find another body, the first
thing I'll look at is the ears.

Saturday, September 29, 1888

Wanted: A New Home Secretary.
When Parliament meets again this most vital issue should attract the immediate attention of our legislators. We have had enough of Mr. Home Secretary Matthews, who knows nothing, has heard nothing, and intends to do nothing.

—*Daily Telegraph*

Mr. Matthews is a feeble mountebank who would pose and simper over the brink of a volcano.

—*The Star*

ᚠᚠᚠ

Michaelmas today and holidays are coming to an end, the city is beginning to fill again. The new Lord Mayor was selected today in the City, the Liberal Alderman Whitehead. The hoppers are hoofing it back to the city with money to spend, and already the gaols are filling up. Parliament opens next week.

A wire early this evening from Higgins at Central News. I went round at once.

"Got this by the next-to-last penny post." He handed me a slim letter.

Dear Boss. Beware. I shall be at work on the 1st and 2nd Inst. in the Minories at twelve midnight, and I give the authorities a good chance, but there is never a policeman near when I am at work.

Yours,
Jack the Ripper

" 'Boss' again. And the hand's the same," Higgins said. "Thought you'd want to see it. Didn't you catch the codder?"

"Er, afraid I had the wrong chap. Did you wire the City police?"

"No, I thought I'd best check with you first. It is a joke, isn't it?"

I turned the letter over and examined the paper. "You got the envelope?"

"Right here." Higgins handed it to me.

"Hmm, Liverpool."

"A scouse, you think?"

"Or a traveller from the north." I tapped the post mark. "Is he coming or going? You didn't show the last letter to anyone?"

"Just you and Inspector Abberline. He didn't think much of it." He looked up at the calendar on his wall. "The 1st and 2nd—let's see, today's the twenty-ninth. Thirty days hath September—that'd be Monday and Tuesday."

"More likely Sunday night and Monday night. I think I'd better wire City. The Minories is their jurisdiction."

"So you think this Jack could be the killer?"

"Aye."

"Why?"

"A feeling. I don't know. Can we hold it back awhile from the reporters? I'd like to talk to the City boss first."

"Commissioner Fraser's on holiday."

I nodded. "And my old friend Henry Smith is acting." I felt better then. Henry is of the old school, a friend of Dolly Williamson's, as frank as his name. "Smith was good enough for my ancestors; it's good enough for me," he always says. I hope for his sake I'm wrong about the letter-writer.

"I don't know," Higgins said, "I've half a mind to give it straight out."

"Maybe you should print it, provide fair warning. Of course, that's what he wants."

"You think he *wants* me to print it?"

"Aye. I think he wants everyone to know. I don't know what game he's playing. Maybe he's only trying to throw us off the scent."

"We certainly can't assume he's honest."

I laughed. "No." I refolded the letter. "Just keep it back until mid-morning—let me talk to City first. You can still make the late edition."

Higgins shrugged. "Let me know."

I walked back towards the station in the rain, drafting the text

of the telegram in my head. The 1st and 2nd at high twelve, the
Minories—just a wee walk from "H."

The smell of mutton from the chop house broke my reverie; I
realized I hadn't eaten since breakfast. I went in for a sup.

I had just taken my first bite of mutton when I saw Mary Kelly
through the window. She was at the curb, ready to cross. I
watched her lift her skirt and negotiate her way nimbly across.
I'm getting old, I thought, putting a dollop of butter on my potato. When I was twenty I would have forsaken my meal for the
chance of a chat. I took a bite of potato and watched her walk up
Whitechapel. She stopped at the steps to St. Mary's, hesitated.
Then she went in.

Michaelmas Mass. And me sitting here chasing after a married
woman in my mind. What madness. I finished my tea and paid
my bill.

Mass was still in progress when I went out. I crossed the street
and sent my telegram. You simpleton, I told myself, if you could
see yourself you'd be ashamed. But my boots did need a shine.
And the lad beneath the street lamp needed a copper. I could see
myself in them when he had finished. I would do the honourable
thing then and go. Just then Mary Kelly came out and down the
stairs. I paid the urchin and crossed the street. She was heading
east. I followed. When she stopped at the corner to cross the
street I caught up to her, but she stepped out quickly and a coach
blocked my way.

On the next block, she reached in her bag and took out an
apple. There was an old roan in a hackney harness; he'd seen
better days. Mary stopped and patted his head, then held the
apple out flat in her hand.

"He's a noble head," I said.

Mary cocked her head and turned round.

"His name is Toppit."

"Known him long?"

"About six months. He likes his apple."

I smiled. She was wearing white gloves and had a Michaelmas
daisy stuck in her bag. "Been to Mass?"

"Do I look like a churchgoer? Not likely, Inspector."

"No?" I laughed. My father used to say that an honest woman
was an aberration of God, that they are naturally and without
reason evasive. And yet my mother never told a lie—it was her
greatest fault.

"But isn't it a feast day, Mrs. Kelly?"

"Michaelmas, that's all."

"The archangel of the sword. The prince who slew Satan."

"Is *he* dead?" she said. "I hadn't heard."

I laughed. "That's because you don't go to church."

"Do you, Inspector?"

"Sometimes. Pretty flower that." I could smell the purple aster's starlike petals from where I stood. I grinned.

"Do you like it?" She stopped and returned the grin. "All right, I did go to church. But I don't make a habit of it."

The clock struck the hour. She looked up. "Oh, I'm sorry. I'm in a frightful rush." She gave Toppit a last pat on the head and dipped a curtsey to me. Then she scurried off.

I went back to the station. Henry Smith's reply was waiting on my desk.

TAKING THREAT SERIOUSLY AND ADOPTING YOUR SUGGESTION STOP AS OF TEN PM TONIGHT WILL HAVE A THIRD OF MY CONSTABLES IN THE CLOTHES OF LOAFERS, COSTERMONGERS, MILKMEN, CHIMNEY SWEEPS, AND ITINERANT WORKMEN—WITH ORDERS TO DO ALL THAT A CONSTABLE SHOULD NOT DO ON DUTY—DRINK ALE, SMOKE PIPES, SIT ON DOORSTEPS, GOSSIP—AND TO QUESTION ANY MAN AND WOMAN SEEN TOGETHER AT THE APPOINTED HOUR. ADVISE YOU DO THE SAME STOP SETTING UP TEMPORARY HEADQUARTERS AT ALDGATE STOP

MAJ HENRY SMITH

And a wire from Central, from the Commissioner himself. Request denied. In the Metropolitan divisions, the dignity of rank will be secure; only detectives will assume disguises. All constables will be in blue, making it easy for a killer to avoid them. Men and women will be stopped, but officers will be instructed not to stop a couple if they appear respectable.

Early to bed with a glass of Beecham's powders to soothe my nerves and stomach. I sleep and dream of angels, wake to the beating of wings above my head. A large horned moth is flying against the pane.

High twelve. As surely as sunrise follows dawn, all the fallen angels are out there now. Down the high street they stroll in their fur and flowers, their skirts fluttering, revealing dainty ankles. And as surely as Apollo pursues Daphne, all of the fine fair men have come riding in their carriages, seeking the fairest angels of the night.

⌐⌐

Long Liz had turned five tricks and spent each on beer. Five more and she might be able to sleep. She turned the corner and stopped at the small stall. She'd had some cheese and farina earlier; now she bought a bag of cachous and ate them as she walked. The rain had slacked off a bit and the streets were filling up.

The man who approached her was a better class than most; though his dark clothes were rumpled, they were of a good cut; he had at least seen better days. He was tall, and Long Liz met him eye to eye, though his face was half hidden under a dark deerstalker hat.

"Looking for me, guv'nor?" She twisted the candy in the pink tissue and rubbed her sticky fingers on her skirt.

"I might be."

"You won't be sorry."

"Won't I?" He shifted the narrow American cloth parcel he was carrying to his other arm and groped in his pockets. He pulled out half a crown.

She was happy now.

He handed her the coin. "We must be quiet," he said. "And you must do it as I tell you."

"Of course, whatever you want. You're the master."

"Do you love me?"

"Of course, guv'nor." She giggled.

"Say it."

"I love you."

He laughed. "You'd say anything but your prayers, wouldn't you?"

She laughed. A coster passed then, and as he did, her jack leaned forward and kissed her. "I love your hard cock, that's what I love," she said, reaching for it. They all loved smut, and as it brought them off quicker, so much the better. Since the *Alice* had gone down, her life had been a succession of nameless and faceless men, the more the better to scrape away at the pain of being alive when her children had drowned before her eyes.

He reached out and touched the fur on her black worsted jacket, let his finger stray to the maidenfern and rose corsage, the unbuttoned bodice of her sateen dress. Then he moved his finger up under her chin, lifted it and kissed her again. "If I . . . ?" He pulled a large red handkerchief from his pocket and held it up. "It's my fancy, will you let me?"

"Let you what?"

"Blindfold you." He laughed. "Just for jolly."

"Well, I don't know—"

"Just wear it then."

"Can I keep it?"

"If you like." He tied the scarf in a bow round her neck and stepped back to admire it. She reached up and felt the pure silk. If he didn't change his mind, she would pawn it.

He took her arm and led her away towards the double gates on Berner Street. She knew the court. It was close on the clubhouse, but the night was dark. The heavy dark green wooden gates creaked softly as they entered.

"Over here," he whispered, leading her towards the right. The fence on the side of the narrow court was high and shut off the light from the buildings beyond. Only a dim light came from the rain-streaked windows of the clubhouse twenty feet off.

"But there's folk inside."

"I know," he said.

"You're a strange one," she said. But she had the half crown in her pocket. Let him get his jollies whatever way he wanted. She stumbled as he led her, almost losing her bonnet. He grasped her arm tightly; his mustache scraped sweetly against her cheek. They were by the fence now; he pulled her to him, smashing the rose she wore at her breast. His cloak smelled of cinders.

"Turn round," he said.

She felt his hands on her bum, and then his cock hard. His hands moved up to caress her neck beneath the silk and she smelled his breath, not sour, but sweet as a baby's as he turned her face round and sealed her mouth with a kiss.

ℱℱℱℱℱℱℱℱℱℱℱℱℱℱℱℱℱℱℱℱℱℱℱℱℱℱℱℱℱℱℱ

In the City Police station Kate woke suddenly, raised herself from her cot, and began to bang with her shoe on the bars of her cell.

"What d'you want? Keep down the noise, you," the blue called.

"I want out."

"Ha! You can barely stand, let alone walk."

She was quiet a moment. She sat back on the cot. Where had the night gone? The last she remembered she and John had been drinking at the Ten Bells. Her feet hurt and she thought about unlacing the boots, but the laces were crusted with mud. Her black straw hat lay on the floor, the jet beads glimmering in the weak light. She reached over, picked it up and stroked the old green velvet of the petals on the brim. Then she smoothed her auburn hair and tied the hat on.

They had made good money at Kent: a shilling for every seven bushels. But now it was gone, in three days she could scarce remember. She grimaced as the spasm hit her in the stomach. It brought a moment of lucidness and a fragment of memory.

Quickly then, she felt her pockets, pulled out a small flat tin and opened it. The tickets were still there. John had pawned his shoes and shirt for the last round. Where was he? She smoothed her dress and brushed at the lint; the Michaelmas daisies on the green field were stained with red wine. When did I drink that? she wondered. When she spoke next, her voice was softer.

"When can I get out?"

"You can get out when you can take care of yourself."

She planted her feet wide and stood. "I'm fine now, see."

"Hmm, we'll see." A few minutes later the sergeant came in and said something to the blue. He brought over a pencil and paper. "All right, what's your name?"

"Kate."

"Married?"

"That I am."

"Who's the lucky man?"

"John. John Fitzgerald Kelly."

"Where's home?"

"Down Fashion."

"Think you can make it back?"

"Yes."

He nodded and went back to his desk. Fifteen minutes later she saw him look at his watch. He came and unlocked the cell. "Well, all right, you can go now."

"You won't see me again, you can wager."

"That's what they all say."

"You wouldn't mind telling me the time?"

"Just on one. Too late to get any more drink."

"Damn! I shall get a damn fine hiding when I get home."

"Serves you right," said the blue. He led her down the damp corridor and opened the heavy station door.

"Good night, old cock," she said, skipping down the stairs.

She was fine now and sober enough to want just one more White Satin before she looked for John. He might be kipping on Flowery Dean. Lucky for her she'd passed out in the City. Metro would have kept her till morning.

Cold as the devil's prick out. She was grateful for the alpaca petticoat, and John's old boots.

She hadn't tricked since before hops picking. It took her but a second, though, to realize someone was tailing her. She stopped by the next lamppost and feigned tying her boots. He came up behind her.

"Looking for me, mate?" she said.

"I might be. What's your name?"

"Kate."

"A nice Christian name. Perhaps I was looking for you."

"You won't be sorry."

He laughed. "How much?"

She whispered the price in his ear.

"What would you do for that?"

"A regular."

"How about if I give you half a crown? What would you do for that?"

"Anything you like."

"Anything?" He put his arm round her waist. "You're a

fine-looking woman. I'd like to see you better. Would you do it with me over there?"

"In the square? But there's lights. I know a private park."

He held the coin out in his hand. "There's always a dark corner. Besides, perhaps I want to see what I'm doing. Will you?"

The copper wouldn't be round for twenty minutes. Any passersby—well, let them watch if they fancied. Besides, she never took long to bring a jack off. She held out her hand. "I'm game."

He leaned towards her and kissed her cheek. "That's an angel." Then he put the coin in her hand and his arm round her shoulder. "I bet you've a fat bum—will you let me pinch it?"

She giggled.

He took a scarf from his pocket. "I'll give you this if you let me pinch it till it's blue." He laughed when she took it; it was all a joke. "Tie it round your pretty neck," he said. "I'll help you." She let him fix the bow. Then he led her through the gates into the square.

"Turn round, Kate. I'll have you from behind." His voice was flat then, matter-of-fact. She knew better than to laugh.

She nodded and turned her back to him.

"Close your eyes now. If you open them before I say, I'll take back the coin."

She squeezed her eyes shut. A fleeting memory surged through her gin-sodden brain: seeing the stallion mount the mare in the pasture, his prick going right out of sight into her bottom, and Mum pulling her away, telling her how people's children came out of parsley beds. So long ago.

"That's an angel," he said behind her. She could hear his moving about. A rustle of paper . . . taking out a sheath?

"You ready?" He put his hand to her mouth and drew his finger across the lower lip; when it was wet with spittle he drew it across her cheek, fingered her ear. "Help me now. Lift up your petticoats—I want to see your bum."

"Hmm." She felt his hands grip her then, felt the power of his need. She lifted her skirts with her hands.

"Open your eyes now, angel."

She opened them. A sharp blinding light filled her as he penetrated her, brought her to endless orgasm.

Sunday, September 30, 1888

⌐⌐⌐

There was only one topic today throughout all England: the murders. A glorious sunny day, blossoms of cirrus clouds on the horizon. Why is it that afterwards the curtain of grey is lifted and the sun shines?

I was still tossing and turning in my cot at half past midnight last night, thoroughly knackered but unable to sleep, my body lathered with sweat, though the night was cold and wet. A freight train rumbled past towards the yards; I counted the cars by their sound in the fog, waiting for the guard's van, following it with my ears till the sound faded into the wet drizzly night. The clock in the hall chimed the quarter hour. Then the door was flung open. Willy's burly frame blocked the doorway.

"I'm awake," I said. "What is it?"

"He's done another! And get this! It's in the yard at Forty Berner Street."

"What? Are you sure?"

"Pinhorn cabled from stationary. I've sent for Philips and Abberline."

I pulled on my trousers and boots and, still buttoning my coat, followed him out to the waiting carriage. Forty Berner. My first thought was that Shaw had lied. He was the letter writer. He was the killer. The red ink. His talk of mad artists, of clipping ears. He'd given fair warning. Well, West, you're a fool for sure now. The story my granny used to tell me about the pig and the wolf and the turnip patch came back to me. The wolf asked the pig to join him at eight to dig turnips. The pig agreed, then went at dawn and had his fill of turnips, laughed at the wolf when he showed up at eight to eat the pig. Bits and pieces all adding up. Shaw had the vision to plan it. He had the motive: Hadn't he said, "If the whole propertied class had one throat, I would gladly cut it"? The pieces fit—until I placed the knife in his hand.

Shaw? Shaw a wolf? No, he was the little pig. I felt my head. It was hot.

I squeezed myself in the seat next to Willy and we set out. The fog was a pea souper; we threw caution to the wind and whipped the horses, aiming ourselves between the dim islands of light and praying we would not hit a pothole. We rolled along like a '74 in a gale, but we made it in under five minutes to the makeshift rough barricade; we went through the scattering of bluecoats, through the tall green gates and into the courtyard. Inspector Pinhorn was manning the door to the club, and over by the left fence a lone constable was guarding a Jewish-looking man, his bull's-eye lanthorn under his coat for warmth. Pinhorn came down the stairs and led me to the corner.

The woman lay facing east, a light film of mist on her face, her right arm squared over her breast. Her features were placid, the jaw slack. A red silk checked scarf was tied around her neck, the large bow turned to the left, a sailor's knot. The knife had cut cleanly and deeply across the lower edge, ear to ear. I leaned down with the lanthorn and looked at the woman's ear. The ear hadn't been severed, but there was a splatter of blood and a nick on the lobe.

"The next job I do I shall clip the lady's ears off and send to the police officers just for jolly wouldn't you."

Higgins had held the letter back. Only a handful knew of the threat. A red rose and maidenfern corsage was pinned to the breast of her black worsted jacket; I knelt and reached inside her bodice, my fingers brushing the soft petals of the rose. The skin was warm.

I rose and shone the light on her full length. Her legs were drawn up and the side-sprung boots placed squarely against the fence; her skirt was pushed up. I lifted it to her navel: a brown snatch, all parts intact. No other wounds. I turned to Pinhorn. "Any footprints? Witnesses?"

"Not a trace. Just the man who found her. He says his horse shied up as he entered the yard. Maybe he interrupted the killer."

"Get a tarpaulin and cover her up," I said. "Don't let anyone touch her."

"We found these, just by the body." The constable held up a thimble. "I've checked her pockets. A comb, piece of Sunlight soap, a lead pencil, a button and a hook. No identification. No money."

"Another kipper," Willy said.

I leaned farther and shone the light on her left hand. It was grasped tightly, and it took me a minute of wrestling to unlock the clenched fingers. A sweet in a pink wrapper was clutched in her fingers.

"What you got inside?"

"About two hundred Jews."

"Christ Almighty!"

"They were having a singsong. Constable Reilly and Sergeant Godley are in there. You'd better go in."

"I think I'd better keep you company," Willy said. "Anyone checking these buildings?" To the left of the court was a row of terrace cottages.

"McCormick went round. Tailors and cigarette makers living there, sweatshops. Just a lot of sleepy people in night clothes. One woman thought she heard a scream."

"Did McCormick check the outside closets?"

"Doing it now."

Willy and I walked up the path and opened the door. Inside the hall were two hundred men and women; they were frightened and angry.

"They call themselves the International Workingmen's Club," Godley said. "Socialists."

"Did you tell them why they're being detained?"

"No."

I went up on the stage and asked for silence. The babble of Russian, Czech, Polish, and English ceased slowly, but then the silence was complete.

"We have had another woman murdered outside this building. I am ordering my men to go round and examine each of you for any sign of bloodstains. As the officers pass down the rows, will each of you stand up and display your hands and arms. After that the women may go."

There were mutters of protest in Russian and Polish and a few more rational voices in English urging calm. I looked at the banner across the podium announcing tonight's speech:

THE NECESSITY FOR SOCIALISM
AMONG JEWS
JOHN ZOZEBRODSKI—SPEAKER

Below it was a notice for the November Hyde Park Sunday Rally—the first anniversary of Bloody Sunday.

"Do you want me to take it down, sir?" Godley said.

"Leave it, Sergeant," I said. "Which one of you is Zozebrodski?"

A short wiry man came forward.

"Any other speakers here tonight?"

"Just me."

"No one named Shaw? Bernard Shaw."

"He's speaking at Hampstead Heath tonight."

I nodded, motioned to Godley to begin, then went back outside to see if Philips or Abberline had arrived. A train went by, into the London, Tilbury and Southern Railway yard. The windows shook. I went over to talk to the man who had found the body. He was scared but he told his story willingly.

"The bells were ringing in St. Mary's and I had just come in—"

"From where?"

"I have a pitch at the Crystal Palace."

"Were the gates open or closed?"

"They was closed. I got down to open them. I clucked for the mare to go faster. That's when she shied up. She don't shy easy. So I poked the ground with my whip. It was dark as pitch."

"Did you hear anything, see anything?"

"No. I had my eyes on the windows. They were still singing inside the hall."

"Are you a club member?"

"Yes. I'm steward of the club. I should have been at the meeting, but I work the Saturday night trade outside the Palace in Sydenham. The firework picture let out early tonight; I thought I might get in a bit of song."

I turned to Pinhorn. "Anything suspicious in his cart?"

"Just the usual: glass brooches, cameos, paste rings."

Philips arrived then with Inspector Edmund Reid.

"Where's Abberline?" I said.

Reid shook his head. "I just got back. Haven't seen him."

Philips knelt by the body. The first thing he did was lift her skirt.

"Surprised?" I said.

"Aren't you?" He pronounced the body dead, stood and wiped his hands with his handkerchief. The clock struck the half hour.

Willy came out. "Everyone's clean, John. And we've pretty much taken the place apart. No one's hiding in here unless they've got a trapdoor. Do you want us to let the women go?"

"Just hold off a minute. I don't want any of them fainting." I turned and watched the two attendants carrying in the shell. "Give us a hand, Willy. Mr. Diemshitz, I want you to go down to the station and make a statement."

"Just a minute," Philips said, turning back to the body. "I want to check something." He knelt and with his handkerchief pried open the victim's jaw. "Yes, I thought so. There *is* something missing. He's cut out her tongue."

As the body was being lifted into its shell, a blue came running up, breathing heavily. "There's been another woman murdered— in the City! Hard on Mitre Square."

"Mitre Square—that's just off the Minories. Christ Almighty, it's him!"

Willy was already in the carriage. I swung aboard. "Edmund, I'm leaving you in charge. Come on, Willy, let's go—fast!"

We galloped into the fog, towards the City.

* * *

The Ancient Square Mile City is an institution unto itself, a place where even Her Majesty the Queen may not enter without the Lord Mayor's key. It is beyond the jurisdiction of the Metropolitan Police and Scotland Yard, outside Warren's warren. I thought of that fact as we crossed the bit of crumbling wall that marks the line between "H" Division and the City, glad that the City commissioner tonight is my friend Henry Smith and not the autocrat Fraser. We sped through the maze of crooked streets; in five minutes we were pulling off Aldgate into Mitre Street. A throng of carriages blocked the entrance. Willy and I added ours to the jumble and went down the main passageway into the square.

The square was once courtyard to a cloister. A plaque upon the warehouse wall attests to its origins: "Site of the Priory of the Holy Trinity. Founded 1108."

Two lamps and a dozen bull's-eyes lit the court, five lights shone from the side of the Kearley and Tongue Tea Warehouse, and the lights were on in a three-storey brick dwelling in the southeast corner. I saw Henry Smith standing in a clump of blues outside the three-storey. The collar of his grey ulster was pulled up to shield him from the rain, but his head was hatless and his silver hair glistened.

"We got here as fast as we could," I said.

"Got your wire. Barely had time to read it. Give a guess who lives up there."

I looked up at the lighted window. Henry gritted his teeth; water dripped from his nose. "One of my best men, P. C. Brown."

"Asleep?"

"No, hanging out in public houses—my orders. Christ! Two in one night!"

"Two *so* far, Henry."

We edged our way to the front of the blues; Willy crossed himself. Next to me I could feel Henry's two-hundred-fifty-pound frame shaking. I imagine we could all have done with a drop of the Glenlivet at that moment.

"I've ne'er seen a body like this," Henry said.

"I *have*," I said.

She lay on her back, a red scarf tied round the neck in a large bow pulled to the left. Her throat was cut just below. She was wearing a pair of men's laced boots, very muddy, and the soles had been placed squarely against the ground; her clothes were pushed up over her chest and her belly had been opened and the intestines pulled from the body and draped over the left shoulder. The sex had been cut out.

"Just like our Hanbury Street Annie," Willy said.

Only this one had been pretty: auburn hair beneath a black straw hat trimmed with green velvet and jet beads, blue eyes, high cheeks. She wore a black cloth jacket with an imitation fur collar. The blood had matted the fur and run down onto the dark green print dress, staining the white Michaelmas daisies and golden lilies.

"She's still warm," Smith said.

"Aye, exactly the same," I said, my mind shrieking, yet my voice remaining calm and simple, childlike. "Only the face is different." He had mutilated her face with the knife, nicking each eyelid, a short gash, straight down, giving her a Pierrot-like appearance. Nothing random about it, more like he had taken time to do it just so.

"He's cut off a bit of her ear," Willy said.

I nodded.

"And a bit of her apron," a blue said. "Hacked right off."

"Someone take off their coat and cover her," Smith said, and one of the constables took off his greatcoat and laid it over the corpse. "Where's Watson?" Smith said.

"Here," said a constable wearing badge 881.

"See anyone?"

"Not a soul, sir," the blue said. "I entered the square as usual, half past one exactly—nothing then. I'd have seen if there was. I left by Church Alley."

"Where?" I said.

Watson pointed north, to the passageway that runs the length of the east wall of Kearley and Tongue, leads to Duke Street. "Then I came round Aldgate and back up Mitre. When I come back at quarter-to she's right there. Fifteen minutes is all—"

"Hear any noise?"

"Not a sound but the echo of my own footsteps."

"Damn it," Smith said. "Nothing? How about the men on fixed point?" His voice boomed back and forth on the walls of the court. "What did he do, just disappear?"

"If only we had bloodhounds," I said.

"Still no duggies, eh?" Smith said.

"Our commissioner says only provincial police use dogs. You've dogs aplenty, Henry. Have you none with noses?"

"My dugs retrieve only."

"Curses."

"Speaking of curses, they say this square is haunted."

"If it wasn't, it is now."

"See that plaque?" He pointed to the wall by the archway. "The story is that there's one spot here where the priory altar stood. One of the monks stabbed a woman who had come to the altar to tempt him, mutilated her face, and cast out her entrails. The monk's ghost comes back at high twelve."

"Holy mother," I said. A shiver went down the centre of my spine. "What's the ghost look like?"

"Raven hair and big bushy eyebrows, wearing monk's garb."

"But why the monk's ghost? Why not the woman's?"

"The woman turned out to be his sister, and the monk killed himself. Quite a tableau, eh?"

"Where was the altar?" Willy said.

"Never knew." He looked back at the body. "Until now. Well,

we're wasting time. Sergeant Hunt, you go back to the station and get a camera. Witherspoon, you telegraph Superintendent MacWilliams. Halse, you head up towards Bishopsgate. I'm going up Aldgate. John, why don't you and your sergeant come with me?" He was already in the carriage. The bells of the church rang the hour. Willy and I climbed on.

"Wait—found something!" a constable said, rising from a squat and bringing a small tin box to the carriage. Inside the box were two pawntickets from a Spitalfields popshop made out to Emily Birrell and Anne Kelly: man's boots, flannel shirt, one and sixpence.

"Well, at least we may be able to pin a name on this one."

We headed east into dense fog but had not gone two blocks before we heard a loud whistle. A gig overtook us and Daniel Halse sprang out.

"They found something, sir—Goulston Street—a message written on the wall!"

We applied the whip and raced back along Aldgate.

* * *

Goulston Street is a broad street running parallel to Commercial Street, about a third of a mile north of Mitre Square, in "H." As we pulled up to the corner of Wentworth, "H" Division Constable Long ran down from the stoop of Flat 108. "Looks like he's heading up this way, sir. If you hurry, maybe you can cut him off." The horses stamped, and steam rose from their sides.

"We were told you found a message?" I said.

"Aye, and a small bit of bloody apron. If it hadn't been for that, I would have missed the writing."

"What was the message, Constable?"

" 'The Jews are the men who will be blamed for nothing.' "

"Where?"

"Over there in the passageway, out of the rain, on the right-hand wall."

"Willy, you'd better arrange a house-to-house. Try at every door. We'll head up towards Lamb."

I turned to Smith as we sped along Goulston. "The Wentworth Dwellings—model dwellings for Jews—think he left the writing there on purpose?"

"I hope he stopped to think about it. I can smell him. We're close, John."

"We're almost back to my office, Henry." We raced north up Goulston, whipping the poor bays into a froth. We had gone but a few blocks when one of my men called out from a small passage off Dorset. We went about six yards down a narrow close and found a small public sink in the closet.

"The water is pink," the constable said.

I dipped my handkerchief and it came up coloured. The water finished draining while I was standing there. My hair stood on end and for a moment I imagined that the Ripper was close, very close, perhaps in one of the houses that lined the court. Then a constable's whistle sounded from the direction we had come. We raced back through the rain towards the sound.

* * *

"We've lost him," I said, when the clock struck four. We were pulled up by the railway yards, and the cars loomed up dark but empty in the night.

"I'm afraid so," Smith said. "Well, let's go back and take a look at the message."

What happened then is beyond my wildest comprehension. A carriage came bearing down on us and from it Willy Thicke emerged, more livid than I had ever before seen him.

"It's the man himself, John," he said to me.

"Who?"

"Sir Charles."

"You must be joking."

"I wish I were. The Commissioner's at Goulston Street—and he's sent for a bucket of water!"

* * *

It is almost midnight now and though I have not slept for forty hours my anger keeps me wide awake. I am under strict orders to keep the Commissioner's act of crass stupidity to myself; I am breaking an oath even to write it here.

When we got to the passageway both Sir Charles and the hand-writing were gone. Only a swash of dampness on the wall above the dado showed us where the killer had written. The message had been at eye level. I lifted my arm as if to write. Yes, about my height. Five feet nine. Had it matched the handwriting in the letters?

"Did you photograph it?" I asked Constable Long.

"Not enough light."

"Why didn't you stop him?"

"Warren's the commissioner, sir. Not even you could have stopped him."

"Hell I couldn't! He had no right!"

"He meant well, I suppose."

"Damnation! What kind of stupid remark is that, Long? He destroyed evidence!"

"No use getting your knickers all in a twist," said Long. "Like the Commissioner said, it's the Jews who would've suffered. By daybreak we would have had a mob. We tried, really. Wasn't just me. Inspector Pinhorn was there; Pinhorn wanted him to just erase that one word, but the Commissioner wouldn't hear of it."

"Did the inspector make a copy?"

The look on Long's face told me he hadn't. Would nothing go right tonight?

When I got back to Commercial Street, there was a light in my office. I opened the door slowly. There at the desk, perusing the papers I had been working on this afternoon, sat the owner of the chair, Superintendent Glenn Arnold. He startled when he saw me. "West. So you're back finally. Bloody awful business, what?"

"I didn't expect you."

"Sir Charles wired me. I'd only just unpacked. Expect you can use a breather."

"I'm glad you're back."

"I can't honestly say that I am. Two at one blow! It must have been quite a night."

"You don't know the half of it."

"Well, sit down and tell me. I've got a meeting with Sir Charles and the Assistant Commissioner at seven."

"But Anderson's in Switzerland."

Arnold smiled. "Yes, well—"

"Isn't he?"

"He's on the train right now from Paris."

"Paris? How?"

"Listen, this is all very hush hush—not a word to the papers— but Dr. Anderson has never actually been in the Alps. He's been in Paris on a Home Office operation this whole while."

"Really? What sort of—"

Arnold held up his hand. "I really shouldn't have divulged even that. But rest assured, by daybreak, we'll have our chief back. Now, tell me about tonight."

* * *

At daybreak I walked back to Berner Street. The newsboys were hawking the morning papers and the cry of murder rang out from every corner: "Murder!—Horrible!—City!—Paper!" The Metro murder had escaped the first edition, so good was Metro's news blackout. It was common knowledge on the street, however, and every newly arisen person onto the pavement was greeted with the official count of the bloody saturnalia.

At the Berner Street gateway there was already a large crowd of onlookers. The house was silent. I went over the yard in the daylight but found nothing new.

I had a coffee, then began the walk to Mitre Square. A half mile from the square the congestion began. At the square itself, the two main entrances were blocked by hundreds as hundreds more pressed from behind. With the help of a City blue, I jostled my way up Creechurch Lane and through the arched warehouse passageway. The body had long been removed to the city mortuary in Golden Lane, but on the pavement a chalk-lined drawing indicated the fatal spot. Costers had set up their barrows at the fringe and were selling nuts and fruit. Many of the Petticoat Lane vendors seemed to be congregated here and I recognized a dip or two amongst them. The blue and I passed one I knew who gave us a bad look. "You frigging police can't find nothink," he said. "What good are you?"

"Suck eggs, McNab," I said.

I saw a mother hold her infant high over her head to see the murder spot. "Does it want to see the blood?" she said. "Does my pretty see the blood?"

I shuddered and was glad Dame Barnett was not there to hear.

When I got back to the station, there was a telegram from Webster Higgins at the Central News Agency. I walked back to the City. Higgins was waiting on the stairs of the squat yellow brick building.

"Took you long enough. Major Smith's been and gone."

"I just got back. Have something for me?"

"I don't know. Anyone hear a scream at Berner Street?"

"Why?"

" 'Saucy Jacky' here says she screamed." He tapped the card against his hand, then held it out. "Mailed in the wee hours—before the newspapers came out. If we'd printed the last letter, those two women might be alive today." He spat.

A red thumbprint was smeared on the front of the card next to the East Central postmark. Rills and peaks blotted the paper. I turned the card over. The handwriting matched the last two missives.

I wasnt codding dear old Boss when I gave you the tip Youll hear about saucy Jackys work tomorrow double event this time number one squealed a bit couldn't finish straight off had no time to get ears for police thanks for keeping last letter back till I got to work again

Jack the Ripper

"I'm making up five hundred facsimiles of the original 'Jack' letter for Major Smith. I'll have copies made of this as well." Higgins reached over and rubbed his finger over the thumbprint. "Do you think it's blood, Inspector?"

"Looks like it. The Yard could tell us. You know, I have often thought that fingerprints might be used to establish identity. They say no two are the same."

"Hmm," Higgins said. "An interesting theory. You could go round and ask every man to give you his print." He laughed. "Might as well take round a glass slipper, eh?"

* * *

At sunset I went back to Mitre Square. As dusk fell, the stream of people began to run the other way. One might venture out by day to view a murder site, but staying there at night was no one's idea of a lark.

Monday, October 1, 1888

Prince Henry of Battenberg, attended by Colonel Clerk, joined Prince Albert Victor of Wales at *Glen Muick* in a drive which Mr. Mackenzie had for black game.
—Court Circular for September 30
October 1, *The Times*

fff

Up before dawn, Venus and Mars large and close on the horizon. Sunny again. If not for "Saucy Jacky's" little games, I would be on leave now somewhere far afield, tramping down the hedgerow, my hunting dog at my heels. Saucy Jack—a sailor. I must speak to Abberline about checking weekend dock arrivals.

I was the first in the mess, finished my tea and crumpet before any other detectives came in. Strange not to have the morning reports to write, to be merely Detective Chief Inspector once again. It is Arnold who will now breakfast with Dolly Williamson, return wearing a rose on his lapel from the bowl of ever-changing-colour blooms. I shall miss my chats with Dolly, miss the gossip and intrigue.

Meetings all day at Whitehall. Is Anderson back? A Home Office secret mission? To Paris? Something is afoot. Has Monro really resigned as AC or is he just waiting for Warren to make a mistake? Well, he's made one now, hasn't he? Will Matthews ask him to step down? But who would replace him? Not Monro; his lameness will prevent his ever filling the Commissioner's spot. Surely not Anderson.

Today the whole cast was on the scene, and I had no excuse to drop in on the set. Perhaps Arnold will fill me in, but will he record the glances and details that tell the real drama? Will he record the colour in Sir Charles's cheeks when the telephone rings in the far hall? It is common knowledge that the germ of the Monro-Warren bout was the acquisition of the telephone. Sir Charles denounced it as a new-fangled horror and refused to have one installed. The military deals in paper, in documentation in triplicate, not in will-o'-the-wisp talk. Sir Charles hadn't counted on technology passing him by, didn't realize for a score of fortnights how insidiously the instrument had changed the balance of power. When he finally assented to having one installed, the receiver Pennefather refused on budgetary grounds. It has been war ever since then.

> One fine day in the middle of the night,
> Two dead boys got up to fight.
> Back to back they faced each other,
> Drew their swords and shot each other.
> A deaf policeman heard the noise,
> Came and shot the two dead boys.

The newspapers have gotten in the fray and are calling for everyone's resignation. A melée and I shall miss being at its centre. Still, there are advantages to being relieved of responsibilities. I walked out the door this morning without ink on my fingers, strolled over to Old Jewry. In Elizabethan days, before the Great Fire burnt it out, the heart of London beat inside the City walls; I felt the throb returned today as I sat over coffee in Henry Smith's office.

"We're going to catch the bastard," Henry said. "The Lord Mayor's going to offer a reward of five hundred pounds for the killer's capture."

I whistled.

"The Corporation of London will pay more if necessary, but it seemed a nice figure. We're going to get him, even if Warren's determined not to. This killer's made fools out of us long enough. There must be someone who is helping him, who sees him come home—for a price, he can be had."

"Do you really think he has help?"

"He must. He doesn't just eat fern seed and disappear in thin air afterwards. He has to be seen by people. I've been thinking that maybe he wears a disguise, discards it after."

I nodded. "I've thought of that too. I think he uses Nero's disguise."

Smith rolled his eyes. "You need some sleep, my lad."

"No, I'm quite serious. Nero's disguise was his innocence. He didn't look like a murderer."

Smith nodded and kept nodding a long time. "Aye," he said at last, "you may have a point there. Some say he's a Dr. Jekyll and Mr. Hyde character, that he leads two lives, has two names, two minds."

"A divided personality?"

"Yes. Two minds. He may suffer blackouts. The one may not even know what the other is doing. Have you seen the performance at the Lyceum?"

"No. Maybe I should make time."

"It's a frightening play. Not for the weakhearted. Not as bad, though, as the postmortem at Golden Lane. One difference from your Hanbury Street victim, John. Our surgeon, Mr. Brown, says the killer took away a little more than a breakfast cupful. There's also one kidney missing."

"Just one?"

"The left." Henry scratched his head. "I can't figure it at all."

"Didn't they used to extract kidneys for divination?"

"I could use one myself then. Damn! We were so bleeding close last night. Well, next time maybe we'll have duggies. I know of a fine pair of hounds in Cheapside. Duggies don't pay no mind to a man's looks, only his scent. Next time we'll track him to his lair."

There was a knock on the door, and Henry got up and answered it. A young detective constable stood there, hat in hand.

"Yes, White?"

"I tried to see you all day yesterday. I had to go down over to Kilburn on a lead. I left a message."

"Oh, yes, you were on patrol near Mitre Square Saturday night. Come on in. This is Chief Inspector West from Metro, 'H' Division. He's on the case."

Steve White took a hard-back chair. "I don't know if I should be telling you this—I'm as loyal as the next man—but it's been bothering me."

"You always do right to tell the truth, lad," Smith said.

The detective nodded. "I'd been five nights on stakeout in Bishopsgate, south of the square. I used to drop over to Aldgate and chat with the constable on fixed point. That last round—and that round only—P. C. Watson would stop and chat with the night watchman at Kearley and Tongue's, have a drink."

"Mr. Morris, the night watchman, used to be a peeler," Smith said. "He and Watson were friends. So he didn't make the round in fifteen minutes that night like he said?"

"No, the killer would have had at least twenty, twenty-five minutes between rounds."

"Which our damsel might have known," Smith said.

"Or the killer," said I.

"Any identity on the woman yet?" White said.

Smith shook his head. "We're working on it."

"Will this get Watson in trouble? I'd like to keep my name out of it," White said.

"I'll talk to him. Nothing on the record. Was that all, Detective?"

White leaned forward in his seat and lowered his voice. "I said good-bye to McGregor on fixed point and went up towards Duke. I stopped to wait for Watson by the lamp. I knew he'd be coming around shortly—I thought I'd wait, shag a smoke from him. I saw this man come out Church Passage. He startled me 'cause he came upon me so suddenly—he was walking quickly. I saw him quite clearly under the lamp."

"How tall was he?" Smith said.

"Taller than myself. Perhaps five feet eight. I took him to be in his mid-twenties. He had a long thin face and delicate nostrils, black mustache, long white hands with long, tapering fingers. I noticed the hands right away. They seemed to shine in the dark—snow white."

"Was he wearing a hat?"

"A felt deerstalker with a peak. I fixed him with a stare, and he half turned and looked at me. I'll swear but that startled me. His eyes were extraordinary. Luminous-like. Glowworm bright." White coughed and looked up at us, shook his head. "I wasn't under orders to stop anyone but couples, but something in me made me speak to him. I asked if he had a match. He stumbled but turned round and said, 'Sorry, no.' 'Cold, isn't it?' said I, and he gave me a surly look and a scowl, but he answered me, 'Yes, very cold,' in a soft, cultured, musical voice—just a tinge of melancholy in it, perhaps something a trace foreign. Just then I heard Watkins call out from the square: 'Hullo, what's this?' When I turned round he was gone."

"You didn't follow him?" Smith said.

He shook his head sadly. "It was just a feeling. I went instead to the square. As soon as I saw the body I ran back to where I'd seen him, but he had disappeared. I thought he had headed north and went after him a short ways, but I'd lost him. Nothing. I just had a feeling, sir, no evidence."

Smith patted him on the shoulder. "It's all right, son. If one acted on intuition, we should have bags and bags of trouble with the populace. But at least you've seen him. If we get as far as an identity parade you'll have your chance."

White left and Smith turned to me. "There goes a brilliant career missed. The man who might have nabbed the Ripper. Well, I've got to clear out my desk. Old Iron Fist Fraser is due back any minute."

"We all go back to the ranks. I'm off to see Fred Abberline. I'll be in touch."

*　*　*

"Abberline's in the interview room talking to an indigo warehouse worker," the desk sergeant said when I came in. "Go on up."

"This here is William Marshall," Abberline said when I took a chair. "He saw our Berner Street victim talking to a man at half past twelve." He turned back to the portly labourer. "Let's see, you say you were heading home to Sixty-four Berner Street, three doors down from the gates to the yard?"

"Yes. I come that way every night."

"What did the man look like?"

"Late twenties, about five feet six, and respectable looking, an educated voice, a little high pitched. He was wearing a dark overcoat and a deerstalker felt hat pulled low over his eyes. And he was carrying a newspaper rolled under his arm."

"So you heard him speak?"

"Oh, yes. He was kissing and cuddling her and sweet-talking her. When I walked by, he whispered something in her ear, and she laughed. Then he said, quite distinct, 'You'd say anything but your prayers.' "

*　*　*

By nightfall both women had names. Two more fallen angels. The Berner Street victim was identified by a woman from the Swedish Church. Her name was Elizabeth Stride, née Gustafsdotter, but on the streets where she lived and sold herself she was known simply as Long Liz. Long Liz—lying lengthwise today in the cold shell. The inquest will begin on Wednesday at Vestry Hall, Cable Street.

The City victim was named Kate; she was identified by her hopper lover, who'd reported her missing: Kate "Kelly" "Conway" Eddowes. Ironically, she spent the hours before her murder in the hands of the Bishopsgate police, not four hundred yards from the place where Sergeant Death arrested her. Had she been arrested in "H," she would have been alive today. Metro keeps its drunks all night, whereas City lets them go after the beerhouses close if they seem sober. Prostitution, of course, is not a crime.

It is long past midnight now and time to say my prayers and go to bed. "Anything but your prayers," he said to Liz, kissing her. "You'd say anything but your prayers."

Not a slimy swarthy phantom creeping up upon his helpless victim but a man, flesh and blood, jovial, jollying it up with his prey, putting her at ease, kissing her—a Judas kiss—before his fingers found their mark.

In my mind's eye, I can see him. Only one question lingers— why? I know how he does it, but the motive is still veiled. A mad Malay seaman? A fanatical vivisectionist? A religious maniac? A scientific sociologist? A Dr. Jekyll and Mr. Hyde? There is even talk that the killer is one of our own, that no one but a policeman could have eluded the police. But why? I look past the veil and see only emptiness. You cannot see emptiness any more than you can prove a negative.

Tuesday, October 2, 1888

Has anyone seen him? Can you tell us where he is?
If you meet him you must take away his knife,
Then give him to the ladies. They'll spoil his pretty fiz.
And I wouldn't give you tuppence for his life.

ƒƒƒ

Will it never end? Will the bodies go on forever? At half past two this afternoon, in the embryonic Metropolitan Police Headquarters at the west end of Whitehall on the Thames Embankment, a Grover and Sons workman by the name of Fred Wildborn walked down a small stairway to the dark basement. He had gone to retrieve his tools, which he had hidden in a small cache behind some boarding in the arched corner recess close to the foundation stone. The Duke of Edinburgh laid the stone in 1875, setting his seal to the plans for the baronial keep of horizontal brick and Portland stone that was to house the Royal Opera, but the project never rose above its foundations.

The workman had picked this spot, not for any historic relevance, but, first, because it was out of the way, and, second, because there was a chink in the flooring above that let in a narrow beam of sunlight. Yesterday he had been in a hurry. Today he stopped and looked twice at the odd bundle at the edge of the darkness. It was about the size of a trunk and wrapped in black cloth; he gave it a prod with his boot but it didn't budge. He went to his supervisor, Mr. Magee, and the pair of them together lifted it up and took it to the floor above to examine it in the light. As they unwrapped it, they saw that the wrapping was a dress of broché silk, a dress with a three-inch flounce. Inside was a human torso. A female torso that had been decaying for at least a fortnight, but one that even now showed exquisite breasts.

Magee and Wildborn were both shaking and shouting gibberish, I am told, when ten minutes later they staggered into the "A" Division headquarters and reported their find. The officer on duty sent round for the forensic surgeon, Thomas Bond, who took one look at the torso and said, "Ah, I've an arm that will fit this."

He was right, for the arm being brought from the Millbank Street Mortuary and placed in connexion with the body, revealed a perfect fit. Bond says the woman was in her early twenties, five feet eight, brunette, fair of skin, and had been suffering from pleurisy. The arm was found on September 11th and had been perhaps three days in the water. That would place the woman's death about the 8th—the same time as the Hanbury Street killing. A double murder that night too?

There is not much hope of identifying this victim, but at least there will now be an inquest. Perhaps she is a duchess whose habits allowed her to be decoyed into some dark courtyard? At any event, finding her within "A" Division has produced immediate results. Extra officers have been assigned to the case and there is finally talk of hiring bloodhounds.

"Well," I said to Willy, "have time to go and take a look at our new police headquarters?"

"Bags of time."

It was coming down in buckets when we went out—not a cab in sight.

"Lovely day for a stroll," Willy said.

"How about we pop in for a pint first? Maybe it'll slack off."

"I wouldn't say no."

We stopped in at Ringer's, the Britannia to those new to these parts. Mrs. Ringer was at the bar, polishing glasses.

"Haven't seen you for a while."

"Yeah, it's murder, this case," I said.

She laughed. "We're taking a beating, that's for sure. Since the killings hardly a soul's in here at night. Well, drink up, it's on the house this afternoon."

We downed our Charringtons; it was still raining, but this time a cab was waiting on the corner. We took the hansom over to the site on The Embankment. The front faces the Thames and is impregnable.

"Anything new?" I asked the tall constable on duty.

"Not a damn thing," he answered.

"None of the workmen saw anyone enter with a bundle?"

"If they did, they're not talking."

"What time do they get off?"

"Five. After that the padlocks go on all the entrances. But they sent them home early today. The place is deserted."

"Mind if we have a look round back?"

"Suit yourself."

"Could we borrow your bull's-eye?"

He shrugged. "Makes no odds."

Willy and I walked round the building. This area was once a marshy fen without roads, and it is still a bit of soppy mush in the rain. Our boots made deep marks. The stink of the river, brackish and fishy, hit as we rounded the corner of Cannon Row; then a gust of wind blew it off. The prevailing London winds blow west to east; it was to escape the fumes and stinks of the East End that Elizabethan London grew westward, away from its heart.

I stopped and pointed up at the high hoarding. "He could have scaled that and then picked his way round the excavations."

"To do that carrying the bundle would have required superhuman strength and agility, don't you think?" Willy said.

Detective White's words came back to me: "eyes like glowworms." Was he drugged? There is only one drug I can think of that would give a man the quickness of mind, strength of body, and fortitude of resolve that the killer must have needed: coca. It was recommended to me two summers ago by my doctor as a cure to overcome timidity in society, and for a while I looked upon it as a magical elixir vitae. I took a three per cent solution three times a day, and my confidence soared, all lethargy and languidness vanished, and I became all at once a tiger, a falcon. The drug took effect almost at once, first a pale acetylene torch of flame in my blood, a voluminous hollow rushing, then the rush of electricity through my veins, the physical well-being, my eyes in the mirror like bright headlamps. For a week I was the most dashing man, but then I found its effects too explosive: my left eye began to twitch quite uncontrollably and two pretty young women, thinking me winking, stopped speaking to me. A third—with a face like thunder—cornered me on a horsehair settee in her mother's parlor. I ceased using the coca that day, whereupon I experienced a profound tiredness that took a full fortnight to diminish. Yet during those days I was a racehorse quivering at the gate. I could have bolted this barricade and carried a *living* woman with me.

The Player's Almanac for last month quotes Othello: "Each man to what sport and revels his addiction leads him."

I wonder.

"Yes," I said to Willy. "Superhuman strength. But we've no bundle. Shall we try it?"

I was over the hoarding in three minutes. Willy, despite his bulk, took only a little longer. We made our way round the construction and down the stairs to the basement.

"I hear this is where they're planning to put the Black Museum," I said as we went down the last flight of steps to the basement.

"Sort of spooky, don't you think?"

A small shaft of light illuminated the far corner of the dank basement, but even if we hadn't had that marker, the smell would have guided us. "Over here," I said.

"It stinks like death."

"Aye," I said, looking round at the hard-packed earth. "Hey, shine that light over here." I leaned down and picked up a crumpled newspaper, unfolded it. The *Echo,* stained with blood. "Looks like he's left his calling card, Willy. Come on, let's get out of here."

* * *

I could not eat supper. I sat in my room and read the papers. They say that this week Prince Eddy, his mother, and the young Princess Alix will all dine with Her Majesty at the Scottish castle. Will they be served in splendour, or will they eat the same spartan meal *she* does? Will he propose? Has he already? There seems little doubt of Alicky's willingness. What Royal Princess would turn down the future crown of England? And she is poor and an orphan. The Queen obviously wants the match. The setting is certainly made to order: the pale stone castle with its turrets and battlements nestled in the Valley of Dee in Aberdeenshire, surrounded by the wild mountains of Cairngorm.

But will Alexandra allow her son to marry a Hessian? Especially one who is prettier than herself?

Wednesday, October 3, 1888

MURDER—£500 REWARD

Whereas, at 1:45 A.M. on Sunday, the 30th of September last, a woman was found brutally murdered in Mitre-square, Aldgate, in this City, a reward of £500 will be paid by the Commissioner of Police of the City of London to any person (other than a person belonging to a police force in the United Kingdom) who shall give such information as shall lead to the discovery and conviction of the murderer or murderers.

> —James Fraser,
> Colonel, Commissioner,
> 26 Old Jewry.

ʄʄʄ

The dogs have arrived. Barnaby and Burgho. They are great magnificent bloodhounds with huge ears, immense flews, and more dewlap than a pair of Renaissance cardinals. Willy and I were at the Serpentine in Hyde Park at dawn when their crates were unloaded.

"Is that the owner?" Willy said, gesturing towards the tall, stooping man talking to Abberline at the park gate.

"Mr. Edwin Brough. Of Wyndgate near Scarborough. A personal friend of the AC."

"Eligible for the reward?"

"No, Metro's hiring them."

"Well, bully for King Stork."

"It was Dolly's doing, actually. Arnold tells me he interceded personally with Pennefather. So, where's Anderson?"

"Coming on foot, no doubt."

"Half expect the Home Office to show up as well."

"Expect they have," Willy said, lifting his chin and indicating the pathway.

I chuckled. Dr. Robert Anderson was striding towards us, walking stick in hand. He paused at the gate and shook Mr.

Brough's hand. The men are the same height, but Anderson towers over Brough. It is the way he holds himself, so vigorously upright. An attractive man, Anderson, a rugged face, silver-bearded, a determined countenance, every inch the barrister.

I lit a smoke and watched as Mr. Brough uncrated his hounds. The AC held one leash and Mr. Brough the other. The hounds snuffled about, relieved themselves.

I can't say I really trust Anderson. An Anglicized Irishman of Ulster stock, he did secret service work in connection with the Fenians, then a Home Office stint, work with the prisons. He is Matthews' blue-eyed boy and I am told the telephone between his office and the Home Secretary's has been in constant use since his mysterious return. I'd almost rather be ruled by a military martinet than a Home Office stooge. Still, he's my chief. And Abberline tells me he dislikes Warren, so he can't be all bad.

"He'd never make a thief catcher, would he, Willy?"

"He's a brief, what do you expect?" Willy spat and patted his pockets. I handed him a smoke.

"He'd be disappointed to hear you say that," Fred Abberline said, coming up beside us. "He fancies himself quite the astute scientific detective. He'll bend your ear if you let him."

"I can't wait."

"Ho, you'll get your chance now. He's calling us over. Remember to speak up."

"What do you think, Inspector?" Anderson said to me as I knelt and patted the nearest foot-long head.

"Nice bloods."

"That's Burgho. She's Mr. Brough's Grand Champion bitch."

"Burgho," I said, stroking the sleek black head. I received a doleful look from red-rimmed droopy eyelids and a wag of her sweeping tail.

"Well," Abberline said. "I've volunteered to be the thief. How much of a head start will you give me, Mr. Brough?"

"Fifteen minutes should be sufficient. Go ahead, we're ready here. Just give me your jacket."

"It's just been cleaned."

"It will do fine. They're clean-shoe trackers."

"I hope they won't rip him up when they catch him," Anderson said. "I need this man."

Mr. Brough laughed. "His greatest danger when they find him is of being licked to death. Go on, get started. See you in about half an hour." Brough turned to me. "Poor bloods. Their name is a frightful misnomer, for they are not bloodthirsty at all but loyal and sweet in disposition."

"Perhaps it is because they are bred to track people, not animals," I said. "And only monsters and giants are supposed to be able to smell blood."

"Wasn't Bruce himself hunted by King Edward's bloods?" Anderson said.

"Yes." Brough reached down and patted the two giant heads. "They don't smell blood, you know. There's so much myth about these animals. They were the first thoroughbreds. These two are descendants of a strain of black hounds bred by the patron saint of hunters. They're bred true; they'll never quit on a trail." He looked at his watch, unfolded Abberline's coat. "Well, I must prepare the dogs. If you'll excuse me."

"And then there are the human hounds," Anderson said. "The City reward has every man and woman imagining himself a sleuth."

"Yes. And many a plan is being laid for its expenditure. A lot of dreams can be bought for five hundred pounds."

"I've been reading over your reports, West. You've been doing a splendid job under very difficult circumstances. Abberline thinks so too."

"Well, we've been busy. Seventy-six butchers and two hundred seventy-nine common lodging houses. Unfortunately, we've turned up very little. If only we'd had the hounds the other night."

"Yes, well." He shifted on his feet and smiled. "Listen, now that you're not so tied up with division matters, you can be an added help to us."

"Sir?"

"I've a special inquiry I'd like you to make for me."

I am not a man to be flattered, but I must admit to feeling a mite proud. I didn't think Anderson knew me from Adam.

"You used to be in 'L' Division, correct?"

"Yes, my first three years I walked the Drury Lane beat."

"So you know theatre people?"

"I've met a few," I said.

"Good. If you'll come round my office after this demonstration, we can talk about it, what?"

"I'm due at the inquest at eleven, sir."

"I promise you won't miss it. It won't take but a minute. You can take my carriage back. Ah, Mr. Brough is motioning us. I think we're ready for the chase."

The bloodhounds took twenty minutes to track Abberline down. From Prince of Wales Gate they led us on a merry romp along Rotten Row to the Achilles statue, then through the crowd at Speaker's Corner to Victoria Gate, where they found Abberline hiding behind a small bush and proceeded to lick him joyously from head to foot with their monster tongues.

* * *

Robert Anderson sat behind his massive desk and toyed with a letter. "I've two birds for you to kill, West."

I smiled and leaned forward. He tapped the letter. "We've had an anonymous letter accusing the American, Richard Mansfield."

"The actor?"

"The same. The writer says his Mr. Hyde is too convincing to be an act."

"You don't think—?"

"I think we should pursue every lead. Those 'Dear Boss' letters to Central News, only Americans say 'boss.' And the murders did all occur after performances."

"More likely a member of the audience."

"I'd like your personal judgement, West. Just talk to him."

"You said *two* birds."

"We've enough murder about without a play scaring the wits out of people and inciting who knows what frenzy in some sick mind. I'd like you to ask him to close down the production. For his own safety."

"I'll be glad to speak to him, but I can't guarantee anything. These theatre people—the show must go on and all."

Anderson took out a cigar and removed the gold label, cut the end and lit it. Then he began to cough.

"Are you all right, sir?"

"What?"

"Your health, sir." I stifled a wink.

"Oh, that. It's a trial I must bear. I've had to take a carriage to work instead of taking my three-mile constitutional. I miss my route: across Kensington Gardens and Hyde Park, then through

St. James—a fine way to begin the morning." He leaned forward and grinned, then coughed several times. The cough was forced. "Would you care for tea, West?"

"Sounds delightful. I missed my tea this morning." I looked at my watch. "But I've an inquest to make—thanks just the same."

"Lady Agnes made me drink mine. But I wouldn't mind another cup. Don't worry, you've time." He poured two cups and set one before me. Then he walked to the window and lowered it. "I hope you don't mind. That Salvation Army band is too loud. Besides, some hymns don't suit my spiritual digestion." He went back to his desk, ashed his cigar in the potted palm. "It is all a bit of a mystery, isn't it?"

"Aye, it is that."

"A mystery that stimulates the imagination. But don't let us go too far afield. I'm convinced we'll find the scapegrace soon and stop all of this silly hysteria."

"Are you? Why?"

"Because we are cleverer than he."

"Are you sure?"

"Oh, very. I think we'll find him in Whitechapel."

I drained my cup and set it down. Anderson hadn't touched his. "But this theory that he's an American?"

"Oh, I haven't ruled out anything, naturally, but I do think he must be a local. How else would he know the streets and alleys?"

"Wouldn't he only have to find a local woman who knew the way to the darkest corner?"

Anderson knocked his ash into the tray. "Ah, but—crucial detail—how does he find his way *out* of the labyrinth?"

"We could use Sherlock Holmes on this case, couldn't we, sir?"

"Do you think?" Anderson laughed. "Sir Charles and I were discussing this just yesterday. Holmes would simply walk onto the scene of the crime, scoop up a bit of ash and say, 'Ah, a black ash, the ash of a shilling cigar, a Trichinopoly. Don't you see, dear fellow, the murderer is Dr. Robert Anderson.' " He smiled. "But then the inventor of the detective story makes both the lock and key, whereas here in Scotland Yard we detectives are given only the lock. We must find the key. Why, if we detectives could have our cases fitted on us like the case was fitted on Sherlock, we could be equally clever." He held his Trichinopoly aloft. "Voilà." He took a deep puff on the cigar and blew the smoke past me. "It is fine and dandy to play at being a detective, but in the end we must have proof, legal proof, not something as insubstantial as an ash. Why, we should simply be laughed at!" He inhaled deeply, blew three smoke rings into the air, and stood up. My audience was over.

"Let me know Mr. Mansfield's decision. I'm counting on you, West." He looked at his pocket watch. "There, you can still make the inquest. Give my regards to Abberline. I hope he got his clothes clean."

* * *

I rode in regal splendor to Cable Street. Anderson was wrong, though; I did miss the first portion of the inquest. Abberline was nowhere in sight, but I was glad to see that Mary Kelly had come here rather than attend the more lurid session being held by Coroner Langham in the City. She occupied an aisle seat, two rows in front of the girl with the sleeping baby.

I went up to her at recess and tipped my bowler.

"Why, it's Inspector West, again, large as life," she said. She closed the sketchbook on her lap and turned towards me. "Don't they ever let you off?"

I laughed. "Actually, I am off, in a way. I've been relieved of officialdom. You can call me 'Tec.' Did I miss much?"

"The police artist's sketch of the scene of the crime. And testimony from a warehouse worker named Marshall. A neighbour of the victim." She smiled. "You know, you had me fooled the first time. I didn't think you were a copper when I first saw you. I thought—" She lifted her hand and the pencil poked the air.

"What did you think?"

"A parson's son."

"But I am."

"A second son?"

"Aye."

"My father was a gaffer." She studied me with her lilac eyes. "I have two older brothers. Henry looks a little like you. He's in the Scots Guards. Did you eat?"

"Not since breakfast. I was just going to get a ham sandwich and sarsaparilla."

"You see, I've brought a mountain of food, and now I'm feeling a little under. It'll spoil before supper. If you're not too proud?" She pulled a wicker basket from under the seat. "I was going to sit out in the park. Do you think it's too cold?"

I laughed. "Not at all. And I could eat a small elephant."

"Splendid, I'll watch." She laughed and handed me the basket. She stood and smoothed her skirts, wrapped her maroon shawl round her shoulders.

"Good baby," I said, as I escorted her down the aisle.

"Laudanum," she said.

"What?"

"Best baby-sitter in the world. Rotten, isn't it?"

I helped her spread out the red-and-white checked cloth under a middle-aged elm. "To tell the truth, Inspector West, I had an ulterior motive. You've an interesting face. I wanted to sketch you."

"Are you any good at it?"

"I just do it for myself. Probably not."

"Will you give it to me after?"

"If you like."

I was hungry suddenly and proceeded to eat with determined concentration the lunch she spread out. Simple fare that had the air of ambrosia: sweet crisp pickles and a wedge of cheese, hard-crusted bread with jam of this year's preserving, butter without stint, a jug of creamy milk, another of frothy beer. She took only a little beer and sipped that slowly. I was only half through when she set it down and opened her book.

"You sure you don't want any? Aren't you hungry?"

She shook her head and began to sketch.

"This won't hurt the picture? Chewing and all?"

"I haven't done the mouth yet, Inspector. I'll tell you when it's time to shut it."

"You could call me something else."

"Like what?"

"Well, my friends call me John."

"You and every second other bloke." She smiled and her face dimpled. "John West, the pilchard." She grimaced and clutched her belly.

"You okay?"

She nodded, forcing a smile. "I'm fine."

I took the tomato from the bag and with my pocketknife dissected it. "A slice?" I said, handing out the wedge on the blade. She shook her head.

"Done yet?"

"Almost."

"Do I have to shut up yet?"

"I'll tell you when. Are you in a hurry?"

"Well, my superior is probably wondering what's become of me. I do have to check in from time to time." I patted my pocket. "May I?"

"Of course."

I lit a cigarette.

"Do you like him?"

"My superior? He's a good gaffer."

"What about Commissioner Warren?"

"I've met the colonel only once."

"What did you think?"

"He is very 'imposing'—very straitlaced—a mustache and a monocle, a teetotaler and a churchgoer, a real military man. If he had his way, we'd all be carrying guns."

"I hope they fire him. Can they fire a knight?"

I laughed. "Yes, but will they?"

"Why'd he get knighted?"

"You don't know? Why, for his gallant attack on two hundred heads at Trafalgar Square. He's very proud of it."

She laughed. "Oh, he's the one who outlawed Sunday meetings. So why do you work for him?"

"I don't, actually, not yet anyhow. I'm C.I.D.—it's all rather complicated. We have a system of checks and balances built in to protect us from ourselves."

She was leaning up against the trunk of the elm and yawned and blinked her eyes. A smile broke on her lips, deep and beautiful, a marvel to behold. "When I was fourteen, just before I married—"

"You've been married so long?"

She shook her head. "My husband, Jack . . ." She paused. "He was killed when I was sixteen, in a mine explosion. He was a collier. I couldn't live on the widow's pittance so I came to London."

"I'm sorry," I said, knowing I didn't sound it. I made my voice casual. "So, you're the Widow Kelly?"

"No. His name was Davies, Jack Davies."

"Oh." I nodded. "I see. I'm sorry if I—"

She stared at me, her mouth set on a hard line I'd not seen on her before. "I wasn't sorry he died—that's horrible, I know."

"No children?"

"No, none. I can't." She cast her eyes down. "When I was fourteen . . . I forgot what I was going to say . . ." She suddenly turned quite pink, then put down the pencil and carefully and studiously retied the pink ribbons of her chablis-coloured straw hat. When she looked back up at me, her face was composed. "I'm going to do the mouth now, Mr. West."

I had the feeling that she'd been on the brink of telling me the story of her life, that I had by the very act of turning to listen—to really listen—scared her, threatened her. She finished the drawing and handed it to me. "You can give it to your missus."

"You've caught me," I said. "And there is no missus, much to my regret." It was a character study more than the rendering of a practised artist. She had drawn me with tousled black hair, my weed hanging lopsided out of my mouth. "You didn't sign it," I said.

She shrugged. "I'd rather not."

I carefully rolled the paper and put a band round it. She gathered the linen up into the basket and tucked a stray wisp of golden frizz behind her ear.

"You cold?" I said. "Your lips are blue."

"A little. Guess we'd better go back."

I looked at my watch. "There's thirty minutes yet. If I guarantee you a seat, will you stop for a cup of coffee?"

"I thought you had to check in with your superior?"

I laughed. "You've a good memory. No hurry. What do you say?"

"If you'll make that tea and get me a centre seat, yes. Do you have that much influence?"

"No, but I've a friend who does. Trust me?"

She laughed. "Are you an honest copper, John West?"

"Aye."

"All right then. I'll trust you." She fell into step beside me, and we crossed the road, walked down Commercial. The street was full of congress. "Turnips, buy my fresh white turnips," a crone called from the corner. Next to her an old Jew had set up his table and tablet and was writing letters. Behind him the shopman in his blue apron set out fat white eggs in yellow straw. At the sweet shop workmen were repairing the pane where a stargazer had cut the glass with his thin blade and gorged himself on brandy balls and barley sugar; I saw her look longingly at the almond bark; then we turned the corner, walked past the chemist's shop with its window of gay red, blue, and yellow globes; past the milliner's with its silk scarves and straw hats; to the small stall. There were two tables outside with wicker chairs.

"One tea, one coffee, black," I said, flipping a coin on the counter. The man served me two steaming crackled mugs. I watched her lift the heavy china as if it were a dainty cup. I drank mine slowly, drawing out the moment. I patted my pockets, found my last cigarette, lit it and inhaled. Then I unrolled the drawing and studied it. "You have talent," I said. "Can I see the others?"

She shook her head.

"Why not?"

" 'Cause I drew the bodies."

I leaned back in my seat, my glance now level with hers. "I *saw* the bodies."

She handed me the pad. Quick sketches of jurors' faces, one of Baxter strutting across the stage. The next page was labelled Hanbury Street. A crude sketch but accurate. I turned the page. Mitre Square, the label said, but the sketch was identical: one hand squared over the breast, the legs drawn up, the intestines drawn out and placed above the shoulder. Not random butchery but rite and ritual, a tableau reenacted. A set stage.

I turned the page. And smiled. There was a picture of me and Abberline. Abberline's body just a sketch, mine shaded in and polished.

"Lots of talent," I said, handing her back the book. "Have you studied it?"

"I told you, I only draw for myself."

"Would you like to draw him?" I pointed down the alley at the barefooted bearded sailor in a tattered straw hat and gold earrings who was hobbling along. The sailor saw us looking and came up. His Guernsey shirt was grey and torn; his black silk handkerchief was tied in a sailor's knot. He held out a hand. "Give a copper to a poor old sailor, as hasn't spliced the main jaw since the day 'fore yesterday at eight bells?"

The man did look wretchedly hungry so I reached for a coin, but Mary gave me a tap under the table. "He's a shade lurk for sure."

"A what?"

"He's no sailor or I'm a monkey's uncle, Mr. West." She turned to the sailor. "Get along with ye. We'll not be fooled by a regular landsman's trick."

The man pulled up his sleeve. "Where do you think I got this mermaid? I been to Yokohama."

"It's a cheap tattoo; more likely you got it in Liverpool." She looked him square in the face, and he met her gaze, then looked away, turned and walked off without a bit of hobble.

"Well, what do you know. He was shamming. How'd you know?"

"He spit to wind'ard," she said. "No real sailor would do that."

"Want to join the force? You've the makings of a thief catcher in you."

She beamed. "Maybe I'll be the one who catches the killer and gets the reward. If I had five hundred quid—"

"What would you do, Mary Kelly?"

She got quite pink in the face, shook her head.

"Well, you saved me a copper." I lifted it and tossed it in the air, caught it square. "A penny for your thoughts."

She laughed. "You're determined, aren't you? All right, I was thinking of a hill. Do I get the penny?"

I placed it in her hand. "What hill?"

"It's a place back home. Just before I got married, I was going to church to say confession, and I turned off on the wrong road, not by mistake, but quite deliberately. I just kept walking up and up, beyond where I'd ever walked before, to where there were high fields. I could hear them singing in the church down below; from up there I could see that my village by the stream was in the crook of a great chasm. I heard the birds singing the hallelujah, and a deer came out and stood in the corn and peered out at me, totally unafraid. They were in the dark, and I was in the light, with God. That's when I stopped believing."

"Or really started."

She smiled. "I got a thrashing when I got home."

"What did the priest do?"

"Made me say a hundred Hail Marys."

The bells of Christ Church began to peal. Mary pushed her half-finished tea to the side of the table, got up and brushed her skirt, mock-curtsied. "It's been lovely. Now let's see how much influence you have with your friends."

I got her a centre seat in the tenth row. I took my seat on the front bench and tried to focus on the testimony, but I kept falling into reveries as the afternoon waned. It was so easy talking with her, and it is so difficult making conversation with any of the young women I call upon. I wanted to look round but felt conspicuous. Perhaps she has a sister, I thought, and had fairly made up my mind to ask her after the testimony. When I did look round, her seat was empty.

Now at midnight I am still rethinking the afternoon, setting in my mind the small nuances: her gestures, her smile, the bell in her laughter, the way she wrinkles up her nose when she is drawing. Do I want her because she is unattainable or because she was made for me?

Thursday, October 4, 1888

ʕʕʕ

Jack the Ripper made his public debut this morning. Five hundred enlarged posters of JR's first "Yours Truly" letter were affixed to lampposts, houses, and fences by City Police. Even those who cannot read are stopping and studying the hand. "Jack the Ripper." How quickly the name has claimed the public fancy.

My rendezvous with Richard Mansfield was set for half past six at the Lyceum, the third pillar. A decrepit hackney let me out in front. I stood there in the windy copper-green dusk, watching the omnibuses, phaetons, growlers, gigs, and clarences coming off the noble granite and stone Waterloo Bridge and onto the gaslit Strand. I was cold and wretched as a fly in winter as I huddled there against the pillar, waiting. The chimes rang out double: half past. A fog was rising up from the river and already the lights on the Strand were misty splotches of yellow. The American was fifteen minutes late. Two ladies in pink parasols and sky-blue bonnets came out of Kenneth's Dramatic Agency, went across to Burleigh Street and into the hash house next to the costumier's. I could smell the mutton and dumplings, and my stomach began to rumble.

The third pillar, Mansfield had said. I studied the bill for tonight's performance. "*Dr. Jekyll and Mr. Hyde*—Curtain: 8.15." I crushed out my smoke and trudged up the red granite stairs with fleur de lis design and peered through the oval windows into the outer red-carpeted lobby. I must have looked sufficiently miserable, for the guard took pity on me and opened the door.

"I'm waiting for Mr. Mansfield."

"Well, come in then." He left me to wander and I went up the staircase and through a set of doors into the darkened theatre. It was a small theatre: a small gallery above me, a pit, rows of dingy stalls. The room smelled of oranges and ginger beer. A dim light shone from the doorway behind me, greenish-grey. I went forward towards the black stage. The pit yawned menacingly.

I jumped when Mansfield spoke.

"You won't get warm in here, Inspector. Best come on back to my dressing room."

I followed him backstage to a white door. Mansfield was of average height with a smooth, symmetrical face and a melodious, accentless voice. Not a feature about him that bore remembering, unless one counted the pistachio-coloured peridot pin on his white tie. He looked older than his four and thirty years, perhaps because of the pince-nez.

"Complete with the latest accommodations," Mansfield said, illuminating the room with a flick of his fingers on the switch. Electric light flooded the room: a couch, two chairs, a long table of makeup, a stove for making tea. Functional rather than beautiful, yet with understated elegance. I took a soft rouge chesterfield.

"I've had far worse," he said, "far worse." He laughed. "Once in Wales I stood with one foot on a brick and the other foot on a brick and the water running all about me, with a little piece of looking glass in my hand, preparing my makeup. And the stage was made of a number of boards laid across barrels. I was Othello that day."

He took a seat, then sprang back up. "Well, now, may I offer you tea? I'm sorry not to offer stimulants, but I make it a rule never to indulge until after."

"My own rule."

"Especially this performance." He sighed. "And then my reward, a nice long Irish and soda."

"Is this performance so different?"

"It is exhausting. Hyde especially. But it is also pride. They have accused me of using chemicals to induce the altered state. Acids, phosphorus. It is none of that."

"I heard someone say you used a wig with a spring."

"Also a lie," he said. "Mine is an innocent wig." He picked up a hairpiece from the dressing table and tossed it to me. "I use only such materials as you will find in every actor's box: greasepaint, pomade, rouge, lining pencils and powders. To use an appliance would be like using a mask; it would not only be inartistic and illegitimate, but downright farcical. Bah! It all originates with actors; it's just professional jealousy—they can't believe there's no trick." He turned and faced me. "I assure you that the change is effected entirely without adventitious aid."

He winked. "Of course, there is that other box each actor draws upon—to a greater or lesser extent." He was brewing the tea and he turned and gave me a bland smile. "Posture and voice, expression of face."

I found it hard to imagine this face and voice being anything other than the man before me.

"Camomile," he said, handing me a small Wedgwood cup. "For my old bête noire." He patted his stomach and sat beside me, sipping the yellow tea.

I drank half the cup, then set it in its saucer. "I've come on Assistant Commissioner Anderson's request."

"Am I a suspect?"

I laughed. "It has been suggested that your frenzy onstage is too real to be an act."

"Well, stay and see. I'll arrange a free ticket."

"Anderson wanted me to talk to you about withdrawing the performance."

Mansfield sighed deeply. "A week ago I would have shown you the door," he said. "Artistic freedom and all that. Oh, I would have been flattered. It's terribly flattering to think one's performance could have such power as to have it censored. But this week I'll listen to you because I'm losing money. Since Saturday the crowds have been off."

Mansfield got up and took a siphon of soda water, drained the glass. "I thought I had it made. Scratch John Bull and you'll find an ancient Briton who revels in blood. Crime draws us in, a veritable lodestone."

"Yes. We love our criminals almost as much as our Royalty. Robin Hood. Spring-heeled Jack—"

"Unfortunately, there are enough horrors out of doors, so there's little appetite for horrors onstage. I can't compete with the ha'penny rag sheets." He set down his glass. "I don't under-stand—*why* is he killing these sisters of the abyss?"

"Ah, that is the question."

Mansfield shook his head, and when he spoke next it was his actor's voice, deep and melodious: " 'I cannot tell, the world is grown so bad, that wrens make prey where eagles dare not perch. Since every Jack became a gentleman there's many a gentle person made a jack.' " He looked up. "A pity, really. We were doing so well."

"I think you might get some favourable publicity. Sort of a public service."

"I'm genuinely sorry those poor women were killed, but I really don't see how it will help."

"It's possible that something like this may be inciting someone. Mr. Mansfield, I wonder, have you noticed anyone strange in the audience?"

He closed his eyes. "No," he said, then opened them and shook his head. "When I did *Pirates of Penzance,* I had such a person, an old lady who came to each performance and sat in the first row. I had to ask her finally to stop coming; she was controlling my performance, upsetting my timing. I found myself playing to her smiles instead of my fellow actors." He shook his head. "No, no one. I would have noticed. Just your usual audience. Do you really think my Hyde has anything to do with this bestiality? If it's true, they'll surely run me out of town. I'm curious, have you been sent to talk to Bandemann as well?"

"I understand Bandemann's Hyde is puerile and tedious. Nothing to upset people."

Mansfield nodded. "That malevolent little dwarf is a thief and an imposter. And he wears false teeth when he becomes Hyde. Imagine!" He set his cup down with a rattle and stood. "I've got to begin my makeup. You may watch, if you like, but then I must be alone totally."

"To concentrate?"

"I must transfuse myself. My mother's trick."

"Your mother was an actress?"

"One of the finest. She was a prima donna soprano. A terrifying woman." He laughed. "I remember one night as a child coming backstage as she was preparing to enter as Lucrezia. She had worked herself into a frenzy of rage, and I was terrified. I tugged at her skirts, and she brushed me aside with a cruel slap. She would not come out of character for anything."

He sat at the table and applied a light base of flesh paint, then took a red pencil and lined the eyes. Bismuth whitened hands. He held them up. "There are a few tricks—when the calcium light is thrown through the green gelatine plate, the hands will glow green." He turned back to the mirror and finished applying the pencil. "You really shouldn't see this, of course. For the sake of art, the footlights should always be between the actor and his public. But—"

He rose and faced me, a kind stranger, perhaps a bit more haggard round the eyes, but a normal man.

"Inspector West, tell your Dr. Anderson that I shall speak to my boss, Henry Irving, about his request. I'd rather you caught the woman queller, but if the box tonight is meager . . ."

"Would you substitute another play?"

"The house is rented. I would have to find something. I'd like to do *Richard III,* the Duke of Gloucester." He struck a pose: " 'Now is the winter of our discontent, made glorious summer by this sun of York; and all the clouds that lour'd upon our house, in the deep bosom of the ocean buried.' No, I think I must wait awhile for that. Not two deformed wretches in a row."

He turned round on his stool. "You know, it would be such a relief to end it. It is a terribly tiring role. Each night it is harder to untwist my body from Hyde's foul shape. My neck becomes each night more corded; my Hyde becomes a little larger in stature—he is upstaging my Jekyll. Poor Jekyll." Mansfield smiled. "It is an interesting play Stevenson has created: giving a man's soul two bodies."

"I don't quite understand."

"Hyde remembers Henry Jekyll as the mountain bandit remembers the cavern in which he conceals himself from pursuit. Hyde has no guilt, no remorse. It is Henry who suffers the hell of knowing the bandit in his soul. It is somehow easier being Hyde. Too easy." He sighed. "I shall miss the crowds. Ask at the front box for a ticket. Just give them my name." He rose and shook my hand. "I am glad you will see the performance. The saddest spot in the sad life of the actor is to be forgotten. Who shall say when no one is alive who has seen what sort of actor Mansfield was? Who will say then how Jekyll and Hyde were played? Yes, I am glad you are staying."

* * *

An empty stage, a cold, grey-green light, silence even in the pit, cavernous, cobalt shadows.

I jumped in my seat when Edward Hyde first howled and leapt upon the stage. No, it could not be the same man. Here was a crouching imp, stunted in stature and misshapen in form, crook-

backed. His eyes gleamed like red coals, and from his mouth
came raucous, diabolical hisses and gasps that cried out of defor-
mity, decay.

I gasped with dismay when in the yellow light Henry Jekyll
woke and saw that his firm white comely hand had become the
corded clawlike hand of Edward Hyde. I was on the edge of my
chair when Edward grasped the potion and drank and writhed
and twisted back into the pale and erect shape of Jekyll. Alas,
Hyde returned; with each draught the devil in him grew stronger,
the taste for blood more keen, the passion of the spirit of hell
stronger. The last twenty minutes I sat spellbound, aware of neither stage nor seat nor audience round me.

They gave Mansfield fifteen curtain calls. When the final curtain fell, the audience rose—reluctantly, I thought—for the fog-
filled night outside had in the space of three hours grown more
menacing.

I walked for a long while with my bill of play clutched in my
hand, my eyes round as carriage lights. The gas lamps along the
Strand flickered like corpse candles; still, I was glad each time I
reached the next island of light. The phantoms of the night in
lace and satin lolled and whispered within the misty circle of each
lamp, reaching out to touch a sleeve, drawing passersby into the
dark shadows.

"Are you good-natured, dear?"

"That depends."

"I could show you a jolly time."

"How much?"

"Five bob."

"What will you do for five bob?"

I would hate to meet Hyde in a dark alley. Hyde was pure evil,
without remorse. Hyde could have his bestial pleasures and then
escape to the mountain hideout, never think of Jekyll. But Hyde
is only a product of an imagination, not a real man. Is my murderer's sleep troubled tonight? Or does he sleep dreamless and
without guilt in a stone mountain hideaway? Man or monster?

Friday, October 5, 1888

But I, that am not shap'd for sportive tricks,
Nor made to court an amorous looking-glass;
I, that am rudely stamp'd, and want love's
majesty
To strut before a wanton ambling nymph;
I that am curtail'd of this fair proportion,
Cheated of feature by dissembling nature,
Deform'd, unfinish'd, sent before my time
Into this breathing world, scarce half
made up, . . .

Have no delight to pass away the time,
Unless to see my shadow in the sun. . . .

And therefore, since I cannot prove a lover,
To entertain these fair well-spoken days,
I am determined to prove a villain,
And hate the idle pleasures of these days.
Plots have I laid, inductions dangerous,
By drunken prophecies, libels, and dreams,
To set my brother Clarence and the King
In deadly hate the one against the other:
And if King Edward be as true and just
As I am subtle, false, and treacherous,
This day should Clarence closely be mew'd up,
About a prophecy, which says, that G
Of Edward's heirs the murtherer shall be.
Dive, thoughts, down to my soul, here
Clarence comes.

—*Richard III*
Act I, Scene 1

ƒƒƒ

Mansfield wired this morning. He is withdrawing the play after tonight's performance. I am glad I had the chance to see the show. As long as I live I shall not forget his genius, but he is right: When all are dead who were witness, there will be none left to speak of his talent.

On my way to the Yard to see Dr. Anderson, I heard two girls skipping rope to a new song:

> Jack the Ripper
> Stole a kipper
> Hid it in his father's slipper

Farther on, a group of children were playing killing games. One lad had a shard of bone and was creeping up on a group of small girls who were shrieking in delight. I shook my head. We've come a long way from hopscotch and ring-around-a-rosy.

At the Yard I had to wait only five minutes in the outer office. Robert Anderson himself came out to usher me in.

"Jolly good show, West. I knew you were our man." He lowered his voice. "We've a new suspect. I'd like you to make another special inquiry."

"Yes?"

"Well, we've been informed that the lead American cowboy at the Crystal Palace's Wild West Exhibit has gone missing. There's a woman missing as well, and the officials suspect foul play. I'd like you to look into it. Today if you can."

I spent the rest of the afternoon and early evening tracking down the Wild West's lead cowboy. I found him happily in bed with the missing woman, the tightrope walker from the circus.

I wired the Yard and then took a cab over to the Lyceum. I wanted to thank Mansfield personally.

I found him removing his makeup.

"Awfully good of you to cooperate," I said.

"Just as well," he said. "I was close to murder tonight. I must be getting old."

"How's that?"

"I'm suffering a decline in patience. We had a cougher. I suggested to the attendant that he treat her ailment by removing her immediately to the Strand and passing a warm steam engine over her chest, a remedy I learned from a critic. I hate coughers!"

When I left, a crowd had gathered round the back door waiting for autographs. I couldn't get a cab, so I started walking, down towards Old Bow Street, my old beat. The gin shops were just closing; I saw a ragged child of six with an old shaving mug getting a dram of gin for her father. I passed a vacant lot; Sir John Fielding, the blind magistrate, once had a house there. St. Paul's chimed the midnight hour. I rounded the bend and walked past the gates of the flower market. Wains and carts were drawn up, unloading milky white turnips and orange carrots. I saw a cab then and hailed it, was just climbing onto the iron step when I saw a strange sight.

"Just a minute, cabbie."

Mary Kelly's hair was down and she was weaving as she walked east along the road.

"Mrs. Kelly?" I waved the cabbie off. "Mary Jane, stop!"

She stopped and turned round, and I saw her face flecked with hectic spots of colour. "The Cross of Christ on us, why are you staring at me like that?"

"Are you sick?" Then I got closer and smelled the gin on her breath. "You're pie-eyed."

"Thank you, but I don't need a lecture."

"Mary, you've no business being out so late. It's not safe."

"Who's to care?"

"It's past midnight. You look terrible. What do you mean, 'who's to care'?"

"First you lecture me, then you insult me, then you interrogate me."

"What do you mean, 'who's to care'?"

"I just need a bit and a sup."

"A sup perhaps. No bit. Did you and your husband fight?"

"Yes, just a wee bit more of the old blue ruin and then a bite of mutton and potatoes softer than the fog." She moved her hand through the vapours, cutting them afresh with each swath of her hand. "Limerick's green pastures lie just beyond. Can't you smell the fresh-mowed hay, the oatmeal stewing in the blue china dishes? Can't you, Tec?"

"Almost." I laughed, shook my head. She was walking steady now, and I fell into step beside her. "You on your way home?"

"No."

"Shouldn't you be?"

"You're not home, are you?"

"Your husband will be worrying."

She laughed. "Not likely."

"Where's your house? I'll walk you home. Is he there?"

"Do I look like anybody's keeper? Joe's out like I am, in search of a drink."

"You've had a drink, Mary."

"I've had three. And not nearly enough."

"I'm walking you home."

"I'd rather a high hanging on a windy day." She pulled her arm from my grip. "Unless, of course, this is official business. You can book me for disorderly conduct."

I laughed. "Suit yourself if you're determined. You're not afraid to be out so late?"

"You mean the Ripper?" She shivered. "I've no fear on me for that Jack," she said, that moment tripping on the curb and pitching forward. I caught her arm and steadied her.

"Do you think I'm drunk?"

"Very."

"Well, I'm not. Not nearly. But I will be."

"Oh, Mary, Mary, it's late to be out, Mary. And you've no coat."

"Did I ask you to be mother to me, did I ever, Tec?"

"Stop calling me Tec."

"Did I ever ask you?"

"Nay. But if you were my missus—"

"Well, I'm not. So mind your own business—and let me mind mine." She stopped and leaned down and tied her shoelace, and I saw her wince as she stood again. A tear streaked her face.

"Did he hit you?"

"I've never seen the like of you. Questions, questions! Don't you ever get tired of detecting?"

"I care—I—"

"Something like that," she said flatly. "We had words. I lost the latchkey to the house last week. Joe had to break the window. He thought I'd been unfaithful."

"Did he hit you?"

She laughed. "Joe? There's not a mean bone in his body, didn't you know?" She shook her head. "It's not like you think." She laughed again then and closed her eyes, reeled. I caught her arm and felt her body press against mine for balance and something else—I sensed a desert within her as dry and barren as the one inside my soul. I felt my body arching forward, and for a moment as I smelled the muted scent of gin and frangipani, I thought I was going to act precipitously.

She opened her eyes. "What is it you're asking of me, Johnny, a kiss?"

"Only my mother ever called me Johnny. Are you making fun of me? You know in a minute I'd—"

"You'd what, Johnny?"

"Kiss you."

"Are you asking?"

I blinked. "I—uh—Yes."

She laughed. Her arms straightened as she set me at arm's length. "Oh, bobby, my bobby, truest of all my true blues." She took my arm and continued walking. "To hesitate is fatal. I'm glad you didn't."

"Let me walk you home?"

"I'm not going home, I told you."

"Where are you going? Are you out looking for him?"

"Who?"

"Joe. Who else?"

She stopped then. "Johnny, sweet Johnny, just go on, all right? I'll get home fine. I've never felt better than I do this moment. I don't want you with me." She took her arm from mine.

"I don't believe you."

"I know. *You* said I looked terrible."

I sighed. "Well, I lied."

She grinned. "Listen, stop following me. I'm going to a place I know. You're not going to get all stuffy because I'm having a good time? And stop staring at me. You always stare at me."

"*Always.* There's that dreadful word women are so fond of using. I just don't want you to get in trouble."

"I already am. Listen—" She patted my shoulder. "If it will make you feel any better, I promise I'll just have one, then I'll go straight home. If you'll just leave off."

"You promise?"

She raised her right hand. "Honour bright. Now go on. I'm not some frail violet you have to protect. Leave me be."

I hung my head.

She laughed. And kissed me, once, on the cheek. "You're a lunatic," she said. "I'd love to be that girl, Johnny."

"What girl?"

"The one you imagine me to be." She sighed. "Godspeed," she said, and left me standing touching my cheek.

I followed at a distance, watched her enter the afterhours house called The Golden Hart. I waited in the alley across the way. It was sheer caprice at first. Would she keep her promise? The cats were caterwauling on the back fence, and the big tom had finished his serenade when the door opened and Mary stepped out, headed east. I nodded and smiled. She was whistling, and as she passed my alley she broke into a song: "Sweet Violets." It would be easy to follow her in the fog.

" 'Sweet violets, Zillah, darling, I plucked them for you . . . ' "

It was not a gentlemanly thing to do, but I did it. Her song lasted as she led me at a fast clip along Fleet Street, past St. Paul's. She began it again as we headed north along Gracechurch Street to Bishopsgate.

" 'Oh, stay, go not away/Violets are blooming love for you alone/Sweet violets, resting in beauty's bower. . . .' "

When she entered the Evil Quarter Mile, she stopped singing. I had to follow her footsteps, the taps distinctive as she made her way in the dark and fog. We crossed one yard, then another, and I lost all sense of streets, a prisoner to the small *tap tap* of her path. Her footsteps changed then as she left the street and went up a small alley. I waited till I heard the sound of a door, then went up the alley, feeling my way against the barely visible white walls. Then through a narrow arch into a court of houses. The windows were dark all round, and I made my way slowly, somehow remembering there might be a closet, almost tripping upon it. I waited by the wall until I saw a faint light from inside the first room on the right. Through the window I saw her. She had lit a candle and set it on the side table, and she was brushing her hair. It hung to her waist like satin. A hundred strokes and then she blew the candle out.

No sound as I skulked out of the passageway with my India-rubber-soled shoes. A worker was walking by, and I stopped and begged a match. "What street is this, man?"

"It's Dorset, guv'nor. That's Miller's Court."

Miller's Court. Now I knew what seemed familiar. The closet had been illuminated by ten bull's-eyes that night, but it was the same one. The water in the closet had been stained pink. And Mary had slept not five yards from the spot.

And I could never ask her if she had heard anything that night, not without betraying my own villainy.

Saturday, October 6, 1888

ʄʄʄ

Though Kate had not seen her family for more than a year, they all came out. Four sisters in black led the two Eddowes children, ages fourteen and eight. The father and the husband, Jake Eddowes, rode together in a black mourning coach. The man Kate had left Eddowes for, Thomas Conway, and whose initials Kate bore tattooed upon her wrist, walked behind. Towards the back of the procession marched the last man to love her, the labourer John Kelly.

The coffin was polished elm with oak mounts, with a block plate with gold letters that read:

CATHERINE EDDOWES
DIED SEPTEMBER 30, 1888
AGED 43 YEARS

The procession began at the Golden Lake City Mortuary with about fifty people. Commissioner Fraser sent a squad of mounted police: four black geldings and the men in full dress; they escorted her to the city line.

A lone Metro constable met the cortège. By then the crowd had swelled to a hundred and fifty, but they marched quietly to Ilford. At the cemetery the sun came out and shone brightly as Kate's coffin was lowered into the grave.

Jake Eddowes was the last to say good-bye. He leaned over and placed a flower on the coffin.

"I forgive you for all you did to me," he said.

Sunday, October 7, 1888

ʄʄʄ

This morning, in a light drizzly mist, the body of Elizabeth Stride, pauper, was buried. There were no attendants, no relatives to come forth as the foreign soil was shoveled over the crude pine box in the pauper's grave. Elizabeth Stride, born Elizabeth Gustafsdotter at Torlandaner near Göttenberg, alias Long Liz, alias Hippy Lip, may she rest in peace.

> Rattle her bones,
> Over the stones.
> She's only a pauper,
> Whom nobody owns.

And yet she had a family once, a husband, two children, dreams for a future. Only since the *Princess Alice* went down, carrying five hundred to a watery Thames grave, has she been a gutter drab. Tonight, perhaps, she is no longer alone.

Monday, October 8, 1888

Fe, fi, fo, fum, I smell the blood of an Englishman.
> —*Jack in the Beanstalk*

ʄ ʄ ʄ

A light hoarfrost covered the ground of Regent's Park this morning as we uncrated the bloodhounds at Clarence Gate. Barnaby and Burgho leapt out and snuffed round, long tails sweeping.

"This is the real test," Mr. Brough explained, kneeling and holding out the AC's black frock coat to his dogs. "Dr. Anderson hasn't walked this path since Saturday." He whistled. "Come, Barnaby. Come, Burgho." The dogs came at once, sat slobbering, their eyelids drooping, the eyes of ravished men. They inhaled the scent of the coat.

"Find him!" Brough said, rising. The dogs bayed and set off.

"Let's go," Brough said, and he, Abberline, and I set out after the pair. They led at a slower pace than last Wednesday, snuffing tentatively at the pavement in spots, then breaking and racing, only to stop and circle.

"It's the true test," Brough said. "A man hates to admit that he leaves a scent behind him like an animal; that, indeed, his scent is so powerful that it lingers on, one, two, even three days."

"Frankly," Fred Abberline said, "Anderson doesn't believe it can be done. Neither does Sir Charles."

"What does Dolly Williamson think?"

"He hired you."

"Yes, that's right. Come on, they've found the scent again."

The dogs led us down Baker Street to Montagu. On the pavement there they stopped and snuffed steamily about.

"They've lost it," I said.

"Then they'll die," Brough said.

"What?"

"They won't quit. You see, it's in their blood. They'll search here till they drop."

"I have a friend with retrievers; they sweep a large area till they pick up the trail again."

"Oh, retrievers are better at that, no doubt. But on the particular trail of a particular man, bloods have no rivals."

"What if Anderson took a cab?"

"Then we might lose the scent. But he promised me that he walked home from Clarence Gate wearing this coat. There, they've got it! Good dogs. Down there."

The hounds led us in and out of back alleys, then along Sussex to Prince's Square. They stopped at the gate to No. 18, tails wagging. We raced up behind them, breathing hard.

"Is this his house?" I said.

"I don't know," Mr. Brough said. "Is it?"

Fred Abberline shook his head in amazement. "I wouldn't have believed it. A scent almost two days old."

"They could still follow it after three."

"Dr. Anderson will be surprised."

"Shall we?"

Together, we went up the path and rang the bell. A butler opened the door.

Mr. Brough handed him his card. "Please tell the Assistant Commissioner that his hounds have arrived for breakfast."

* * *

The mail had just come in when I got back to my desk at headquarters. I watched Sergeant Godley dump the cloth bag on the table.

"More than usual for a Monday," said I, picking up my silver knife. "You want to help?"

Godley shrugged. "I'll open; you can sort."

"Fair enough." I handed him the letter opener.

"Any official word on the Queen's reply to Dame Barnett's petition?" he said.

"Nothing so far."

"Hey, look at this!" He handed me a sheet of foolscap.

Dear Sir—you had better be careful how you send those bloodhounds about the streets because of the single females wearing stained napkins. Women smell very strange when they are unwell.

                                                        Jack the Ripper

Godley had already cut the next envelope and taken out the letter. "Oh, no," he said.

Dear Boss,
    Keep an extra lookout in Whitechapel tonight.

                                                    J the R
P.S. There is one old whore who I have got my eyes on so look out. J.T.R.

He kept opening letters and handing them to me. Half of them were signed Jack the Ripper.

Dear Boss—I have pleasure in telling you that I am the man that has committed the disturbances in London by killing everybody.

                                Yours truly, Jack the Ripper

"This one's from Chelsea."

Dear Boss,
    I hope when you get home you will find your mother murdered that is what you deserve.

                                Yours truly, Jack the Ripper

"And one from London Central."

Dear Copper,
I am master of the art. I am going to be heavy on the guilded whores. Oh, we are masters. No animal like a nice woman, the fat are the best. My mouth waters when I think of the next nice fat partridge. They'll find nice little partridge breasts some day in their cupboards.

                                            Jack the Ripper

I set that one aside. "Hmm, guilded whores. Or does he mean 'gilded'? This one is nasty enough to be the real thing. Let's wire Higgins, see what he has." While I was waiting for my reply, I got a wire from Williamson.
    "Listen to this, Godley. They've a deluge of letters at the Yard, too. All signed Jack the Ripper. No doubt about it, that poster

has inflamed some sick twist in our John Bull's mind. Damnation! How do we pick out the real killer from the counterfeits?"

"I dunno," Godley said. "Compare the hands?"

"Here comes our reply from Central News." I read the message:

RECEIVED ONLY ONE LETTER SIGNED JACK THE RIPPER—
ADDRESSED TO ME PERSONALLY STOP

W HIGGINS

"Here it is," Webster Higgins said, twenty minutes later. "Handwriting certainly looks the same." He handed me a grey envelope addressed in red ink.

Dear Boss,
    Think I'll quit using my nice sharp knife. Too good for whores. Have come here to buy a Scotch dirk. *Ha! Ha!* That will tickle up their ovaries.

Jack the Ripper

I turned the envelope over. "Glasgow?"

"Someone who works up north and comes down on weekends? That would fit."

"And the Liverpool letter would fit as well. While the train stopped in Crewe, a letter could be given to the guard to post. It's often done."

I went back to the section house and I took down my worn *Bradshaw's,* consulted the timetables. It all fit.

Just before eleven tonight I went to Victoria, walked down to Platform 8. From Platform 9 came a deafening roar as the engineer opened the valves to clear the boiler; steam hissed up and drifted over the tracks; then the apple-green engine chugged out, pulling the long train into the murky night. The *Gazette* has been running a series of articles on the *Flying Scotsman/Great Westerner* railway race; each day impossible minutes are shaved off the old records as the two great trains fly back and forth between London and Glasgow.

I waited ten minutes more: the *Flying Scotsman* pulled in, discharging about forty passengers.

"Mind the step," the conductor said, helping the last passenger, an old man, off the train and giving his luggage after him to the porter in the bottle-green velvet uniform.

"Way there," the porter said, wheeling a cart of luggage past me. The old man in a tartan traveling rug and walking stick hobbled past me. I went over to the conductor and tipped my hat.

"Excuse me, sir, where does this train go after?"

"To the shunting yards, sir, in the East End."

"When does it return?"

" 'Fore dawn, gov'ner; it goes out at eight."

I tipped him a tuppence, then walked down the track and into the station. There were five men in the gentlemen's bar and I went in, ordered a hock and soda, sat sipping it and studying the weekend schedule. There were railway shunting yards just north of Buck's Row and Hanbury Street, just west of Bishopsgate.

A man might go out hunting for the weekend, take a train instead to Victoria, hide himself and continue on to the East End, hunt another prey, get back on the train and ride it back to Victoria, ride the morning train back to Scotland—and appear at breakfast Monday morning, having slept in his own bed, refreshed, with all the cinders washed from his hair.

A Scotsman? I think not. The letter said: "to buy a Scotch dirk." A Scotsman would buy a *Scottish* dirk. *Scotch* was what you put in a spirit flask, a remedy for what ailed you.

All work and no play makes Jack a dull boy. I ordered a wine-glassful of the Glenlivet and drank it down. Then I walked home. What ails me cannot be cured so easily but the whisky helps.

It is one now and I cannot sleep. The sky is clear and I sit and stare at the stars cutting the sky. He has gone to buy a knife. He will be back. I have my work cut out for me. He cuts his work out.

Thursday, October 11, 1888

A very strange, startling rumour as to the manner in which Sir Charles Warren performs the duty of Chief Detective of Scotland Yard is current this morning in the city. The rumour is that rather than face the danger of allowing a crowd to assemble in a public thoroughfare, Sir Charles deliberately destroyed a clue, the only clue which the City Police believe to afford any guidance as to the identity of the assassin.

—*Pall Mall Gazette*

ʄ ʄ ʄ

"The handwriting is on the wall," the City coroner, Langham, was saying, tapping the board with white chalk. "The Metropolitan Police Commissioner destroyed valuable evidence. We have no choice now but to rely on the memory of those who saw the writing."

I looked round but didn't see Mary. I took a seat in front next to Superintendent Dunlap of "A" Division, faced front.

"The Crown now calls Detective Alex Outrum."

A sandy-haired detective with a red handlebar mustache came forward.

"Now, to the best of your ability, please show the jurors just what you read upon the wall." He handed the young man the chalk. Next to me, Dunlap leaned forward intently.

"I'll try." Outrum pushed back a shock of hair and lifted his hand. "The writing was about here on the wall, four or five lines, as best as I can recall, like this:

> The Juwes are
> The men That
> Will not
> be Blamed
> for nothing.

The Coroner stared at the blackboard. "You are very sure? Not the Jews are the men who *will* be blamed?"

"No, because that puzzled me. Definitely the double negative."

"What about that spelling there. It wasn't *Jews*?"

I leaned forward now too.

"No, sir."

"What did Sir Charles Warren do when he saw the lettering? And remember, Detective, you are under oath."

"He said he was afraid a crowd would gather and begin persecuting the Hebrews. He wanted the message erased. Someone said, 'Why not cover it with paper?' Someone else said, 'Why not erase that one word?' That's when he sent for the bucket of water."

"He's gone too far this time," Dunlap muttered.

"What?" I said.

"Damnation!" He rose and brushed by me, left the room. I leaned forward and tapped Abberline on the shoulder. "You heard this before?"

He shrugged. "I didn't place much importance on it. *Ju, Jew, Juden.* Yiddish."

I wonder. I have asked the scribe on the corner. The Yiddish word is *Yidden,* not *Juw.* Surely Abberline knows that.

Williamson's homey advice sounds in my ears: A cat can usually catch a mouse, but not if he is wearing gloves. Something is queer here. Abberline knows Whitechapel like the back of his hand; he even speaks a little Yiddish. Why would he make such a mistake? But then, why would Baxter create a stupid hoax about an American doctor? Why did Warren erase the writing on the wall?

The writing on the wall spelled doom for the last king of Babylon. And all the walls came tumbling down.

Saturday, October 13, 1888

"The Handwriting on the Wall." "Mene, Mene, Tekel, Upharsin!" Sir Charles Warren at least will recognize the words of the Prophet Daniel. Strange that it should have been the blood-red hand of the assassin which should have traced upon a wall in the East-end a message the obliteration of which has supplied the last conclusive demonstration required of the utter unfitness of Sir Charles Warren for the place which he holds.

—*Pall Mall Gazette*

ƒƒƒ

St. Edward the Confessor's Day, and I must confess that strange things are afoot. Superintendent Dunlap resigned today after thirty-six years in the service and twenty-two years as Superintendent of "A" Division. No official reason given, and Arnold refuses to discuss it at all, but the word at Whitehall is that the departure was more than sudden. Up until last week Dunlap was Warren's staunchest ally, one of the few risen-from-the-ranks policemen who supported his military reign, one of the few who had backed up his five-year ban on public meetings. They were friends, belonged to the same club, the same lodge. Now, it is rumoured, they are at sixes and sevens.

What had Dunlap said at the coroner's court? "He's gone too far this time." Something is queer. The more I think about it, the queerer things become. Anderson's strange sickness and miraculous recovery. Warren's bucket of water. Baxter's hoax. The never-to-be-found leather apron. Absences, mysterious missing pieces. My head is in a muddle. Is it all politics? Are they covering up for someone?

The Queen has answered Dame Barnett's petition. There is to be no Royal aid forthcoming. Informally, she has conveyed her regrets. She is aware of the problems of this class of "bad women" and regrets their plight. She suggests that the weekend cattle boats be searched, as the killer is obviously a depraved madman who must be hiding in the midst of beasts.

It is Prince Eddy's Name Day today, but there was no mention of him in the paper, no mention of the Royal romance. I have gotten used to weaving the *Court Circular*'s daily dose of information on them into a full-scale romantic drama. What a full, rich scenario I spin from each dry entry, what vicarious pleasures I receive from playing out the characters in my mind; I feel cheated when the *Circular* does not mention them.

Even their foibles seem romantic. The Curse of the Coburgs, pronounced by an angry monk in a churchyard at midnight: "Then verily shall I pray to the Lord Almighty to visit the sins of the fathers upon the sons to the third and fourth generation of the Coburg line." Then followed mad King George III, blind and deaf, conversing with oak trees, his only real virtue that he spoke like an Englishman and was able to father sons. The second generation, sexual reprobates all, unable to father anything but bastard sons: the profligate George IV, said to be "a bad son, a bad father, a bad husband, a bad monarch, and a bad friend"; his brother, William IV, a weak, ignorant, commonplace buffoon. And now, the next two generations of Saxe-Coburg-Gotha men: Our Prince of Wales, "Spuds," fat and greedy; the young heir, Eddy, hardly the scholar. And yet we forgive them all—they are our fairy tales, our link with the divine. Look at the young German emperor, Willy—a withered arm and yet he rules supreme. In contrast, there stands poor mortal James Monro, banned forever from the role of Commissioner because of a crushed thigh acquired in the line of duty when a horse fell upon him. Reality.

It is time, I suppose, to banish romance and banality, to concentrate on the case at hand. Such a strange, baffling case. What was it Holmes said about such cases? I consult my copy of *Beeton's Christmas Annual:* "Strange details, far from making a case more difficult, make it less so. . . . When a fact appears to be opposed to a long line of deductions, it invariably proves to be capable of bearing some other interpretation."

I have been blaming my superiors for incompetence and stupidity. Have I been reasoning from a false premise?

* * *

I sleep fitfully, dream of mad monks in courtyard squares. Measured squares with heavy gates. I am locked within and cannot find the key. The hooded monk comes towards me with ravished blood-red eyes. . . .

Monday, October 15, 1888

ʄʄʄ

Two weeks now without a body, a week since we have heard from Jack. I am still carrying out special assignments for the Assistant Commissioner. Today he had me going round the cattle boats interviewing skippers, as per the Queen's suggestion. Tonight I smell like a cow, and no amount of Sunlight soap helps; even Willy says so.

All quiet on the Royal engagement, which leaves ample room for speculation. Yesterday's Court Circular reported the departure of Princess Alix; she left Balmoral Thursday last, took the messenger train from Ballater to Buckingham Palace, departing Friday from London. Did she leave with a proposal? When the Prince of Wales returns to London next week will he announce the forthcoming marriage of his firstborn son?

Several clues in tonight's paper. Young Prince Eddy's equerry has been replaced with a Captain G. L. Holford of the First Life Guards. As Greville was far from the age of retirement, we can make certain assumptions: Such a change often occurs when a match is to take place. Greville, it is rumoured, was something of a gay blade; the change may foreshadow a domiciling direction for our young Prince. Yes, all looks ripe for the Royal romance.

My own life is singularly devoid of such drama. Just as well, at least until I can wash the stench of cattle from my pores.

Thursday, October 18, 1888

f f f

St. Luke the Evangelist's Day. A telegram this morning from Henry Smith to come to City headquarters. I went round Old Jewry at once.

Henry pulled out a cardboard box about three and a half inches square and set it on his desk.

"The chairman of the vigilante committee received the package Thursday eve. This came with it," Henry said, unfolding a sheet of foolscap. He smoothed the sheet open.

From hell

Mr. Lusk
Sir

   I send you half the Kidne I took from one women prasarved it for you tother piece I fried and ate it was very nise I may send you the bloody knif that took it out if you only wate a whil longer

signed Catch me when
You can
Mishter Lusk

The ink was smeared, and the characters were thick and jagged, as if the writer had pressed too hard with a cheap point.

"Is there a kidney in the box?"

Henry nodded. "I think so. Mr. Lusk says at first he thought it was a medical student's hoax, someone trying to frighten him—he's had some prowlers lately; he's rather nervous to begin with. Want to see the thing?"

"Not really."

Smith lifted the lid and brought out a stoppered jar sealed with white wax. Inside was a piece of meaty substance swimming in pink liquid.

"Looks like a sheep's kidney to me."

"That's what Mr. Lusk thought—wanted to throw it away, but some other committee members convinced him to bring it to me."

"Do you think it came from Kate Eddowes?"

"Her killer did take away a kidney."

"Do you have the wrappings this came in?"

Smith brought forth a sheet of crumpled brown paper. The package had been addressed with the same cheap pen to Mr. Lusk, Head Vigilance Committee, Alderney Street, Mile End. The penmanship on the wrapping, however, was clearer, more familiar. And there were no spelling mistakes. Two penny stamps were affixed.

"How about inquiring at the Post Office?"

"No use," Henry said. "You see the postage. It must have been dropped in an ordinary post-box. Wouldn't fit through most slots, would it?"

"No. Unless—unless it was mailed from Gracechurch Street or Lombard. They've oversize pillar-boxes there."

"The postmark is smudged; I can only make out the letters OND."

"Only one postmark. It will have been sent in this district. Well, let's go round and see Openshaw. If it is Kate's kidney, then it's proof positive that our Jack the Ripper letter writer is one and the same as the killer."

We went round to the hospital together and gave the jar to Dr. Openshaw. After a short examination he nodded gravely at us.

"It is definitely a human kidney, a left kidney. Not only that but it is of a female about forty years of age and it is divided longitudinally as was the half in Eddowes' body. And even more conclusively, it's a ginny kidney."

"Aye?" Smith said.

"The kidney shows deterioration such as is found in a person with the advanced stage of Bright's disease, just as Eddowes' right kidney demonstrated. But there is more evidence. Attached to it is a portion of renal artery three inches long. The average renal artery measures five inches; two inches of renal artery were found in Eddowes' body."

"But," Henry said, "didn't you tell West here that such organs could be had for the asking? Couldn't this be such an organ, selected to match the information given out at the inquest?"

Openshaw shook his head. "Such organs are available only after the body has gone to the dissecting room; this kidney was put into spirits within a few hours of its removal from the body. Besides, no one ever told the papers the killer extracted the *left* kidney."

"He's gone to a lot of trouble to prove himself author of his name," I said.

"Aye," Smith said.

"And he's waited long enough to send it, hasn't he?"

"Maybe he was just waiting till the publicity died down. Holding something back to get himself back in the news. Well, I'm off to speak to the reporters." Henry took his hat from the rack. "Sometimes I wonder why I do it. The papers will only make him out to be more invisible, more invincible, more unfathomable."

"Only until he's caught, Henry."

"Aye. And then they'll forget him."

"I never will."

I said good-bye to Smith on the stairs, went back inside, and climbed the spiral staircase to John Merrick's room.

* * *

I had a smoke on the landing before knocking. I feel myself in the midst of some strange fable, pitted against a mind beyond human comprehension, a mind that has set itself above the rest. The Divine Mind come to earth? The final irony? Why not, when we live in a world where saints are born into monsters' bodies?

I knocked on the blue door and John Merrick opened it, bobbed his head for me to enter. I came in and shook his small, dainty hand. The touch of perfect human flesh belied the scaly epidermis of the reptilian form before me. There but for the grace of God. . . . And I thank God each time I see Merrick that it is not me. I would have slit my own throat, jumped from London Bridge, anything. Merrick alone of all the men I know has enough humanity to bear his load.

"Well," I said, when the tea had been drunk and I had lit a cigarette. "Have you heard from the Belle Alexandrine?"

"She is very busy, Mr. West. I wouldn't trouble her by taking any of her time. She is home safely, though. She sent me a note and a photograph." He jumped up and produced a large 11x15 photograph framed in mauve velvet. It had been coloured in with a fine stroke: ivory skin, deep blue eyes, a lavender dress. "It is of her in the drawing room at Sandringham. She'll be there soon. But first she must visit the Queen. She has promised to send me a picture of the *tableaux vivants* at Balmoral. They're doing Shakespeare this year."

"Enchanting," I said, looking past the lovely face to the contents of the room in the photograph; the colouring was French, pale blue and pink, cream and gold with a hanging of gold silk and a crimson screen. A great number of animal heads—lions, tigers, bison, elephants—looked down from the walls at the jungle centrepiece: a forest of palms and flowering plants set in rock work and surrounding a sculpture of Venus and Cupid. Rubies, emeralds, and diamonds glowed from the scabbards and dagger belts that hung on the walls.

"She doesn't like the room, she says. It has a musty smell. But her husband is a great hunter—the sons, too—they keep bringing home trophies."

"Now, if only the daughters took after their mother—" I kicked myself as soon as I had opened my mouth. The homeliness of the "whispering Wales" is a common joke, but Merrick was hardly the audience for telling.

He leaned over and touched the door in the corner of the photograph. "She prefers the small conservatory through these doors. She takes tea there in basket chairs in front of the statue of the swan. Her Cocky perches above, and the scent from the flowers, she says, drifts out." He sighed. "I've no sense of smell, none at all."

I changed the subject for fear he would penetrate my present thoughts. Despite attempts at daily bathing and fumigation, a sour animal stench exudes from Merrick. "So, you must be following the papers? Do you think there will be an engagement soon?"

"That is a difficult question. I think it depends on the young folk themselves. Have you seen any new pictures of Princess Alix in the cartographers' shops?"

"Yes. Just last week. I'd say she has a good chance. She is lovely as a day in May. But I wonder if Alexandra will approve."

"Oh, she wants her son to be happy first. They are very close, you know, she and her firstborn. Of course, now he is growing up, she cannot see him always. She misses that, you know, misses the babies."

"Have you met the heir?"

"Oh, no. She comes alone always. But she likes to talk of him." Merrick watched me carefully as I lit a new cigarette off my short butt. "He smokes too much. She worries for his health. He was a frail infant, premature, quite fairy-like—though he is very strong now. Do you know, in her room she had a small button and when she pressed it the ceiling above opened and his cradle lowered down to her."

"No steps to climb. The nanny must have loved it."

"No, not at all. The nanny hated to part with the Prince. She adored him. When he lost his first tooth in a railway carriage his nanny begged for it, then had it mounted in gold with turquoises and wore it round her neck. Oh, but I *am* going on. I must be boring you."

"Not at all. One never tires of our Royal Family." I handed him back his framed picture.

Merrick took it and lovingly replaced it on the table. "She likes to talk about her children. Do you know, Prince Eddy has a tattoo on his arm—from when he sailed on the *Bacchante*."

"I thought his brother was the sailor."

"No, they sailed together twice—the *Britannia* and the *Bacchante*."

"Wasn't his mother upset?"

"She might have been. As it was she was quite relieved. The rumours had it that he'd had his *nose* tattooed. His dragon is at least hidden. And it was done by a Yedo Bay master, very intricate blue and red scales, a gift of the Mikado himself."

"Well," I said, standing, "speaking of tattoos, they'll be bugling for me soon. And twilight falls at five-fifteen. I'd best be on my way."

We had sat for thirty minutes and not talked once of the murders, I realized when I hit the evening streets. I felt relaxed for the first time in a fortnight. So safe to sit above the crowd and sip tea and talk of the niceties of matchmaking. It might almost be a normal day.

Friday, October 19, 1888

ƒƒƒ

A short-lived calm. Henry Smith wired me to meet him at two at 25 Alderney Street, Mile End. Mr. Lusk's house.

When I arrived, Henry was standing at the table, reading a postcard. Mr. Lusk was huddled in a large chair, holding his infant daughter; his wife stood next to him, clutching his shoulder.

"I never would have gotten involved if I'd known it would lead to this. I never wanted to be chairman, anyhow; they talked me into it. I just want to live in peace. I'm frightened for my family."

"We just want that he not come here again," the wife said.

"The card wasn't posted," Henry explained. "No stamp. Someone *placed* it through the slot in his door this morning."

"Did you see who put it in?" I said.

Mr. Lusk shook his head. "It was *him*, wasn't it? I told you we had a prowler."

I raised an eyebrow. "You see," Henry said, "Mr. Lusk complained last week to the police about a prowler: a bearded fellow in a long black coat. They didn't take it seriously."

"He's watching me. Oh, what if he comes back?" Lusk held his child tighter; his wife began to cry.

"Here," Henry said. "Looks like his hand." He gave me the postcard.

Mr. George Lusk, Head Vigilante
25 Alderney Street, Mile End
 Say, Boss, you seem rare frightened. Guess I like to give you *fits*, but can't stop long enough to let you box of toys play copper games with me, but hope to see you when I don't hurry too much. Bye-bye, Boss.

Jack the Ripper

"Box of toys, eh?"

"You've got to find him and stop him," Lusk said.

"Could we take this postcard, Mr. Lusk?" I asked. "If it was the Ripper himself who delivered it, maybe Metro's bloodhounds can track him."

"Take it, take it. I hate it. I wish I'd never seen the evil thing."

"You don't mind, Henry?"

"You've got the duggies ready, go ahead. Just don't give it to King Stork."

"I may have to. Sir Charles has taken charge of the hounds."

"Very well, but make a copy first."

I laughed. Then I took the card over to the Yard and presented my idea to Williamson.

"I'll take it up with the Commissioner, West. He's got a trial planned for St. James's Park tonight. Full moon. Wait here. I won't take long. Cut yourself a rose while you're waiting. There are lapel pins on my desk. And put that card in an envelope. Don't let anyone else touch it."

He was back in five minutes. "No problem. The Commissioner says you can talk to Mr. Brough tonight during the trial and set a time to use the dogs tomorrow. Says he may even attend the trial himself."

"I hope it's not too late."

"It's worth a try, isn't it?" He leaned back in his chair and studied the card. " 'Can't stop long enough to let you box of toys play copper games with me.' Hmm, that's the true criminal mind speaking. That's all we are, all of us. A box of toys."

"We'll catch him."

"Do you really think so, West?"

"Yes. And soon. He's giving too much up, becoming more and more daring. It's like he wants to be caught."

"I don't know. The stakes keep getting bigger, don't they? But I'd not wager he'll give himself up."

"He's got to trip up soon."

"Let's hope you're right. Well, good luck tonight."

"Aren't you coming?"

"Sorry, I've Mansfield's benefit for the East End poor to attend. The Commissioner's box."

"A light farce, I hope."

"*Prince Karl.* You wire me if you get on to something."

* * *

"A fiasco tonight in St. James's Park," I wired Williamson just
before midnight. "Barnaby and Burgho are lost!"

Mr. Brough is distraught. Barnaby was for sale, but Burgho is
a priceless bitch, touted to take top honours in this year's show.
And they have disappeared into thin air! "Crapulous decrepitude," the newspapers will write and again call for Warren's
dismissal. I am not so sure.

Tonight I met King Stork head on.

"We don't know if they can track a man by night," he told me
as we walked from the Yard to the park. "We need this trial
before we can be sure of them." He squinted at me through his
monocle. "And then you have a body to chase, don't you?"

"Night or day, makes no nevermind," Mr. Brough said.
"You've rented them twenty-four hours a day."

On the pond in St. James's, white ducks were tucking their
heads in for the night. A full moon, the harvest moon, bringing
with it the first taste of clear cold, all of the stars in the universe.
The Commissioner breathed deeply.

"Just look at those stars. Makes a man feel pretty humble,
doesn't it?"

"Sure does," I said. I looked at my watch. "As dark as it's
going to get tonight."

"Best be off, Commissioner," Mr. Brough said.

Warren held out his hand and shook Brough's. Then he set off
at a respectable clip. We waited ten minutes, and then Mr.
Brough knelt and held his palm to the dogs, talked to them. The
two hounds snuffed and licked the palm, locking Sir Charles Warren into their finely bred brains.

"Find him!" Brough said, giving his bloods their orders and
their heads. We followed, but even with the moonlight, we fell
behind. By the time we reached the Mall, we could not hear
them. We stopped and Mr. Brough whistled.

"That's strange," he said. "They should be baying. They
couldn't be that far ahead. Barnaby! Burgho!"

Nothing.

We found Sir Charles in his office at Scotland Yard an hour
later, smoking a cigar. He adjusted his monocle and smiled benignly. "Don't worry, Mr. Brough, they'll turn up. They proba-

bly went off in pursuit of a rabbit. Never trust a hound when there's a full moon."

"I never should have taken the chance," Mr. Brough said. "I never should have risked them. It was a personal favour for—if they're harmed, Commissioner—"

"Mr. Brough, Mr. Brough, didn't I just say they'll turn up? Two trials out of three is not bad. At least we'll be able to find our Jack if he strikes in broad daylight. Dogs always come back when they're hungry."

"It wasn't the night. It couldn't be. I'm going back out. They're out there still tracking."

"Suit yourself," he said petulantly. "I told you, don't worry. How about you, West—you going to be sensible and get some sleep?"

"I guess." I turned to poor Mr. Brough. "Wire me if you find anything, will you?"

I walked back to headquarters under the big bright moon. The streets were full. Men out for a sup, women in satin and lace and ready smiles. As I got closer to Stepney, the quality of the cloth declined and the boldness of the women increased. There was a time when I would have been tempted, perhaps there will be a time when I succumb. Tonight I am too deep in thought. Something is rotten in the state of Denmark.

Thursday, October 25, 1888

✞✞✞

St. Crispin's Day today. The weather has changed to cold, true cold, no longer autumn but winter. Half-holidays were reinstated today. Arnold told me, "in all confidence," that he believes the murders are over. Strangely quiet all round. I keep thinking of Pepys' description of London during the plague, how the grass grew upon the streets and how the bells tolling was the only sound from morning to night.

Monday, October 29, 1888

ᚠᚠᚠ

A message this afternoon from Thomas Openshaw to come round the hospital. When I arrived, he thrust a dirty envelope at me. An East London postmark. I opened it and took out the sheet of foolscap.

Dr. Openshaw
Pathological Curator
London Hospital
Whitechapel

Old boss you was rite it was the left kidny i was goin to hopperate agin clos to your ospitle just as i was goin to drop mi nife along of er blooming throte them cusses of coppers spoilt the game but i guess i will be on the job soon and will send you another bit of innerds

Jack the ripper

O have you seen the devle
with his mikerscope and scalpul
a lookin at a kidney
with a slide cocked up

"His spelling seems to be deteriorating again," Openshaw said.

"Notice, though," I said, tapping the envelope, "that he spelled your name and 'Pathological Curator' just fine."

"Very sly. The mail must get through."

"And he reads the newspapers."

"How so?"

"The postscript: the 'devle with his mikerscope'—that's you. The *Echo* ran a sketch yesterday. Didn't you see it?"

"I don't read the *Echo*. And yesterday I was away."

"But *he* wasn't. He was in London yesterday. Right outside

your window. I'll have to check the men's log books for occurrences."

"Speaking of books, don't go away without letting me show you one. Were you planning to see Mr. Merrick today?"

"How is he?"

"I'm afraid he's had a bad night of it." He sighed. "Someday the weight of his head will simply crush him. He's resting now."

I looked at my watch. "I really should be going anyhow." I folded the letter into my handkerchief and placed it in my inside pocket. "Got to see a man about some dogs. Please give him my regards when he's better."

"Did you find the bloodhounds?"

"Didn't you hear? They turned up last night in their kennels, fat and happy. Mr. Brough took them home to Scarborough this morning. Now I've got to find some new ones." I took my bowler from the lab table and set it on my head.

"Oh, the book," Openshaw said, turning to the large shelf behind his desk. "Something you said earlier set me thinking."

"Yes?"

"The way the bodies were laid out. The arms squared just so. The feet drawn up. You said they looked *arranged.*"

"Yes. Exactly so."

Openshaw took a red book with a tasselled marker off the top shelf. "I had a funny feeling I'd seen something like that before." He opened the book upon the desk. "Never know what you'll find in a doctor's library."

The chapter heading was "Concerning the Existence of Mantric Signs Throughout History." There were pictures:

THE SIGN OF PRESERVATION:
By my trust in Thee and fidelity to Thee, I
pray thee, O Lord, to preserve me.

THE SIGN OF FIDELITY:
Faith, Trustworthiness, Fidelity.

THE SIGN OF DISTRESS:
Death. All hope is abandoned.

"Holy smoke!" I said. "The bodies! What is this book?"

"A tract on ancient religious customs. I bought it because it has a chapter on circumcision rites." Openshaw turned several pages and showed me a crude sketch of a man with arms and legs drawn up. "You said the legs of the victims had been drawn up . . . like this?"

"Yes, just so. Soles flat on the ground." I shook my head. "But what does it all mean? A circumcision rite?"

Openshaw pulled at his lower lip "That's a thought. They circumcise women in some African countries. Cut out the clitoris so the woman cannot feel pleasure. The killer did cut out the sex."

"And then some."

"But I was thinking more about the arrangement of the limbs. It's some sort of hieroglyph."

"But why?"

Openshaw shook his head. "I can't imagine. Take the book with you if you want. But take care; it's out of print."

I walked back to Commercial Street and entered the station. I knocked on Arnold's door.

"Sir, you in?"

"Come in, West. Where've you been?"

"At the hospital seeing Openshaw. He got this letter in the mail today."

Arnold read the letter quickly. "I'll send it over to the Yard if you like. But it's not likely it's from the killer." He put the letter under his Stourbridge magnum paperweight.

"Why not?"

"It's been three weeks. If I were a betting man, I'd wager that the killer is under lock and key. His family's on to him and is keeping him back. I don't think we'll see any more of him."

"Openshaw also gave me this." I took out the book and opened to the pictures. "The Berner Street victim—her hands and legs were just like this. And at Hanbury Street and Mitre Square, the women were arranged just so—like this mantric sign. I think the killer arranged the limbs, that they didn't just fall randomly. Openshaw thinks maybe he's giving us some sort of hieroglyphic sign. It's too much of a coincidence to be—sir, is there something wrong?"

Arnold's face had gone white, and his hands on the back of the chair were clenched tight.

"Sir?"

"Where'd you get this book?"

"Openshaw gave it to me."

Arnold's hands relaxed on the chair. "Thomas Openshaw, you say?"

"Yes."

"Hmm."

"Do you want me to follow up on it?"

"Certainly not. We don't have time for such fiddlefaddle." He handed me a stack of papers. "I need this robbery report by five, that's what I need. Hieroglyphs indeed. And take a little time with it. Your writing's beginning to look like an algebraic problem."

"But, sir—I—"

"Coincidence is exactly what it is. You know the first thing the policeman does when he finds a body is to lift the wrist and feel for a pulse. All of those bodies were disturbed."

"The first, yes. But the others—"

"Besides, you're wrong. The Berner Street victim's hands weren't like that. Look at the police sketch. Better yet, get that report finished."

I went back to the files and pulled the case file. Arnold was right. One hand had been moved by the time the police artist had arrived on the scene. Or perhaps my memory was slipping.

The report took me two hours; I couldn't concentrate. The pictures in the book kept coming back to me. And something else: Arnold's face. Why would pictures of ancient mantric signs upset him? Something was not on the square. I added his white face to my mental list of strange occurrences.

Wednesday, October 31, 1888

ℱℱℱ

All Hallows' Eve. Tomorrow is the day on which the Church glorifies God for His saints, known and unknown. A day of feasting. A day for martyrs. It begins tonight: a night of fires, of retellings of old truths, strange foretellings of new ones. This is Midsummer's continuation: a pagan night to be passed in the dark out-of-doors in masquerade.

The day began with heavy rains. Arnold had a meeting at the Yard, left me in charge of the "Morning Report of Disturbances." I sat at his desk and prepared the report, signed it, then had a smoke, stared into space. Gradually I focused on the desk. It was as barren and impersonal as the man. There was nothing of the man there, not even a photograph. He was all business. I shall never get on with him, I thought, and then chided myself. What did I really know about Glenn Arnold after a year of working with him? He has a wife, four children; he attends St. Paul's every Sunday; he is a Freemason, an orchid grower; he loves Regency antiques. This is a job to him; he has some other life. Not like myself.

Sour grapes? Perhaps, but there was something more. He has been treating me differently lately, watching me more closely, burdening me with paperwork a clerk could attend to. The investigation had stagnated; if not for the City actions, there would be no real investigation. The thought kept coming back to me: Something is not on the square. I took up my pen and made a list:

Insp. Frederick Abberline: missing evidence: leather apron in Hanbury Street tap, bloody newspaper and trail of blood on escape route.

AC Anderson: mysterious illness and departure. Switzerland or Paris? Wild goose assignments.

Coroner Baxter: American doctor hoax.

Commissioner Warren: Message erased, missing blood-hounds, general obfuscation.

Then I began jotting down what I knew about each man:

Abberline: son of a schoolmaster, married, four children, Freemason, Church of Scotland Calvinist.

Anderson: Doctor of Divinity, barrister, Irishman, Scottish extraction, married, two children, third son of Crown Solicitor, secret service work—Fenians, Trinity College, Freemason, White's Club.

Baxter: Londoner, widower. St. Mary the Bow Bell Church, barrister, doctor, Freemason.

Warren: G.C.M.G., R.E., second son of a Protestant minister, married, three children, King's College, Hall's Club, Founder—Quatuor Coronati Lodge, Grand Sojourner of the Supreme Masonic Lodge.

I put down the list and sat a long time in the cold, dank room. There was only one thing they shared. None was a Catholic. And they were all members of the Masonic Order.

In a while I put on my hat and went out into the rain. I walked west, past the new Tower Bridge, a steel skeleton with two half-completed Gothic towers, then turned north. It was the De Goncourt scandal over again. Williamson and me and the Catholics in the dark against the brothers of light. Did the Home Office know? Monro was a Catholic, wasn't he? How far did the coverup stretch? I couldn't ask a Mason. Didn't all Masons take an oath on pain of death not to reveal a word of their secret rites?

My friend Hopkins was my only hope. He was much too poor to be a Mason. But if someone somewhere had once written about it, Hopkins would know.

Hopkins was in; the flat was cold. He greeted me with a smile, put down his pen, and listened keenly. When I finished, he nodded. "I can tell you a little about the order. They call themselves the Free and Accepted Masons; they're organized along the lines of a medieval guild with three degrees: apprentice, fellowcraft, and master. Each degree has its own secret signs and passwords. The lodge is a national organization, not international, and charity is its principal purpose. No Catholics or Jews admitted."

"What sort of charity?"

He shrugged. "The custom is that donations be anonymous. I believe each individual determines for himself how best to relieve the suffering of others."

"Do you know any of the signs or the rites?"

"All secret. Supposedly, it's all based on fertility mysteries handed down from the time of the Pharaohs—something of a Hermetic-Cabalistic tradition."

"Mysteries?"

"Souls make their way to Salvation through the reenactment of the ancient dramas of Isis, Osiris, and Horus. Reenacting the sacred rites keeps the old gods alive. Did you know Mozart was a Mason? So was Robbie Burns."

"Did he write about it?"

"I'm afraid not. That's part of the problem with secrets people take seriously. I hear the Queen abhors the order because of that fact."

"I imagine the Queen abhors being left out of any secret."

"Which is probably why the men in her family insist on joining —just to have one."

"No, I think they just like the uniforms."

Hopkins laughed. "That reminds me—" He lifted one finger in the air. "A minute and it will come to me . . . ah!" He went to his bookcase, the only piece of furniture in the room besides the table and bed, and took down a fat volume. "This has a passage on the present-day drama. It's only recently been translated," he said, riffling through the pages. "Here," he said, "start here."

I sat on the edge of the bed with the book, *War and Peace*, read:

> Taking a handkerchief from the wardrobe, Willarski covered Pierre's eyes, catching his hair painfully in the knot as he tied it behind. Then he drew his face down, kissed him, and taking him by the hand led him away. . . . After leading him for about ten paces, Willarski stopped. "Whatever happens to you, you must bear it with fortitude if you are firmly resolved to enter our Brotherhood. . . . When you hear a knock on the door, you will uncover your eyes. . . ." Left alone, Pierre went on smiling in the same way. Once or twice he shrugged his shoulders and raised his hand to the handkerchief as if wishing to take it off, but let it drop again. . . . Loud knocks were heard at the door. Pierre un-

covered his eyes and looked about him. The room was pitch dark, except in one place where a small lamp was burning inside something white. Pierre went nearer and saw that the lamp stood on a black table on which lay an open book. The book was the Gospel; the white object in which the lamp was burning was a human skull with its apertures and teeth. . . . The door opened and someone came in. By the dim light he saw a rather short man. The man paused, then with cautious steps approached the table and placed his small, leather-gloved hands on it. This short man was wearing a white leather apron. . . . The Rhetor cleared his throat, crossed his gloved hands on his breast, and began to speak. "Now I must reveal to you the principal aim of our Order," he said. . . . "The first and chief aim . . . is the preservation and bequeathing to Posterity of a certain solemn mystery . . . which has come down to us from the most ancient times, actually from the first man, a mystery upon which perhaps the fate of mankind depends. . . ."

The third time the Rhetor came back sooner, and asked Pierre whether he was still firm in his intention and resolved to submit to all that would be required of him. "I am ready for everything," said Pierre. "I must inform you," said the Rhetor, "that our order teaches its doctrine not by word alone, but by other means, which may perhaps have a more potent effect on the sincere seeker after wisdom and virtue than mere verbal instruction. Our Order follows the example of the ancient societies that made known their teachings by the means of hieroglyphics. A hieroglyph is a design for something not cognizable by the senses. . . .

"If you are resolved, I must proceed to your initiation," said the Rhetor, coming closer to Pierre. "In token of generosity, I ask you to give me all your valuables . . . watch, money, rings. . . ." When this had been done, the Mason said: "In token of obedience, I ask you to undress. . . ." The silence was broken by one of the brothers, who led Pierre to the carpet and commenced reading to him from a manuscript book an interpretation of all the figures delineated on it: the sun, the moon, a hammer, a plumb line, a trowel, a roughhewn stone and a cubic stone, the pillar, the three windows, and so on. After this a place was assigned to Pierre; he was shown the signs of the Lodge, told the pass-

words, and at last was permitted to sit down. The Grand
Master began reading the statutes. . . . "In our temples we
recognize no other distinctions, but those between virtue and
vice. . . . Fly to a brother's aid, whoever he may be. . . .
Forgive thine enemy, avenge not thyself upon him except by
doing good. Thus fulfilling the highest law, thou shalt regain
traces of the ancient dignity which thou hast lost. . . ." The
meeting was over, and on reaching home, Pierre felt as if he
had returned from a journey that had lasted for decades,
that he was completely changed and had left behind his for-
mer habits and way of life.

I put down the heavy book. It was all there: the kerchief blindfold, the kiss, the leather apron, the teaching by hieroglyph, the
pockets emptied of metal and rings. It was all there but the bequeathing of the "certain solemn mystery."

"Does it help?" Hopkins said.

"Yes, I think so."

"You can borrow it if you like."

"Thank you."

He wrapped the book in oiled American cloth and placed the
package in my hands. I walked back to the station in the heavy
rain, absorbed in thought. The key was not there, but the keyhole
beckoned; I could see a glimpse of light. So much fit. Of course,
there were missing pieces: Why had the killer arranged the intestines over the victim's shoulder? Why had he cut out the sex?

I didn't have proof yet, but my instincts told me I was on the
right track. The killer was carrying out a rite of Masonry, and his
lodge brothers—my superiors—were carrying out their oath to
protect him and the secrets of their Order. I felt as Williamson
must have felt, only I had been betrayed by those above me
rather than those below. Could I trust anyone? Would anyone
believe me?

I had to have proof. Hopkins had said there were degrees in
Masonry. Pierre was just an initiate. All the men on my list were
high Masons. Somewhere within the confines of the highest and
most sublime degrees lay the key.

* * *

Just before teatime, I knocked on Arnold's door and told him I was feeling ill. He sent me to quarters.

I went to my room, changed into dark clothes and my new gum shoes, then lay on my cot until the men had finished their tea. I went out to the hall closet, took the crowbar out, and secreted it in the deep inside pocket of my long black travelling coat. Then I walked into the mess and stole two candles from the drawer; I went down the back stairs and slipped out, went over to the library, and spent an hour in its basement copying floorplans for two of London's venerable buildings. It was dark when I got out, and the rain had let up. Venus an evening star. Tonight, I thought, I will break the oath sworn on the Bible to obey my superiors and uphold the law. "The truth will out." Tonight that credo is my only master. "And hence one master passion in the breast, like Aaron's serpent, swallows up the rest."

I waited in the shadows outside the temple until the constable had passed, then rose and tiptoed to the cellar door and applied the crowbar. The lock came on the third try. I fixed it so it would not fall, then lifted the door, stepped inside, and let the door down slowly. I listened in the dark, then lit a taper. A cavernous roughhewn cellar loomed before me. Off to the left a rat scurried out of my light. I made a slow circle and located the staircase. The top door was locked, but my police skeleton key worked, and soon I was in a small dank corridor with a faint breeze. I cupped the taper and walked ten paces, held my candle along the wall until I found the door. It opened into a large and windowless gallery filled with meeting chairs. At the far end was a door. I crossed the room and passed into a second chamber filled with chairs. A second door and then I was in the inner temple's Sanctum Sanctorum, the Holy of Holies.

I held the taper high; it flickered up and cast long shadows of light upon the wall. There was the altar. On it lay a gavel and a mortar and pestle. It took me but ten minutes more to find and open the carved mahogany chest; it yielded up a chalky white human skull, a trowel and a white kid apron, three smooth stones.

In a half hour I had found nothing more. I waited five minutes, for the constable to pass on his beat. Then I went back to the cellar door. I lifted it a crack and listened. Nothing. I lifted the door farther. No one in sight. I smiled, thinking of something Pizer had told me one day in his cell. "When I come to your country, I hear this word and think it the most beautiful I have ever heard. I ask someone, *cellardore*? What this word mean?"

A skull, an apron, an odd coterie of symbols, hieroglyphics to me. Where was it all written down? Words, that was what I had not yet found. Symbols galore, but no words of explanation, no passwords, no prayerbooks. Was it all passed down verbally? I could secrete myself within a lodge and attempt to observe the rite of passage, but lodges met only from May to August. There would be no performances until spring.

I had used only half my candle. I hailed a hansom and gave the address of the public house next to the Quatuor Coronati Lodge of Masonic Research. Over a half pint I studied my notes on the floorplan. Then I broke in.

It was there I found the library that contained the book that contained the key that unlocked the secret. It was a little book with a crumbling blue leather binding, entitled *Getting Light*.

The candidate for the sublime degree of Master Mason is stripped and hoodwinked, then conducted to the altar of the Sanctum Sanctorum to pray.

"What do you desire?" the hierophant asks the candidate.

"More light."

"And God said, let there be light, and there was light."

The candidate then relives the most sacred drama of the days of Solomon's Temple; he personates Hiram Abiff, Solomon's Grand Master Architect.

Once upon a time, in the days of Solomon, there lived a man called Hiram Abiff, Grand Master Mason and Builder of Solomon's Temple. There was only one Temple in those days, and only one Master Mason. Only Hiram knew the secret sign of the Sanctum Sanctorum; only Hiram held the key to the plans.

One day at high twelve as Hiram was rising from prayer at the altar in the Sanctum Sanctorum, three of his workmen, Jubela, Jubelo, and Jubelum, accosted him and demanded of him the Master Mason's plans. "Have you the Master Mason's sign, or the magic password?" Hiram asked. The three Juwes had not the sign nor the magic word; thus, Hiram denied them. They replied by attacking him with blows, each blow fiercer than the next. First, Jubela; second Jubelo; until Jubelum struck the final blow and the Grand

Master lay dead. Then the three ruffians stole the Master's plans and hid them. They buried their Grand Master and ran away. When the Master was discovered missing, a roll was called. The three Juwes did not answer. A search was made, and the three ruffians were tracked and brought to trial. Each pleaded guilty and each was sentenced to be punished.

"Jubela, vile and impious wretch, hold up your head and hear your sentence. It is my order that you be taken without the gates of the Temple, and there have your throat cut across, your tongue torn out, and your body buried in the rough sands of the sea.

"Jubelo, vile and impious wretch, hold up your head and hear your sentence. It is my order that you be taken without the gates of the Temple, and there have your throat cut across, and your breast torn open and your vitals taken from thence and thrown over your left shoulder and carried to the valley of Jehoshaphat, there to become a prey to the wild beasts of the field and the vultures of the air.

"Jubelum, vile and impious wretch, hold up your head and hear your sentence. It is my order that you be taken without the walls of the Temple, and there have your body severed in two, and divided to the north and south, your bowels burnt to ashes in the center and scattered to the four winds of Heaven."

When the sentences had been carried out, the brethren searched for the grave of their Master; they found it near the brow of Mount Moria. They unearthed the stinking body and searched it for the plans and for the Master Mason's password, or a key to it, but could find them not; they discovered only a faint letter G marked on the left breast.

"Thus, all give the grand hailing sign of distress, for the Master Mason's word is lost forever."

Solomon's Temple represented the world in miniature: measured justice. Symbol and symbolic, layers of meaning superimposed upon the other. Jubela, Jubelo, Jubelum: the three pillars of Masonry, the Juwes who are to blame. Only by punishing the Juwes can the Master Mason's plans be recovered and the Temple rebuilt. Symbol and symbolic, the Evil Quarter Mile as the Temple, each victim playing a role in the drama as the candidate himself—perhaps this very summer—played the role of Hiram Abiff in his initiation into the Holy of Holies, the Sanctum Sanctorum. Each victim taken beyond the gates into a measured square and stripped of all metal—"not a hammer nor an ax was heard"—each victim hoodwinked and then made to open her eyes and face east, hear her sentence.

It was all there in the small, blue leather-bound book, the key to all the mysteries.

Polly was Jubela, Pillar of Beauty, representing the Apprentice stage of Masonry, the Life Force, carnality. Her sentence: throat cut across and tongue torn out. Her sign, Isis's: Fidelity.

Annie was Jubelo, Pillar of Strength, the second step to Masonic light, Fellowcraft. And her throat was cut across and her body torn open, the vitals taken and thrown over the left shoulder. The sign of Osiris, Perseverance, was made.

I don't know the name of the third victim; her name is as lost as the Master Mason's word. She stood for Jubelum, the Pillar of Wisdom and Knowledge, the third and most sublime step to light, the Worshipful Master in the East. In the Sanctum Sanctorum, Horus was reborn from the severed body.

And then he started anew: mirror images of murder. Polly and Liz, Annie and Kate, Torso and Next Victim.

First, second, third. "1st, 2nd . . ." Christ! He warned us in his own deceptive way: "Beware, I shall be at work on the 1st and 2nd . . . at high twelve."

Will he warn us next time? What is to prevent an infinity of reflecting mirrors? Jack the Ripper. A Mason, a pillar of society hiding a monster behind his mask. And the rest of the Masons, carrying out their oaths to protect each other and the secrets of Masonry. He must be very important if they are willing to risk all for it. Is he one of us? I must tread softly and listen carefully. I cannot trust them to stop the killings. I must learn his name before he completes the trilogy.

Thursday, November 1, 1888

ʄ ʄ ʄ

All Soul's Day's Eve. Tomorrow is the day on which the Church prays for the souls of those in purgatory. The proper office is of the dead, and the Mass is a requiem. Indulgences are granted. Tonight candles have been lit on graves so that the souls can rise.

It is midnight and I have just returned from the Haymarket Theatre, a performance of *Captain Swift*. When I sat down this morning at my desk, I found an envelope with my name on it, two tickets within. There was a note from Fred Abberline, with his compliments.

"A little toothful, I imagine. You want to go, Willy?"

"Me? I don't go to theatre. Find some lass."

"I wish."

"Oh, stop moaning."

"I don't know. I had some things to do tonight."

"You're working too hard. You look like you need a rest." He cocked his burly head. "Haven't seen much of you, John. You're not on to something, are you?"

I shook my head. I could use Willy's help, but what I was about wasn't legal. They could take away my badge if they found out about the break-in.

"I have a lot on my mind, that's all, Willy. The investigation doesn't seem to be going anywhere."

"That's putting it mildly. Notice there was nothing in the papers today. That's a first."

"You think it will just all die down?"

"It's possible."

"And the killer? You think he's done?"

"That sod? Not unless he's dead. But it has been a while. I think you could afford to take one night off in a month and a fortnight."

"I saw a play not two fortnights ago."

"That was work."

I took Willy's nephew Martin: a rousing musical performance.
And we had an extra surprise. Ten minutes into the performance,
a whisper went round the audience; the actors seemed to freeze
onstage. The young leading lady looked up at the boxes and
smiled, dropped a curtsy. I looked up. There in the Royal Box sat
a stout man with pointed beard and protruding eyes, our future
King, the Prince of Wales, the man I so contemptuously called
Spuds. I'd seen so many pictures but never the man. And in that
instant my heart swelled over. Here was my sovereign. Look at
him: magnificent in his kingly bearing, splendid in his robe and
medals. I almost cried for loving him so.

When I could tear my eyes off of him, I saw that he was not
alone. Two men stood behind him in the shadows, and next to
him sat a young man with dark receding hair and a trim mustache, dazzling white collar and cuffs. He sat stiffly, looking neither left nor right nor at the stage, but focused somewhere beyond. I lifted my glass and had a closer look. I made out a gold
Jubilee medal and a gold star on his left shoulder, a horseshoe
diamond breast-pin on his cravat. That would be Eddy, staying
this week with his father to help close up Marlborough House.

Father and son, out for a night on the town, just like real
mortals. How perfect I felt tonight as they shone their counte-
nances down on me.

Monday, November 5, 1888

ʄ ʄ ʄ

Guy Fawkes Day. The bonfire boys made a big blaze and bashed a few blue heads. A massive public rally was called for next Sunday, Martinmas Sunday. The anniversary of Bloody Sunday.

At headquarters Arnold had me remaking rosters; Warren has cancelled all Sunday leaves. The Commissioner plans to fight this one out; he will not rescind his five-year ban against public meetings. He shall quell the crowd if it takes all of Metro to do it.

"But," I protested when Arnold said I must take a half dozen men off the murder investigation, "this could just play into the killer's hands. If all our men are assigned to Hyde Park—"

"Save your breath to cool your porridge, West. You'll not get round the Commissioner on this one."

"I've half a mind to attend the rally myself. He's ruining the department. And we all just accept it." I clenched my fists. "I need those men. There's a murderer still loose."

Arnold came into my office and closed the door. "I've been wanting to talk to you, West. I've been waiting for the right moment. . . ." He coughed. "We're all convinced," Arnold said, looking directly at me for the first time in days, "that the murderer has been locked up by his family."

"Who is all?"

"Those at the Yard. Myself. Fred Abberline."

"I think I understand." I paused, looked him square in the face. "A family of brothers."

Arnold raised an eyebrow.

"And the family coat of arms is an arc and compass." I kept my gaze level on his eyes. He knew I knew.

"I can assure you everything is under control, John." He used my Christian name for the first time. "We all can. We've had assurances. He is being treated."

"Treated?"

"With mercury and iodine. There is talk of paresis—what matters is that he is no longer a danger."

"And we are to just go about our own business, Glenn?" The name felt oily in my mouth.

"Yes."

I shook my head. "I understand but I can't accept. Not blindly."

"Precautions have been taken. There will be no more killings."

"Do *you* know who he is?"

He looked at me a long time, then shook his head slowly.

"You won't tell me?"

"Never."

"Then I shall have to find out."

"It is a rugged and dangerous path. If you are wise you will avoid it at all costs."

"I have taken an oath too."

Arnold shook his greying head. He got up and walked to the window, head down, hands behind his back. He shook his head several times, then turned and faced me. "John, I shall say this only once. Give it up. It is better not to know."

"How can it be better not to know?"

"It is, I swear it. Leave well alone."

"I swear only by the truth. You are covering up for someone who has killed. How can you justify *that*?"

"I can."

"Then tell me how you sleep at night."

"I sleep praying for the Empire."

"And harbouring a killer?"

"And if—" He broke off and pursed his lips.

"Tell me."

"And if the killer *is* the Empire?"

"What are you—" My mind suddenly grasped his meaning and all the pieces fell sharply into place. A Royal. No wonder they are scared, all of them. It is the Prince.

Prince Albert Victor—the only prince in history to be given a double name—has another identity as well: Jack the Ripper, master killer. This summer his own father, the reigning Master, initiated him as Worshipful Master of the Royal Alpha, No. 16, Supreme Master of the most royal lodge in the land. He was Hiram Abiff then. *He* took the saloon carriage from Ballateer to Aberdeen, went out hunting humans instead of deer. In the East End he pursued his destiny, to restore the Temple.

The dates all fit. And the descriptions, down to the slight trace of German accent detected in his voice. The father obviously knows. A new equerry, guards in the Royal Box.

My mouth opened and then shut. If you had all the pieces it was obvious.

I looked at Arnold. "I have taken no vow of silence to your order," I said.

"No, but you have taken an oath to your Queen."

"Does she know?"

"Of course not. And she mustn't, not ever. Think about it, John, that's all I ask. Don't act harshly. You'll be taken care of—"

"Who's to take care of my soul?"

"John—I—" He buried his head in his hands. "God save us. God save the Queen."

I walked to Clerkenwell Green after, my mind still reeling, and watched the rowdies hang Sir Charles. The crowd hooted and applauded; when they were done, they hanged the Ripper. An old woman spat on him. The two straw-filled effigies dangled from thin ropes, their black coats flapping in the breeze. A gawky pimple-faced lad shinnied up the elm and grabbed Sir Charles's chimney-pot hat; he shinnied up the next elm and deposited it on Jack's head. The crowd roared its approval, individuals no more but some massive inhuman form. Would they believe it if I told them? Would they rise up like a giant bug and storm the Mount of Olives? The mood was ugly—Bloody Monday, Bloody Sunday, they would not be beaten back forever. Once that raw energy erupted, there would be no going back. If they knew, not all the king's horses and all the king's men could put things back together again.

Tuesday, November 6, 1888

𝄃𝄃𝄃

A bloody tyrant and a homicide,
One rais'd in blood and one in blood establish'd. . . .
A base foul stone made precious by the foil of
England's chair, where he is falsely set. . . .

—*Richard III*

The house is surrounded by a high wall and stands well back from the corner of Pall Mall. Built by Christopher Wren for the Duke of Marlborough, it is more often remembered for the tragedy of Princess Charlotte. I hear it has false doors and windows used by its present occupant for midnight trysts.

I stood in St. James Park for an hour in the wind and rain and watched the windows of the house, but all the curtains were pulled and I saw not a shadow. My legs began to cramp and my resolve crumbled. I shall catch my death of cold, I thought. What was I doing there anyhow? Some crazy idea that I could single-handedly catch him leaving by a back door in his deerstalker? That I could prove his guilt?

I retreated to Piccadilly and the roar of omnibuses, walked in glum silence. When I reached the photography shop I stopped. The pictures of the Royal couple had all been withdrawn. I went in and asked to purchase a print of the young Prince in the grouse butt with his father. "I'm sorry," the clerk said, "those have all been sold."

"I understand," I said. "You have none at all of him?"

"Just the official coming-of-age portrait. Before he grew his mustache."

"I particularly wanted the one of them together."

"Sorry," he said. So was I. The portrait displayed a little-known public fact. The young Prince shoots his Purdy left-handed.

I am in bed now with lemon tea and the chills. Willy has brought me his hot-water bottle and the paper, and I am almost comfortable. Stag season opened today. *The Times* news column announced that Prince Albert Victor has been granted a leave of absence from the Hussars to accompany his mother home to Copenhagen, effective immediately.

Since his graduation from Cambridge, the Prince has been the focus of the public eye: called on to open public functions, to dine and ride with Her Majesty, to woo the prettiest princess in all the land. In the last few weeks the *Court Circular* has shared even the more mundane happenings in his life: his arrival at Sandringham, his attendance on Sunday at Divine Service in Mary Magdalene Chapel.

Of course, everyone knows that the *Court Circular* is often shaded, manipulated to spare us certain realities: the words, "The Queen rode out . . ." often a euphemism for an attack of her sickness. Since the *Circular* is always published in the past tense, it can easily alter memories. Royalty might be naked and the people would still see them in their royal garb.

But his Royal Highness Albert Victor Christian Edward is splendidly garbed, a shining paragon of sartorial convention, groomed daily for the throne he will one day occupy. He belongs to us, our Prince. He inhabits every imagination in the kingdom. And none, save the few who have enough pieces of the puzzle, suspect what imagination inhabits his own. No wonder everyone has scurried *not* to be in charge; no one wants to be the one left holding the bag when the cat is out.

"The sky is falling!" said Duckey Lucky and Goosey Loosey and Turkey Lurkey. "Who shall tell the King?"

"Not I," said Duckey Lucky.

"Not I," said Goosey Loosey.

"Not I," said Turkey Lurkey.

Chicken Little stepped forth. "I shall tell the King."

I know only one man brave enough to face the old woman in the black antediluvian bonnet. I can just see him, cap in hand, hair tousled. "Your Majesty," Shaw would say, "I have come to tell you the sky has fallen."

I wish it were all a fairy tale, that I would wake and say, like Alice, "I've had such a curious dream," and someone would say, "It *was* a curious dream, dear, but now run in to your tea; it's getting late."

* * *

Four A.M.: A bad dream wakes me. I am in a tartan-walled room lying on a tartan rug. Above me a blonde woman with cornflower-blue eyes is laughing. A party is going on, and the music keeps getting louder. They are dancing now, the blonde woman, too, and matador music is blaring. The matador comes towards me; I can only see his eyes behind his cape; they are glowing red. He pulls a red handkerchief from his pocket and flourishes it. All around me people are laughing, laughing and prodding me. I bellow and charge the red eyes, wake to the sound of the bull, sweat streaming from my cold body.

Wednesday, November 7, 1888

I have now in my hands all the threads that were before tangled. Yet I hold no proof. Not a shred. It is all circumstantial. Age, physical description, clothing, whereabouts—it could be any young stag.

I cannot even prove that the murderer is a Mason. It is details that prove, and there are no details. No apron, no photographs of the bodies as found, no handwriting on the wall. Detail by detail the evidence has been destroyed.

I went to Leman Street today when I knew Abberline would be at the Yard, told the officer on duty I needed to consult the map, then slipped in and unlocked the case file with a skeleton key. The Liverpool letter and Glasgow missives have been removed. I picked up the bloody postcard. It will be gone soon, I thought, then remembered the copies circulated. Posterity at least has that, the rills and peaks of his bloody thumb, the print of Cain upon the page written with the victim's blood. If only it were proof.

In the bottom of the file I found a sheet of foolscap, a poem written in red ink. There was no envelope, no way to date it.

> Eight little whores, with no hope of heaven,
> Gladstone may save one, then there'll be seven.
> Seven little whores begging for a shilling,
> One stays in Henege Court, then there's a killing.
> Six little whores, glad to be alive.
> One sidles up to Jack, then there are five.
> Four and whore rhyme alright.
> So do three and me.
> I'll set the town alight.

Ere there are two.
Two little whores, shivering with fright,
Seek a cozy doorway in the middle of the night.
Jack's knife flashes, then there's but one,
And the last one's the ripest for Jack's idea of fun.

Thursday, November 8, 1888

🖊 🖊 🖊

I was at Hyde Park Corner when they announced the new American President today: one Benjamin Harrison, a Republican. He is a Civil War veteran, General of the Indiana Volunteers, and though not the popular choice, the Electoral College will vote him in. And the Americans will accept it. Strange that such a disorderly nation should succeed in such an orderly transition of rulers, but they have done it now twenty-three times. Here leaders are deposed only through upheaval.

At the tip of my tongue is Salisbury's political demise, the desecration of the Royal Family, perhaps even the destruction of the Empire as we know it. I have sworn an oath to all that is sacred to speak the truth. Yet I must not speak the truth lest hell come tumbling down.

Or so I would think. Would anyone even listen? Does anyone really want to know? More likely they would cart me away to Bow and toss the key in the Thames. I could climb up on that box there and shout his name. I could find out right now. Why don't I? It is the truth! My mind shrieks inside my head: Yes! Stop him! But when I imagine the words they are suspicions, suppositions. Where is my proof? It is I who was in command during the investigations, and it is I who let valuable evidence slip through my fingers.

I am walking in purgatory. What if he escapes and kills again? He has managed to send letters—so their security is not absolute. What guarantee have I? I feel so inexorably twisted within this tale. I have no more volition: Fate has taken over and is pulling the strings. I cannot speak his name. I cannot act. I am only a pawn, a small dispensable person, no lord, no prince, no king. *They* must stop him.

Mary must have seen this cast of the shadow of hell on my face this afternoon on Commercial Street.

I didn't even see her, so sunk was I in my own torpor. She touched my arm and brought me back.

"What's wrong, John West?"

I shook my head.

"Did someone die?"

"No. Not really. I've—" Suddenly my body ached like death. You can die from lack of human touch, I thought, I'm sure you can. A miasma of the soul can be as fatal as drowning or a pistol to the head. I looked at her. Her face was concerned and gentle.

"You can tell me. Come on, I'll buy you a pint, Johnny. Is it a woman?"

I smiled.

"Go on, you can tell me," she said.

The world reeled suddenly into focus. There were no guarantees. No guarantees even that I would still be alive tomorrow. I was forty and well lived-in; I'd burned my candles a bit too often at both ends. I felt strangely clearheaded. There were no promises. And Fate gave you only one chance; in rare cases, two. I loved her. I'd loved her since I first set eyes on her.

I laughed. Mary smiled and cocked her head. Save for my mother no one really cared what I did as long as I did not disturb history. On a personal plane I might do anything.

"If I'm thinking of any woman, it's you, Mary Jane."

"Oh, go on."

"Do you love Joseph?" I said.

"Joe?"

"Do you love him?"

"Oh, Johnny. What can I say? Not that way. There are some things I—I can't tell you. I tried once."

"Mary, I think I know."

"Know what?"

"Why you hide so much. Listen, I don't care. I only care about one thing."

"What?"

"Are you happy?"

She looked at me. A tear slid from her eye.

"Leave him."

She started laughing. "Oh, Johnny, Johnny."

"Are you laughing at me?"

"Oh, of course I'm not. It's myself I'm laughing at. Don't you know, Joe walked out on me—last week."

"He left you?"

She nodded.

"Your husband left you? Why didn't you tell me?"

"Sometimes I think you came down with the last shower, Johnny West. Costers never marry." Her voice was bitter then.

"Why didn't you tell me. You said *Mrs.*"

"I lied."

"Why?"

"I didn't want you to know the truth."

"There's only one truth I want to know."

"What truth?"

"Do you love him?"

"Christ, won't you stop? It's not so simple. I lied about a lot of things."

"I don't care, Mary. Just don't lie now."

"Love? Don't you know, I have a past."

"We all have pasts."

"No, *you* have a history. I have a past."

"Do you love him, Mary?"

"Johnny, I was gay."

I didn't flinch. The word stabbed my mind, but I still loved her. At least it was not a "Yes." She looked at me, her gaze breathtakingly levelheaded. Then she went on. "It was a long time ago, before I was twenty. He was the uncle of a friend, he bought me presents. Then he bought me."

Mary's lower lip was quivering, but she went on. "I lied to myself and told myself it was love, but I was a kept woman, Johnny. Until—" She drew a breath. "*Afterwards* he sent a friend, to tell me he was to be married and that it was over, but that if I liked, the friend would continue to keep me."

There were no more tears in her eyes. Her eyes were hard and flat. She blinked and looked me square in the face.

"That doesn't make you gay," I said.

"Doesn't it?"

"Do you love Joe, Mary?"

She sighed deeply. "There's no future with me, Johnny. Can't you see. One day it would matter and then I'd hate you. Besides, you're wrong, Johnny, I didn't say no to that friend. Oh, Johnny, you're so blind. Why do you think Joe left? He found out."

"About before?"

She laughed. "You *did* come down with the last shower,

Johnny. No, Joe knew about before. Who do you think it was
made me quit?" She touched my arm, then drew her hand away.
"Joe left because I—strayed—or he thought I did. What's the
difference now?"

"I told you, I don't care. We could get away, Mary, go some
place new and start over."

"I live here, Johnny. I like my life. These are my friends and
I'm not ashamed of it. I am what I am. I'll always be. Do you
think people are any better in your fancy clubs and parlors? Any
more moral? Oh, they have bigger bankrolls, more pretense and
games—I'm sick of games. At least we down-and-outers are honest about our vices."

"Like you were with me?"

"That's not fair."

"You still haven't answered me."

"You can't go back, Johnny. You can never go back. When a
man's lost caste, he may as well go whole hog, bristles and all.
Ah, it's in need of a drink I am. Are you coming?"

"The future's not written, Mary. I've got a little money saved.
I know a man with a shop. You'd move up quickly."

"Make an honest woman of me? Unsoil the dove?" She
laughed till the tears blinded her. Then she lifted her head and
put on the lilt strong. "Didn't you hear me, John West? Cage me
up in a shop? I'd rather go down on sailors."

She left me standing with my jaw aslack, and started off down
the street. At the corner she stopped and turned round, shook her
head. Then she came back and gave me a kiss on the cheek.
"You've room to let in your attic, Johnny, but I'm still touched.
Listen, if I win the reward, I'll give it all up. Maybe if I could
make an honest woman of *myself* . . ." She grinned, left the
promise hanging. "You don't know anything new do you?"

I smiled. If I could give her proof, she could collect the reward.
"Would you marry me then?"

She lifted her hand and grinned. "Honour bright, John West."

I stared at her. If Fate hadn't intended her for me, why had it
made me feel this way? I wanted to protect her, keep her by my
side, kill anyone who might touch her.

"Be careful, Mary, promise me?"

"Yes. I will." A dark look clouded her face. "Are you sure
nothing's wrong? You can tell me."

"Only this woman I know."

"You don't know something, do you, Tec? Did you arrest someone already?"

"No," I said, and made the rest a joke: "The killer is still at large. But I have deduced that he is a tall man who smokes Trichinopoly cigars and sports a Japanese dragon running down his left arm. You're the tattoo expert, you should be able to find him in no time."

"You're a caution, Johnny. And no help at all. I shall have to find him myself."

Friday, November 9, 1888

As we go to press, intelligence reaches us of another murder
in the City. The City Police state that a woman was found
cut to pieces in a house in Dorset-Street at a quarter to
eleven this morning. No particulars have yet been received,
and it is at present impossible to say whether this crime
belongs to the same category as those which so recently startled the civilized world. Details will appear in our next edition.

—*Pall Mall Gazette*

ℱℱℱ

The bells rang, the trumpets brayed, and the cannons boomed
from the Tower of London and from Horse Guard Parade as the
baroque gilt coach of the new Lord Mayor the Right Honourable
James Whitehead left Guildhall and made its way down the
Strand to Charing Cross. Six brewery shires pulled the coach; six
footmen in scarlet and gold completed the crew. As they came to
Victoria Embankment, a phalanx of red-coated, beplumed
knights on black horses—the 19th Hussars—saluted. The low
and the high lined the street, and all traffic save the Lord Mayor's
procession came to a standstill.

It is an old ceremony, this ritual, complete with crystal and
gold mace and a ceremonial offering of a gold purse, of aromatic
incense and myrrh. This year the pageantry was, by the Lord
Mayor's wishes, muted: There were heraldic shields aplenty, ban-
ners proclaiming *"Labor omnia vincit,"* but no elephants or cam-
els or buffaloes. There were also, by order of Sir Charles, no
public speeches or placards, not even should they chance to be in
support of the new Lord Mayor. All in all, a small event in
comparison to the sideshows of the past.

I had found a place near the stands under a fig tree where the
rain hadn't penetrated and was just settling in when Willy's burly
form appeared before me.

"The Ripper's struck again! Dorset Street."

"Dorset? On the street?"

"No, inside some crib—a woman. Two men turned in the report; Reid's on his way over. A place called Miller's Court, McCartney's Rents. He's a ship chandler; his office is just round the corner."

"Do you have the woman's name?"

"Aye. The name is Kelly, Mary Kelly."

There are people you know for years and would not miss for minutes if they suddenly ceased to occupy your life. There are others who in minutes capture a space in your heart. Like children, they are bone of your bone and blood of your blood, entwined forever in some giant skein of fate. All the way to Miller's Court, I prayed that fate had spared her.

Inspector Reid met us at the barricade and escorted us down the narrow passage into the court. A constable was getting sick against the whitewashed wall.

"Where's Abberline and the Super?" Willy said.

"Dunno," Reid said. "Maybe bringing the dogs."

I looked past the freshly whitewashed wall to the small corner doorstep. "Have you gone in, Edmund?"

"It's locked," Reid said. "You can see it through the window. It's not pretty." He motioned to the boy sitting pale-faced in the corner. "He saw her first, came over to collect the rent. Didn't you, boy?"

"Is it the Kelly woman, lad?" I said.

The boy looked up at me and nodded gravely.

"We've questioned him," Reid said. "Seems the woman and man were six weeks behind on the rent. The man Barnett moved out last week."

"Joseph Barnett?"

"That's the name. A fishmonger. Anyhow, McCartney sent the boy over to collect this morning—found this."

"Are you sure?" I turned to the lad. "Was she behind on payment?"

"That she was, twenty-seven shillings worth: four and six a week."

"Why did you go over today?"

"What do you mean?" He gave me a lean, cynical look, and I saw now that he was older than ten, a street-smart, peeler-shy blackguard.

"Today is not rent day. If she was six weeks in arrears, what made you think *today* she might pay?"

"There was a rumour," the lad said.

"What sort?"

"That she'd been in the money."

"How do you mean?"

He shrugged, and I saw I would get no more out of him. I turned then and faced the window. My hand was shaking. Six weeks behind on the rent. Since . . . I counted back. Since the night of the double murder. Since the night the killer washed his hands in her sink, stained the water pink. Since the night Mary lost her key. If it was Mary. A tiny ray of hope went through me. It might be another woman, a friend perhaps. Mary Jane might be safe somewhere with her Joe.

I took a step towards the small window where the grey curtain fluttered. The wooden ledge was worm-eaten and cool to the touch as I leaned forward and peered through the dirty window-pane. Steel yourself; if the Prince has murdered Mary to complete the ritual, then there may be no Mary.

I peered into the murky darkness, into the twelve-foot-square room. The first thing I made out was an open corner cupboard, a piece of bread on a blue pottery plate, an empty ginger beer bottle. On the mantel, half of a red candle in a wine bottle.

Then I saw the post of the maple bed below and reeled back. Mary lay on her back on the blood-soaked bed, staring at the ceiling. Her legs were drawn up and her left arm was squared across her chest. The rest was pure Apache: Except for the pristine arm and her golden hair, there was nothing else human. She had been skinned, head to heel.

"Do you have an ax, West?" Reid said.

I had to come from a long way away to answer him.

"Why not reach in the window and push up the latch?"

"I told you, it's locked, not just bolted."

"It can't be." My mind cleared a little then. I took a step and though my legs were rubbery, managed to reach through the window to slide the bolt. The door would still not budge. Strange. It couldn't be locked because there was no key. Mary had lost the key.

"Killer must have taken the key away with him, don't you think?" Willy said. "Ah, here comes Philips. Why didn't he bring the ax?"

George Philips nodded solemnly and came to my side, looked in. He made a funny squeaking sound and stepped back. He took a deep breath and said, "Have you a pencil, Inspector?"

Reid gave him a nub, and Philips drafted a ciphered telegram. About a half hour later, Abberline arrived. He was carrying an ax, but he set it against the wall.

"We going in now?" said Reid.

"Not yet, Reid. In a bit." Abberline took out a pack of smokes.

"Where's Superintendent Arnold?" Willy said. "Where's the damn dogs?"

"On their way," Abberline said, lighting up.

It was three more hours before Arnold arrived. The AC came with him. There were no dogs. Grave-faced, Anderson gave the order to break down the door. I was the third person in the room.

There are frontiers to the mind which, once crossed, afford no return. I stepped over the threshold, and a chasm cleaved behind me. I faced the dark side of the moon.

Mary had no nose, no ears, no mouth, no breasts, no sex, and yet it was surely and without a doubt Mary. The white capped sleeves starched so diligently, the hair that was always glistening clean, the crook of her arm where the small hairs gleamed, the violet wells rimmed with green that were only Mary's eyes.

The bedclothes had been turned down and on the chair lay Mary's day clothes, a linsey frock and red knitted cross-over, neatly folded. At the side of the bed was a small table. A table of shewbread it was today: heart and kidney and small mounds of flesh which on examination revealed themselves to be her breasts. The blue *Fisherman's Widow* print had been taken down and turned against the wall. On the nail hung a ripped piece of flesh.

"The ashes are still warm," Anderson said. I turned and watched him kneeling at the grate. "Look at this," he said. He held up the teakettle. "The spout and handle are melted."

Ashes, ashes, all fall down. The Plague Song, sung so sweetly and obliviously by little children. I wonder what he burned. . . ?

"Jubelum, vile and impious wretch . . . it is my order that you be taken without the walls of the Temple, and there have your body severed in two . . . your bowels burnt to ashes in the center and scattered to the four winds of heaven."

In the corner were more ashes, black ashes. I knelt and scooped them up in the small silver snuffbox I carried in my pocket. I didn't look back at the bed; I just put the snuffbox in my pocket and went outside. Willy was questioning a woman at the door to No. 20 Miller's Court; I listened.

"It was about half-past three," she said. "I was awakened by my kitten walking across my neck. I heard a woman scream: 'Murderer!' She screamed it twice. Then all was silent. I went back to sleep."

A white-haired crone poked her head out of the doorway across the passageway. "I seen her too, sure as I'm standing here. Round midnight I was just going out to the Ten Bells and she was agoing in. She says to me, 'Evening, Widow Cox,' and then she and him went on up the passageway. The man was carrying a quart pail of beer.'

"Did you hear them speak?" Willy asked.

"The man, he was too drunk for that. But Mary, she was in fine form. 'I think I'll have a song now,' she says to me. Then she starts singing. 'Sweet Violets,' it is. When I came back to my room at one she was still singing it."

"What did this man look like?" Willy asked, pencil poised over pocketbook.

"Oh, he was a big beery man with a blotchy face and a carroty mustache and beard—and a billycock hat. I'd know him if I seen him again."

At a quarter to four a one-horse carrier pulled up, and Mary's body was placed in the wooden shell and covered with a rag cloth. Women and men lined up to watch as the van wheeled the shell to Shoreditch Mortuary.

I followed. "Sweet Violets," the Widow Cox had said. The song Mary sang the night I followed her home.

> Sweet violets, sweeter than all the roses,
> Ladened with fragrance, sparkling with the dew.
> Sweet violets, from mossy dell and rivulet.
> Zillah, darling one, I plucked them, my darling, for you.

"Sweet Violets," the song of the wild songbird. Never again would she be caged.

* * *

Friday, November 9, a day of celebration. In the East End this afternoon, three thousand meat teas were distributed, compli-

ments of the new Lord Mayor. Three thousand pork pies with
bread and butter and cake, a quart of tea, and an apple.

The new Lord Mayor ate turtle soup, partridge, grouse, pheas-
ant, turkey, rib of lamb, sirloin of beef, ham, capon, chicken,
lobster salad, braised lamb, orange jellies, Italian crèmes, past-
ries, meringues, compotes, and ices. Only a slight furrow creased
his handsome expansive brow as he delivered his celebration
speech.

"Pray charge your glasses," the toastmaster said, "that we
might drink a toast to the Prince of Wales on the occasion of this,
his forty-seventh birthday."

The Lord Mayor stood and mounted the platform, splendid in
his red silk and ermine and sable. He turned to the Chancellor
and nodded gravely, then held up his chalice for a long time as he
considered his words. I am told that there were a number of
pauses in his speech and that certain words were expressed with
peculiar irony:

". . . It frequently occurs in large families, even where there is
a good father and mother, that there are some who are not alto-
gether what could be wished . . . but in the case of our own
Royal Family it is impossible to say that there are any who are
not a credit to their parents, a credit to the nation, and worthy of
the exalted position they occupy. . . ."

He lifted his chalice and drank.

At Sandringham the birthday festivities were only beginning:
two hundred and fifty joints of beef had been roasted and were
now being laid on the table alongside giant prawns, oysters, Italian truffles, hothouse grapes. As dusk fell, a bonfire blaze of lights
flared up and the guests began arriving along the circular drive.
Prince Albert Victor arrived late.

* * *

It is midnight now, outside and in my soul. My brain and body
are numb. Why her? Because of me?

"Zillah, darling, I plucked them for you. . . ." Never to hear
her voice again . . . if only I could cry.

Zillah is Hebrew for shadow. And she dwells now in the valley
of the shadow of death.

Four A.M., the hour of the wolf, the hour when spirits depart
the earth. Fearing for my own, I struggle up from the mire and

sludge of my body and grasp my first cigarette since Miller's
Court. I reach in my pocket for a match. My fingers touch the
intricate silver scroll of the snuffbox, and I feel a tear roll down
my cheek, warm and gentle as Mary's touch.

It is dawn now and I have begun to think. With the light
comes clarity. I open the small scrolled box and stare at the black
ash. It had been a joke, what I told her about the dragon. As this
ash was a joke. He didn't even smoke the brand. "He's gone too
far this time." Dunlap's words in the courtroom echo in my
memory. He hadn't been talking of Warren but of the Ripper's
message on the wall.

And now it all begins to unravel. The elaborate joke, layer
upon layer of meaning, enough myth and fable to please any
faction. Rich man, poor man, beggarman, thief, doctor, lawyer,
Indian chief. It is we who have created Jack: he is a product of
our fears and prejudices, our desires. He has made himself in the
image of our nightmares, our fantasies, a criminal for the most
fastidious connoisseur. Masonry for the Masons, religion for the
churchgoers, justice for the socialists, literature for the common
folk, a dash of Shakespeare for good measure. A murder mystery
complex enough even for Sherlock Holmes, just in time for
Christmas.

In my desk side table is the copy of *Beeton's Christmas Annual:*

It was a large square room, looking all the larger from the
absence of all furniture. . . . Opposite the door was a showy
fireplace, surmounted by a mantelpiece of imitation white
marble. On one corner of this was stuck the stump of a red
wax candle. The solitary window was so dirty that the light
was hazy and uncertain, giving a dull grey tinge to everything. . . .

The door was locked on the inside. . . . The window of
the room was open, and beside the window, all huddled up,
lay the body of a man in his nightdress. . . .

In one place he gathered up very carefully a little pile of
grey dust from the floor, and packed it away in an envelope.

A box of toys for the coppers, tied up in red ribbon. There's the
lock. There's the key. Open it.

"It's elementary, my good fellow." Mary knew her killer. She
was the one who harboured him the night of the bloody saturna-

lia. So many clues—the ginger beer bottle—"I saved up some of the proper red stuff in a ginger beer bottle. . . ." He was there at Miller's Court that night; my hair had stood on end—my body had known. He was there inside No. 13. He knew her. But something that night saved her. He left, taking the key.

And then, waiting, the key in his pocket, awaiting the final curtain. His chance came; he escaped his captors and returned, found her. And when he was done, he let himself out and locked the door behind him, leaving the Trichinopoly ash upon the floor, the half-consumed red wax candle on the mantelpiece.

Did he know us all, select us out one at a time from his box of toys to play out his drama? Was he watching? The bearded man outside Lusk's gate? The bearded shade lurk sailor who hobbled past the table where I sat with Mary? I can never be sure. I saw a mermaid, but perhaps it was merely the curl of the dragon's tail.

Saturday, November 10, 1888

ℱℱℱ

Detail is everything. My mind has taken over from my body, feeding it while it goes without sleep or food or drink. The cigarette lies half finished in the ashtray on my desk. I am John West no more, I am detective no more, I have no desire, not even for vengeance. A film has lifted from my vision, and my brain lies naked against the world. I can only remain awake and watch, take in, my senses blended, sharpened. I can smell Arnold's flowers beginning to decay within the brackish water; I can see each ridge and whorl in the fingerprint on the glass of whisky he serves me; the whisky is peat in my mouth, dry molten earth.

"Drink that down, man," Arnold said.

I complied. Then I shivered, and looked up slowly, feeling for the first time today a body sensation: the glass, warm against my blue fingers.

"You look completely knackered," Arnold said. "Didn't you get any sleep at all? And where's your hat?"

"I feel fine."

He poured another dram. "Listen, West, I think you'd better take some time off. You can't go on like this and not crack. I've seen it."

I shook my head.

"You're released from duty as of this moment, Inspector. Go to bed. Come back in three days."

"And do what?"

"Lie low. This isn't over yet. You're not involved yet. You might just come out with a promotion."

I laughed, a sick, rattling laugh that made him cock his head, and look again at my eyes.

"Something I don't know?"

"I am involved. I knew Mary Kelly. I wanted to marry her."

"I would never have given you permission to throw away your life like that."

Yesterday I would have hit him. Today it did not matter. I no longer saw the world with eyes that faced the future. It was over for me. I smiled.

"Good, John. I'm glad you're seeing the light. It's especially crucial if you're involved. Frankly, you're a danger to us all if you let feelings get in the way. Does anyone else know of your relationship? Detective Thicke?"

"No, I never talked about it."

"Good. We're safe then. I'll arrange your leave papers. I'm meeting this afternoon with the Prime Minister. I'll make sure he knows you've cooperated."

"It doesn't make any difference, you know."

Arnold nodded. "Well, I'll just go tell the clerk to make out your papers. You finish that drink, I won't be a second."

I watched him go out the door, then I stepped to the desk where the morning report lay drying. My eyes scanned the report: "Joseph Barnett, fishmonger, 24 New Street, Bishopsgate." I downed the whisky and stood waiting. Arnold came back in and handed me the papers.

"Go to bed, West. Or go get roaring drunk. Get a little distance from your pain."

"Pain?"

He looked at me, then shook his head. "Promise me you'll not play copper in your condition."

I shrugged. "Sure."

"You'll get some sleep?"

"Aye."

"Good lad."

He let me out, and I walked towards the stairs that led to the section house. As soon as he closed the door, I turned and went the other way, out the front door.

The sign over the doorway of 24 New Street read BLACK-BURNE'S RENTS: GOOD BEDS AND ACCOMMODATIONS FOR SINGLE WOMEN. I found Joseph Barnett sitting stiffly on a cotton flocked mattress, staring into space. His flashy coster clothes were wrinkled, slept in, and his guinea boots were caked with mud. I took out my pack of smokes and set them on the table before him. He couldn't have been more than thirty, but the eyes that met mine were older than my own.

"My name is John West," I said.

"What do you want from me, copper? The Yard's been here. Want to see the cuff marks?"

"Mary Jane was a friend of mine."

His eyes narrowed. "That's a good one. Mary *Jane,* eh? What sort of friend?" He snorted and spat. "The paying kind?"

"I gave her a penny once—to ask for her thoughts. She cried on my shoulder when you left her. My God, was it only two days ago? That's all, I swear it."

"You saw her Thursday? When?"

"At teatime."

"She was with *you*? At the Elephant and Castle?"

"No, I saw her on the street, quite by chance."

Joe breathed in sharply, reached for the pack of smokes and took two out. I shook my head; he pocketed the second and lit his own. "I was waiting at home—" The last word strangled in his mouth. He closed his eyes. "She came late, had no time for me. I left in a huff. I didn't even say good-bye."

"Why did you go to Number 13? To take her back?"

"No."

"Why?"

"I don't know. I'd been the night before and given her money. Not much, and I didn't have anything to give her this time. Just to see her. I'd been so angry with her."

"Did you know she was in arrears on the rent?"

"What? She wasn't."

"Six weeks."

"That's not possible. I gave her the money."

"Perhaps she spent it on something else?"

"What?" He scratched his head. "I wonder. I thought she'd gone back to her old ways, that's where she got the money. That shawl for the Widow Cox, a meal every day for that dying bitch Harvey. That's when I started to get suspicious. She's always been generous, but this month, she was spending like there was no—" He stopped; his face had turned a shade greyer.

"Was the door unlocked when you got there?"

"The other inspector kept asking me that. If I had the key. I kept telling him it was lost. She wasn't there; neither was that bitch friend of hers. I let myself in like she does, reaching through the broken pane and pushing the bolt."

"Why did you leave last week?"

"It's none of your business."

"Listen, Barnett, she as much as told me. You thought she'd been with another man . . . you accused her. Was it the night she lost the key?"

He shot me a look of pure hostility. "You are the one, aren't you?"

"The one what?"

"How d'you know about that night if you aren't the one? You been talking to Maria?"

"Maria? You mean the Harvey woman? The report says you and Mary fought over her being there."

"She's the one to blame, putting ideas in Mary's head. I kicked the bitch out, that's what I did. It's what she deserved, filling her head with fancy ideas—and filling her belly with—" He stopped and spat. "I mean it, Detective, are you the one that did it?"

"What?"

" 'Cuz I'll cut your throat if you are. I'm not blind, you know. Mary denied it, but she can't deny getting sick mornings. I'm no idiot. It wasn't mine, that's for sure."

"What wasn't?"

"She was with child and it wasn't mine."

"But I thought—Are you sure of that? She told me she couldn't have children."

"I'm sure as a man can be."

"Whose was it?"

He glared at me. "You didn't poke her?"

"No. I didn't."

"Ask the bitch then. Ask her about the night she lied to me at the Fish Hill Public House. Ask her about the night Mary lost the key. If I ever find the bastard that poked her—"

"Are you sure she was with child?"

"Oh, she was with child all right. I've sisters. I know when a woman's in the pudding club."

"Did *she* know?"

"Whu'?" He blinked. "I don't know. I figured her denying everything, she knew." He buried his head in his thick hands. "If she'd only just admitted it to me, I would have stuck by her. She wouldn't have gone out drinking that night." He shook his head and smiled a crooked smile. "Boy, but she was a ripper when she got to drinking, my Old Black Mary, she was. Oh, Christ, I need to get pissed as a drowned rat in a bottle. Detective, do me a

favour. Come back here the day before the funeral and help me
sober up? I want to be there."

"I promise I will."

He stood on shaky legs and stepped into his boots. From his
pocket he drew out a small blue envelope. "Would you do me one
more favour? Hold this. I don't want to lose it where I'm going."

I nodded and took the envelope, placed it in my pocket. When
I got outside, I opened it. Inside the small glassine packet was a
lock of golden hair.

* * *

I went down the long hill in the mist to Billingsgate, to the
great market, which since Saxon times has sold fish from out of
the "Great Stink." I passed the fisherman's church, St. Mary at
the Hill, my mind dredging up the fact that Sir Thomas à Becket
was once priest there. Strange that the memory for odd facts still
works alongside the automaton that the rest of the body has
become. I wasn't in a hurry; I walked slowly along the slippery
cobblestones to Old Swan Pier, my hands in my pockets. Five
wooden eel boats rocked against the spars.

"Yarmouth herring, three-a-penny! Yarmouth herring, three-a-
penny!" The costermonger's voice rang out from Lower Thames.
No wonder Mary knew all about fish. No wonder she liked that
maudlin print of the widow with child.

"Looking for something, mate?" The coster stopped his bar-
row and eyed me. Costers are a clan, trusting none but their own;
they spend their money on clothes and drink, owe the world
nothing. Still, this one hadn't taken me for a copper. Maybe I
didn't look like one anymore.

"The Fish Hill," I said.

"You're looking at it," he said, wiping his hands on his shirt
and indicating the building across from me. A violet riband of
smoke rose from the black chimney of the yellow brick public
house on the corner. I touched my hand to my bare head and
went across the street, opened the door, and entered a dim room.
I ordered a Newcastle Brown.

"You're new around here, aren't you?"

"Looking for a girl."

"Maybe I can help you." The publican gave me an oily smile.

He was huge and fat and six-foot-four, with a bulldog face and a weed in his mouth.

"Name's Maria Harvey."

"Oh, that one. 'Fraid I can't help you, sir. You a copper or a reporter?"

I shook my head. "A friend of a friend."

He shrugged.

I laid a shilling on the counter; he eyed it. I put down a second.

"You might try back here round half past five," he said. I nodded, watched him take up the coins.

When I returned, the gas jets had just been lit; they flickered against the marble pilasters. The misty rain had stopped and the bells were ringing. The evening was cool and opal-grey, with pale melting shadows.

The publican drew me a pint and nodded once at the solitary woman at the end of the bar drinking Mother's Ruin. I moved down and took the stool next to her. "Maria Harvey?"

"What's it to you?"

"I'd like to talk to you. Do you mind?"

"Yes."

"I was a friend of Mary Kelly's," I said. "Name's John West. I saw her the day she died."

She stared at me, then looked back towards the bar.

"Can I buy you a drink?"

She shrugged. I held up two fingers to the publican; he brought a round. I watched her down the gin. She couldn't have been more than twenty-four, and she was fine of form and face, but I sensed death on her, knew it when the coughing began. She covered her face till the seizure passed.

We drank two more rounds in silence, me looking into the eyes of the stag over the mirror, her into her tumbler. Then I caught her staring; our eyes met in the looking glass.

"Do you still mind?" I said.

"What do you want to know?" She turned on her stool towards me.

"Joe Barnett said I should ask you about the night Mary lost the key."

"Frig Barnett."

"Maria—it is Maria, isn't it?"

"Sometimes."

"I'm asking you: What happened to Mary the night the key disappeared? What really happened?"

"Did Joe send you?"

"I only met Barnett today. I was Mary's friend."

She took a large swallow of her gin. "It was a big mistake ever getting involved. I was only doing her a favour—frig them all." She took another gulp. "What's it to you, anyhow?"

"I was in love with her."

"Mary?" She shook her head. "Poor you."

"I need to know. It's important. What happened that night?"

She sighed. "Why not? I had a top trick that night, a sort of lucky fluke. A friend of a friend, from the old days. Five quid I was promised if I could guarantee the client the whole night and a private room. He gave me some honest money and arranged a place to leave the message when I'd made the arrangements. But I got sick bad." She tipped back her glass and drained it. I lifted my finger for another round.

"Ta." She wiped her mouth on her sleeve. "Mary and me, we knew each other way back when, back when we were both eighteen and living off Haymarket in a posh house. Wasn't nothing to make five quid then. Rich men with fancy carriages, silk dresses, once even a trip to Paris—top of the tree, we were. We looked like twins then, we did. People used to stop us on the street. Mary was always one to help out a friend. I couldn't miss this chance."

"Go on—that night."

"I knew she and Joe were hard up. I mean, I owed her one, all she did for me. I asked her to take my place."

"Did she?"

"She said no at first, but then she agreed. I gave her part of the honest."

"What about Joe?"

"Mary said she could take care of Joe, get him away for one night. He'd never know. I left my friend her address; figured the client would be none the wiser. Frigging frig-up instead. Mary, she changed her mind."

"She what?"

"Changed her mind. Picks a fight with Joseph to get him out, then up and panics, just scoots out at two in the morning, leaves the door unlocked. The trick comes and finds nothing so he don't stay. Only he takes the key and locks up neat-like. When Joe comes home, there's hell to pay. First he thinks she's locked him out, so he smashes the window. Then he sees she's not home; he thinks she's been out cheating. Never did trust her after that—wouldn't let her out of his sight. And he blamed it all on me!"

"You sure she didn't stay that night—and say she hadn't?"

"Mary lie? Maybe you didn't know her. She even gave me back her share of the honest."

"Did you see your friend again?"

"After that cock-up? He'll not be looking me up again." She coughed, a small spasm, then took another gulp of gin.

"When did you see Mary last?"

"The day before she died. At the Elephant and Castle—one of our old haunts. She brought me back a dress she had borrowed. She'd mended it for me. She was always doing things like that for me, cooking me soup and making me eat it." Maria started crying, but she didn't look away.

"Did she love Joe, Maria?"

"Joe?" Maria laughed. "Like a brother. Mary loved everyone, to a fault you might say. Too generous, she was. She even bought the drinks that day."

"What did you talk about?"

"Woman things. Nothing in particular. She was in a hurry, said she had to go over to Leman Street to find a man. Someone called Johnny." Maria smiled. "Funny, Mary's face lit up when she talked about him, like she was over the moon about him. I teased her about it—she just said it wasn't in the cards for her and him."

"Did she say why she was going to see him?"

"I don't think so. No." Maria screwed up her face. "Something about a letter, I think—I don't remember."

"Maria, one last question. Did Mary ever say anything to indicate she might be in a family way?"

"Mary?" Maria laughed. "Mary was lucky. She was barren as an old bone."

Monday, November 12, 1888

ⲅⲅⲅ

There were huge crowds outside the hall when I arrived at the inquest this morning. I had to push and jostle my way up the stairs and into the room. Abberline and Arnold were in the aisle, surrounded by an army of reporters. I took a seat in the back.

"Oyez! Oyez!" the bailiff called. "All rise." The crowd rose, but the talking did not die down as the Liberal Coroner Roderick McDonald entered and took his place.

"I must object, this is not our jurisdiction," one of the jurors said.

"Yes," said a second juror. "We protest."

"The body lies in Shoreditch Borough; therefore you are called to hear the evidence," McDonald said. "Will you choose a foreman, gentlemen."

"But the body was found in Stepney Borough, Spitalfields," the first man insisted. "Coroner Baxter should be heading the proceedings."

"Jurisdiction resides where the body *lies.*" He took out the Bible and handed it to the first man. "Each kiss the Book and pass it round, gentlemen."

Reluctantly the jurors did so.

"Thank you, gentlemen," McDonald said. "Now, we shall go round to the mortuary to view the deceased."

I made the procession with them in my mind: walking single file past the rusty iron wicket-gate, past St. Leonard's churchyard of sooty stones, down the path and sharply to the left into the brick mortuary, looking down into the wooden shell at the waxen body.

When they came back, their faces were ashen; they listened to the testimony of the Dorset Street neighbors in silence. Then George Philips entered the witness-box and began giving the autopsy results. "Rigor mortis had set in when I arrived at two P.M.

and increased during my examination. I found arterial blood on the wall in splashes; the sheet had been placed over her head and he had cut through the sheet. . . . Her right hand had been severed and placed inside her stomach cavity. . . . Her breasts and . . ."

And then he had taken away the sheet and arranged the limbs, set out the table of shewbreads—"nice little partridge breasts in their cupboards"—

McDonald's gavel brought me swimming back to the sea of hushed faces. He would clear the room now of women and children. He should have done it before. "I think we shall not ask that the next portion of your report be read," McDonald said. "We have established the cause of death. Thank you, surgeon, you may step down."

There were murmurs from the audience; the *Globe* reporter stood. "What about the missing parts? We've not been told all."

McDonald held up his hand. "We shall resume at ten tomorrow. This inquest is adjourned until then." He rapped the gavel.

"All rise," the bailiff called.

It was then that Arnold saw me. He turned and whispered to Abberline, then came down the aisle and took my arm, steered me aside.

"You've still not slept."

"I'm not tired."

"You look like hell."

I nodded. "It's where I've been."

"Here comes Philips. Let me talk to him. He could prepare you a sleeping potion."

I shook my head. "I've things I must do."

"You don't have any sort of crazy plan for retribution, do you? If you do, get rid of it." He leaned over and whispered, "Besides, *he* leaves this evening with his mother for Copenhagen."

"Is it far enough?"

"They'll go to Russia if they have to. He won't ever come to trial."

I caught up to George Philips on the pavement outside the courtroom. I grasped his sleeve and made him stop.

"She was with child, wasn't she? It's that missing part you're hiding, isn't it?"

He stopped in his tracks and stared at me. Then he turned his

back and began walking. I followed him and grabbed his sleeve.
"I know she was," I said. "Can you deny it?"

He wheeled and glared at me. "Damnation! No, I can't."

"How far along?"

"Six weeks, two months. Maybe three. How did you know?"

"Is that what he burned?"

"I don't know. Honestly."

"I believe you." I stepped back, let him go. Whose child if not
Joe's? And how?

There was one more thing nagging me: "a rumour that she'd
been in the money." Joe hadn't any money to give her, certainly
not enough for arrears. Why had the lad been sent that morning
to collect? If he hadn't gone, the body might have lain there all
day. The Lord Mayor might have had his parade and repast in
splendid ignorance; there might have been no talk of murder at
the Prince's birthday ball. Someone had told the landlord. Who?
The Ripper himself? I went back to my office and took out the
files, read McCartney's statement twice, then grabbed my hat.

"Who?" McCartney said, puffing on a fat banded cigar. "Why,
it was this fellow, that's all I know. A dark-haired, wiry sort of
man. He came by here round nine A.M. and asked me if I'd seen
Mary yet, said he was a friend of hers. I'd never seen him before."

"Did he give you his name?"

"George," he said. "He was quite the dandy. Wore a peacock
blue waistcoat and tight pegged trousers, and rings on his fingers.
He asked me to give her his greetings when I saw her, apologized
for not leaving a tip. That's when he let drop that he knew for a
fact she had come into some money the night before. He said she
had promised to help him out. Told me where he'd be waiting
when she got up."

"Where was that?"

"In Ringer's. He said he'd wait till noon, but then he had to be
going on down to Romford." McCartney shrugged. "That's all I
know. I never saw him again."

"Would you recognize him?"

"I'd recognize the coat." He laughed. "Yes, I believe so."

I walked down to the Britannia and asked Mrs. Ringer for
help.

"I know a lot of Georges," she said. "What's he do?"

"Don't even know that. He may be from Romford."

"There's a George Hutchinson from Romford. He's a groom over at Foley's."

* * *

"I saw her with a swell. That's how I knew she'd be flush," George Hutchinson said when I located him at the back of Foley's stables. "This was the genuine article, Tec."

He brushed the black mare a few more strokes and then patted her sleek rump. "Mary liked horses; that's how we first started talking. Sometimes she confided in me, and—" He set the brush on the ledge and came out of the stall. He was a short man but so proportioned that he appeared quite manly. "Sometimes she loaned me money. She was the most generous woman I ever met when she was flush." He laughed. "That night she was stone broke. In fact, she asked me for a loan of tenpenny. I didn't have it."

"What time was this?"

"Just past two. I'd got off the bus from Romford at ten till. Then it started raining. That's when I saw Mary. She had her hair down—sort of wildlike—but she wasn't caring."

"Was she drunk?"

"Nah, just a mite spreeish. Had a glow on her, though. We chatted a few minutes and then she said good-bye; she seemed in a hurry to be off. She started on down Flower and Dean."

"And the swell?"

"At the corner of Thrawl, this man stepped out and tapped her on the shoulder. The genuine article: diamond stickpin, thick gold watch chain with a big ruby seal, a bunch of medals on his chest. I mean, this is a swell." Hutchinson took his coat from the hook and put it on. "I know about clothes, and this one, he's dressed to the nines. He's got maybe five hundred quids' worth on his person, not counting the jewels."

"What sort of clothes?"

"Very formal. One of those new tuxedo suits, high linen collar and cuffs, gaiters with white pearl buttons. His coat's trimmed with Astrakhan lamb; he's got it kind of thrown over his shoulder."

"Gloves?"

"Yes, brown kid. Everything but the top hat and stick. He says something to Mary and I see she knows him. They both start laughing. Then he puts his hand on her shoulder and pulls her close, whispers. 'All right,' says Mary. Then he says, 'Don't worry, you'll be all right for what I've told you.' And he gives her a hug and they walk down the street a little, towards Queen's Public House. Then she says, 'All right, my dear, come along, you'll be comfortable.' And he says something I can't hear. She shakes her head. 'I've lost it,' she says. So he reaches in his pocket and pulls out a red scarf and waves it at her like a bullfighter. She laughs and grabs the scarf and ties it round her neck. Then they turn round and start back towards Miller's Court. She gives me a wink when she passes, and he gives me a surly scowl—he's got his hat pulled down low over his face, but I'm standing in the lamp and they have to pass quite close. The man, he's thirty maybe: pale face, dark hair, thin mustache curled up at the ends. Looked Jewish to me."

"Why didn't you come forth and give this description?"

"I don't owe you coppers anything. Besides, I was the last person to see her. More than likely you'd try and nab me for it."

"We'll need a statement, Mr. Hutchinson."

"If I must."

"What happened then? You waited outside?"

"She winked, didn't she? I waited till the Whitechapel bells struck three, then called it a night."

"You didn't go up the court? Peek in the window?"

"What do you think I am?" He shook his head. "It's a bad business this, very bad. Sorry I can't give you more. That's all I know."

"Would you recognize the man again?"

"Yes, I think so."

"Anything else? Any detail you haven't told me? Have you any idea why she wanted to borrow tenpenny?"

He shrugged. "If I knew more, I'd be off collecting the reward, wouldn't I?"

"Anything at all you haven't told me? A word, a gesture, anything?"

Hutchinson closed his eyes. "I can see him. I've a good memory for faces. Brown eyes. A black cravat; the stickpin was horseshoe shaped—diamonds—looked genuine, same as the ruby. He's got a bunch of ribbons on his left chest, and one of those gold Jubilee medals on a little blue ribbon."

"Gold? Are you sure?"

"I'd not mistake that."

I smiled. "I think we'll go down now to the station."

I sat at my desk and took his statement in thick black copperplate on a blue special report sheet.

"Thank you, Mr. Hutchinson, you've been a great deal of help."

"I can go now?"

"You can go now. But you'll have to appear at the inquest tomorrow."

"Well, if I have to, I have to. Sorry I can't give you more."

I showed him out, then stood on the stairs in the cold starry night. You don't know it, but you've helped a great deal, Mr. Hutchinson. You've supplied the only concrete detail that links the killer to the castle: a gold Jubilee medal.

Silver and bronze Jubilee medals with the diademed and veiled effigy of Her double-chinned Majesty are quite common—I myself have a special Policeman's Jubilee medal, issued for my work in crowd control that day last summer when the Queen celebrated fifty long years—but only members of the Royal Family wear gold.

Yes, George Hutchinson, it should be very interesting when you give your testimony to the public. You may even find yourself a rich man.

It is all in the report. Only a few questions remain to be answered. Why was Mary out that night, seeking tenpenny? Did she meet him by accident or by design? Tenpenny is the price of a telegram. Did she know something? Was she on her way to wire me and ask my help?

Tuesday, November 13, 1888

Murder: Pardon.

Whereas on November 8 or 9 in Miller's Court, Dorset Street, Spitalfields, Mary Jane Kelly was murdered by some person or persons unknown, the Secretary of State will advise the grant of Her Majesty's pardon to any accomplice not being a person who contrived or actually committed the murder who shall give such information and evidence as shall lead to the discovery and conviction of the person or persons who committed the murder.

Sir Charles Warren has resigned at last, and King Stork follows the Dodo into retirement. . . . We have reason for rejoicing and for gratitude that on this, the anniversary of the Battle of Trafalgar-square, we should be able to welcome the news of his sudden and irreparable overthrow. Never before have we had to insist upon the removal of a public officer for whom personally we had a profound respect. Seldom has so good a man made so lamentable a fiasco of a task which he honestly attempted to perform. He fought his fight with the stubborn tenacity of a true British soldier, and we gladly unite in paying our tribute of homage to our fallen foe.

—*Pall Mall Gazette*

Today is the anniversary of Bloody Sunday. The carnival of roughs ringing Trafalgar Square cheered their approval when Sir Charles's resignation was announced, their anger defused. He has dated it Thursday last—before the murder. The official reason given is strife with the Home Office over the autonomy of the Commissioner; references are made to obscure passages in the Official Secrets Act. The papers appear to be buying: they are applauding themselves for having brought about his demise. If only they knew.

At the inquest today the wheels of justice ground to a stop.

There sat George Hutchinson, hat in hand, ready to give testimony.

"There is other evidence which I do not propose to call," McDonald said, "for if we at once make public every fact brought forward in connexion with this terrible murder, the ends of justice might be retarded." He rapped his gavel. "I now declare this inquest closed. The jurors have more than sufficient evidence to return a verdict of death from foul play."

For a moment I thought the world would erupt. "What about the evidence?" a woman shrieked. "They haven't heard but half the witnesses," said another. "Where's the photograph? We hear there's a photograph!" But the clamour died and the jurors rose and went out. In ten minutes they were back with their verdict: murder by person or persons unknown.

My own resignation I placed this afternoon upon Arnold's desk. It is dated today.

"One scapegoat is enough, don't you think? Besides, there's no danger staying now," Arnold said. "It will all blow over. You've cooperated; you'll only rise because of this."

"I'm no longer a thief catcher. I've lost the art of it." I placed my badge and police Jubilee medal on the table atop the papers, turned away.

Arnold picked up the medal. "This is yours to keep," he said. "You earned it."

I shook my head.

"You're an abject fool, West."

"Perhaps."

"Will you go away?"

"I don't know."

He shook his head. "Godspeed," he said softly.

Monday, November 19, 1888

ʄʄʄ

Mary's funeral today at Shoreditch Church, a beautiful service with at least a thousand people in attendance, including Mary's family from Wales. An anonymous donation paid for the coffin and plate. It read:

MARY JANE KELLY
AGED 25
DIED NOVEMBER 9, 1888
GOD FORGIVE HER

Those she had befriended did not forget her. I only recognized a few. Mad Jack O'Brien had a shirt on for the occasion. Mrs. Flower-of-the-Flock, the woman who makes toy whips for children and has carved up three lovers, left her knife at home. Tommy No-Legs had his stumps securely fastened and was sober, or nearly so. The Ten Bells and Britannia had taken up collections. A floral cross of heart's ease and a crown of violets graced the ash coffin.

Joseph Barnett was not there. I called at Bishopsgate for him, but he had checked out. Two crones occupied the narrow cot. I have kept the lock of Mary's hair.

Kneeling among those who had known her, I recited the words of the rosary:

Hail Mary,
Full of Grace,
The Lord is with thee.
Blessed art thou amongst women,
and blessed is the fruit of thy womb, Jesus.

And now the grave doth open its mouth.

Saturday, November 24, 1888

✦✦✦

The ministers today selected James Monro as the new Chief Commissioner of Police. Our cautious canny chief, despite a smashed leg and crippled thigh that will ever prevent him from riding a horse, let alone stand without great pain, has won the battle. Frederick Abberline is on the new list of Yard promotions for Chief Inspector; it is rumoured Robert Anderson will be knighted.

Prince Albert Victor, accompanied by his mother and sisters and his equerry, Captain Holford, arrived at Marlborough House today from the Continent. They leave this evening for Sandringham after a brief visit with Her Majesty the Queen at Windsor.

Tuesday, December 25, 1888

The winter hoarfrost is thick on the pane. I am home in my father's house in Norfolk on the bank of the sandy Wash, in the great bed in which I was born. Mother has taken over the small room facing the rectory; she comes up the stairs no more. I hear her moving about below me in the kitchen, preparing my porridge and eggs as she once prepared father's. Soon I will get up, go into the village for the paper and rolls.

I am not far from *him* here. I am told he is kept sedated. When the sedation wears off, he begins to cry and pray, to plead with God to save him. I find in my heart a small grain of something that is almost compassion. Driven by the symbol and symbolic, driven by addiction and obsession and excess—to arrive at the ultimate damnation.

In the room where he slew Jubelum was his punishment. In this room with the Magdalene who was to be the world's redemption, he met Fate. He slew Mary, opened her belly with his clean, sharp knife. Within was the child. With the first slash of his knife, he severed the innocent babe from life; the Dragon licked the blood from its body. And God's chosen, the Avenging Angel, was plunged forever into the abyss. The flames spit up blue and yellow shrieks as the Divine Mind laughed its way back to heaven.

Since then he has been truly demented, thoroughly doomed. The beautiful princess who was to be his bride turned down the greatest honour in the land. Only her kiss would break the curse and she was gone, out of reach. And none lived happily ever after. Nothing would ever again be as it was.

We will never know all of the story. Did Mary meet him that night by chance or by design? Had she known him before? Only he might tell us, and he is beyond mortal men. Does he carry within him the memories of each victim? Did Mary love me? Did she know she was with child?

She must have known him before she met him that night out-side Miller's Court. "I've lost it," she said. And from his pocket he pulled the red handkerchief, flourished it like a matador before her, made her laugh. "I've lost it." Had he left a scarf that night her room harboured him from the pack of blues? Had she been there? Was he kissing her as I dipped my white handkerchief in the bloody pool of water? Why hadn't he killed her then? What had saved her?

"I've lost it." Or did she mean the key? The key he at that moment had in his pocket, the key he later used to lock the box of toys for us coppers, the key that proves Mary was no random victim.

In the room, the second time, he lingered in the candlelight, drinking sticky ginger beer, having a cigar, then another. Did he watch her undress, watch her as she folded her garment and shawl neatly on the chair? The candle must have still been burn-ing when he disrobed.

And then Mary saw the Mikado's gift: the blue and red crea-ture of hell slithering down his left arm. She saw the Dragon and cried out, "Murderer!" He wheeled and lunged for her. "Mur-derer!" she cried again, before he had her mouth and throat, before his fingers found their grip and made the stars dance be-fore her eyes.

There are some answers we will never have. Had she not met me that night, had I not let slip the horrible "joke" about the tattoo and the Trichinopoly, might she not be alive today? If not for truth, might Fate have again spared Mary and the child in her womb?

The mystery of the child shall remain with me to the end of my days. "I can't have children," she told me. "It's not mine," said Joe. "Barren as an old bone," said Maria. "Changed her mind . . . just picks up and scoots out at two in the morning. . . ." Who was lying? Joe? Maria? Mary? If not Joe's seed, then it must have been the murderer's: Mary must have been there, taken the Prince to her bed the night of the bloody saturnalia. The Prince thus slew his own unborn child.

But what if Mary told the truth about that night? What if until Joe accused her she had truly been straight? "I strayed—or he thought I did. What's the difference now?" she said to me. An Irish-Welsh Mary with violet-green eyes and golden hair, living in a crib within the citadel of crime? A coster Joseph, salty as the crust of the earth? A crib instead of a manger? All the difference in the world.

I miss Mary and find myself going to church of a Sunday and staring at the Madonna with Child, fancying she will begin to speak to me with a soft brogue.

I read poetry now, meander some days through the woods with a book. The world seems changed.

In a flash, at a trumpet crash,

I am all at once what Christ is, | since he was what I am, and
This Jack, joke, poor potsherd, | patch, matchwood, immortal
       diamond,
Is immortal diamond.

Sometimes all at once I will hear a noise behind my ear like the beating of wings. Then music will flood my head and Mary's voice will ring out like a bell:

   Oh, stay, go not away
   Violets are blooming love for you alone
   Sweet violets, resting in beauty's bower
   Crouched all unnoticed I did pluck that flower
   Sweet violets still looking up to heaven
   Zillah darling, I plucked them and brought them to you.

Monday, December 31, 1888

ƒ ƒ ƒ

And so Time swallows itself up. The year of the Divine Mind comes to a close. Today a man's bloated body was dragged from the Thames, a season's ticket for Blackheath in his pocket. The name was Montagu Druitt, a schoolmaster who disappeared in November. Of good family, but there was talk of a scandal. He had been dismissed from his duties at Michaelmas. The Yard has told the papers it believes the man was Jack the Ripper.

And so we have our scapegoat.

I shall keep a journal no longer. But as long as *he* is alive, I shall be watching. And the fate of this journal? My legacy of truth? Shall I burn it? It is after all only one man's impressions, one man's memories. As soon as I write a word I am afraid I have lied. "The Prince went out hunting that day"—that is what history will record. The *Court Circular* does not lie.

And then he lifts the bottle and drinks, and when he kisses her next his lips are spicy and sweet with the ginger beer. She stares into his brown eyes, and then her violet-green eyes widen. . . .

I was not there. I will never know. I know only that now she has no lips with which to kiss, and her eyes cannot see. I have only dry words, inadequate tools to describe what sight and senses have etched upon the brain and heart. Only death can dull the impression through the shattered pane. How many times has it come unwilled to haunt me? Enough now that it is almost endurable? The small square white room, the simple maple bedstead, the puff of a starched sleeve, the sun striking the amber bottle of ginger beer upon the sill. So many times that it is these mundane man-made items that are the grotesque. How horribly artificial they are against the muted impressionistic rose-and-mauve pallet of the rest of the scene.

I squint and all the soft specks of colour merge and flow into an animated picture. I step into the room and over and round that which has been a woman, not taking my eyes from the left arm which emerges clean and perfect from the white sleeve. Only the arm weds the abstract to the real. I cannot decide if it is hideous or beautiful: the small golden hairs gleam in the sunlight; the white half-moons are even beneath the nails; the flesh at the crook of the elbow is clean and supple. I can't take my eyes from it: so perfectly it is arranged—a strong squared line of white leading the eye to the centre of the picture.

Above the square are Mary's open eyes, startled, knowing. I peer into them but see only what I have seen before: my own face, my own forever horror. She hadn't a prayer.

The final key is placed in the lock and turned; the puzzle falls away. And I am too late, too late to save her. And now my complicity is sealed. Who will tell the Queen the sky has fallen? Not I. No, I—like the others—will hold the silence under dark cover. My Queen and country are at stake, and I am only a man like any other, no hero after all, no rescuing knight, no prince. I have made bright the truth, and the truth is dark and ugly.

And he, the inbred saurian child of hell, the Prince of Darkness, he must rise like any man and walk out on the path beneath the sun. Oh, poor puzzled Prince, to have to see his shadow as he passes!

We have only Salisbury's word that he will never hold the Throne.

January 1892

At 9:35 A.M., Prince Albert Victor, Duke of Clarence and Avondale, and second in line to the Throne of England, was pronounced dead of influenza.

—*The Times*
January 14

F F F

He is dead at last—on the cursed 14th. Killed as the third Duke of Clarence was? Not drowned in a wine butt of sweet Malmsey in the Tower, but dispatched with prussic acid by the Royal Physician as he awaited Princess May and the bridal bower, once again the toast of all London. Society's pillar lies cold upon the marble slab. They say he died cursing Salisbury.

The Jack the Ripper file in New Scotland Yard was closed today to the public for a hundred years. The Prince's letters and diaries have all been burned.

His death chamber at Sandringham is as it was when he was living, a shrine attended by his mother. New-cut flowers are placed on the bedside table as soon as the old ones wilt. A fire burns always in the grate. His dressing table is preserved as it was that last morning: the comb and brush arranged neatly, a few black hairs entwined in the bristles. His watch upon the glass top keeps perfect time. Fresh water is poured daily into the china jug and a clean towel laid out; the bar of soap he used lies in its blue dish next to the toothpaste.

His deerstalker hat, the one he wore the last morning when he went out to hunt, hangs on a hook behind the door. On the bed is draped a Union Jack. His medals lie on the bedside table, the gold Jubilee medal on a blue garter ribbon the centrepiece.

A copy of the funeral poem, written by the Poet Laureate, is propped beside the pillow:

> The bridal garland falls upon the bier,
> The shadow of a crown, that o'er him hung,

Has vanish'd in the shadow cast by Death.
So princely, tender, truthful, reverent, pure—
Mourn! That a world-wide Empire mourns with you.
That all the Thrones are clouded by your loss,
Were slender solace. Yet be comforted;
For if this earth be ruled by Perfect love,
Then, after his brief range of blameless days,
The toll of funeral in an Angel ear
Sounds happier than the merriest marriage-bell.

His body lies in a marble crypt at Frogmore, Windsor, not far from the house where he was born. At Mary Magdalene Chapel in Sandringham they have erected their own monument: a stained-glass window depicting him as Saint George. He is wearing shining armour and a halo, slaying the Dragon.

In the street the little children sing songs while skipping:

Jack the Ripper's dead
And lying on his bed.
He cut his throat
With Sunlight soap:
Jack the Ripper's dead.